BOATHOUSE MURDERS

A gripping crime thriller full of twists

PAULINE ROWSON

The Solent Murder Mysteries Book 11

Originally published as *Shroud of Evil*

Revised edition 2022
Joffe Books, London
www.joffebooks.com

First published by Severn House Publishers Ltd.
in Great Britain in 2015 as *Shroud of Evil*

This paperback edition was first published
in Great Britain in 2022

Cover art by Dee Dee Book Covers

ISBN: 978-1-80405-425-3

CHAPTER ONE

Friday, 19 October

'Good result.' Tim Shearer, the lean and dapper Chief Crown Prosecutor, addressed Andy Horton outside the court room on the Isle of Wight.

'Would have been better if they'd pleaded guilty to begin with instead of wasting everyone's time,' Horton replied.

Shearer nodded in agreement. 'I'd give you a lift back to the ferry, only I'm staying over to discuss a couple of other cases.'

And thankfully they weren't Horton's. The Isle of Wight was not his patch. That was under the control of the acerbic stick insect DCI Birch, who was currently off sick following a hernia operation, and his fat sergeant, DS Norris. But a robbery from Northwood Abbey, on the northern coast of the island, at the end of June had resulted in the villains being caught by Horton and Sergeant Cantelli, as they were trying to sell the stuff on in Portsmouth, five miles across the Solent, at the beginning of July. And that *was* his patch. The thieves, Jamie Maidment and Lewis Foreland, had been advised by their solicitor to plead not guilty, but thankfully they'd now seen the light — though not before going to the Crown Court and a jury being sworn in.

Horton told Shearer he had his Harley. As he collected his leather biking jacket and helmet from the witness waiting room, he thought what a breath of fresh air the new CCP was. The last one had been counting the days until his retirement and had become disillusioned with the criminal justice system. Not that Horton blamed him for that: he often despaired of it himself. But Shearer was clever, cooperative and keen. He'd recently arrived from London and had told Horton that the loss of his wife, killed in a car accident, had prompted him to make a fresh start in a city where not every street, shop and restaurant would remind him of his Jenny. It was the same name as Horton's mother, except he always thought of her as Jennifer. And while once he'd tried very hard to obliterate all memory of the woman who had abandoned him at the age of ten to the mercy of children's and foster homes, now he thought of her constantly, or rather as frequently as his workload permitted. The change of heart had come about as a result of a case in December when he'd discovered that her disappearance just over thirty years ago was not because she'd got sick of having a kid in tow and had run off with a man, but because someone had wanted her to vanish. He didn't yet know why or what had happened to her but he was getting closer to discovering the truth.

The October sky was overcast, threatening rain, and a brisk, chilly wind had sprung up. In the blustering gales Horton caught the smell of the sea coming off of the River Medina which fed down to Cowes and into the Solent. He headed out of Newport on the Harley and made for the abbey, pleased for once to be able to deliver good news and relieved to get out of the stuffy overheated courts. Even stopping off at the abbey he would easily make the one o'clock sailing to Portsmouth, which would get him back to his office by about two. Time enough to clear up some paperwork and see what else had come in over the last few days while he'd been preoccupied with this case. But as the houses gave way to fields, he sensed in himself a reluctance to head straight for the abbey. There was somewhere en route that he wanted to see. There would be another sailing at one thirty and again at two o'clock. Cantelli was more than capable of handling anything that had cropped up and, if it was urgent, the sergeant would have rung him. Or their boss, DCI Lorraine Bliss, would have been squawking down the line at him.

He indicated off the main road and turned onto a narrow and deserted country lane. Perhaps it was reading that newspaper article while waiting to be called into court that had made him think of Lord Ames who, it was reported, was leading a trade delegation to Russia. Or perhaps it was the fact that one of the stolen items recovered from Jamie Maidment and Lewis Foreland had been a wrought-iron weather vane made by the famous sculptor Albert Trostley and donated to the abbey by Lord Richard Ames, one of the abbey's generous benefactors. But Horton didn't need any article to conjure up thoughts of the trim and aloof aristocrat. Since meeting him in August he'd mentally replayed the conversation that had taken place between them in the exclusive Castle Hill Yacht Club in Cowes. Ames had denied any involvement in Jennifer's disappearance but Horton didn't believe him. Getting proof of that though was another matter. And he didn't think he'd find it at Ames's Isle of Wight holiday property, which was where he was heading.

He pulled up at a junction by a small copse and withdrew an Ordnance Survey map from the inside of his jacket. After consulting it and putting it back he swung right, heading towards the sea. The lane was narrower now, barely wide enough for one car to pass. The trees hadn't yet lost their foliage and the leaves were deepening to a blaze of red and gold.

Soon the tarmacked road gave way to a gravel track. A sign on his right said: 'Private Road. No access.' Horton ignored it. He noted a group of stone buildings in the fields on his left. They looked uninhabited and the tall chimney on one of them hinted it might have been used as a furnace at some stage. There was a small track on his right.

The trees closed in again on either side of him and within seconds he was pulling up in front of a solid grey stone wall and a pair of sturdy wooden gates, behind which were more trees. The house was obscured from his view. Were there security cameras? If so then they were well hidden. Perhaps even now someone was inside the house viewing monitors and a police unit would arrive to ask him what he was doing here.

He could press the intercom and see if Lord Ames kept a housekeeper or security guard on the premises, but he didn't. Instead, he swung the Harley around and returned along the track until he came to the fields now on his right and the track on his left. He took the track heading north, towards the sea. After about a third of a mile it petered out and in front of him was a dense wood. He silenced the engine and again consulted his map. There were no public footpaths and a sign bordering the woods told him they were 'Private' and that 'Trespassers would be prosecuted'. He stuffed the map in his jacket and climbed the low fence.

As he trekked through the undergrowth his mind roamed back to what he had unearthed about Jennifer since being given — or rather discovering — a photograph on his boat left by a man who had called himself Edward Ballard and who had alleged he'd been attacked while mooring up in the same marina where Horton lived. Since then, Ballard had vanished — that is he'd never existed to begin with, certainly not with that name. Horton had checked all the databases. He'd since learned that the black and white photograph had been taken on 13 March 1967 during the first sit-in protest at the London School of Economics, where Jennifer had been working as a typist. It was a picture of six young men, with one of them being Lord Richard Ames. Horton recalled their confrontation in the yacht club.

'Where did you get this?' Ames had asked him lightly, but behind the jocular tone Horton had sensed anger.

'From a friend,' was all Horton had been prepared to say. Ames hadn't asked which friend. 'It's a long time since

I've seen it. I hardly recognized myself,' Ames had to admit it. There was no denying it was him.

Horton had asked if Jennifer had taken the picture but Ames claimed memory loss. Convenient. He'd told Horton that she'd been friendly with one of the men in the picture, James Royston, who, Horton had since ascertained, had died of a drugs overdose in 1970. The coroner's report said Royston had been found dead in a sordid bedsit in London with puncture marks in his right arm and enough heroin in his system to knock out a rhinoceros. No one claimed to have known that Royston had been a drug addict, but then no one had denied it either. The sister who had raised her younger brother after their parents had died hadn't seen or heard from him for five years.

Ames had told Horton he'd come down from Cambridge, where he was a student, to the London School of Economics that day to visit a friend called Timothy Wilson. He was the man beside him in the picture and had later been killed in a motorbike accident in 1969 on a deserted road across Salisbury Plain on a calm, clear April night. It hadn't been obligatory to wear a crash helmet back then, so Wilson had stood little chance of surviving. But what had caused the crash, Horton wondered. Wilson *could* have been frightened by an owl, except there weren't any on Salisbury Plain, and neither had there been any army manoeuvres across the plain that night. The autopsy report confirmed that there was no alcohol or trace of drugs in Wilson's system, and nothing was wrong with the bike. The coroner had put it down to a moment's lack of concentration. That was possible. Perhaps Wilson had been upset or angry about something. Perhaps he'd even had a row with Ames and had been returning from Ames's Wiltshire estate, which Horton believed to be likely. Horton had travelled that route himself three weeks ago.

The third dead man, Zachary Benham, had no living relatives. In fact, like Horton, he'd been illegitimate. But unlike him, Benham had been a product of a wartime romance or perhaps just a one-night stand, and his mother had given birth and handed him over to the orphanage. But Zachary Benham had proved himself to be resourceful and clever. He must have been, thought Horton, to have earned himself a place at the London School of Economics in 1966. But he had died along with twenty-three other men in a fire that had raged through their ward in Goldsworth Psychiatric Hospital in Surrey in 1968. The hospital had closed in the 1980s. The two night nurses on duty, Sheila Grover and Malcolm Bellings, were both dead. Nurse Sheila Grover had sounded the alarm ten minutes after the fire had started, allowing it to get a stronghold and it had spread rapidly, trapping the men inside the ward. They had evacuated the building but too late for those twenty-three men, including Zachary Benham.

Horton pushed aside a menacing-looking shrub that blocked his path through the dark woods and pressed on. During the last two months he'd checked the Police National Computer, and the databases of the Inland Revenue, National Insurance and vehicle licensing authority for traces of the last two remaining men in the photograph. Both had long hair and beards, and Antony Dormand had his right arm draped around the shoulders of the man on his right, Rory Mortimer. There was no record of Antony Dormand or Rory Mortimer ever having married, divorced or died, paid taxes or worked, in the UK at least. He didn't have access to international databases unless he enlisted the help of Agent Harriet Ames, who was based at Europol in The Hague, and he couldn't do that because he was certain she would report back to her father, Lord Richard Ames.

Suddenly Horton was out of the trees and on a shingle beach. Across a choppy grey sea he could see a small sailing yacht heading west towards Cowes, a motor boat going east towards Fishbourne, and further out, a container ship and a fishing boat. In the distance, he could also see the buildings on the shores of the mainland of Gosport and Portsmouth.

He turned westwards, keeping the line of the woods on his left, which after a short distance gave onto a wall beyond which were more trees and clearly the rear of Ames's property. Ahead Horton found his progress impeded by a long and sturdily constructed pontoon. It was almost high tide and the sea was lapping under and against it. The pontoon was roped off on both sides with a sign that declared it was a 'Private Beach' with 'No Permitted Entry'. He guessed the sign on the other side and at the end of the pontoon said the same. The pontoon led up to a sturdy wooden gate in the wall. Horton knew that anything below the average high-water mark belonged to the Crown and therefore anyone was permitted to walk on it. Unfortunately though, the length of the pontoon prohibited that, because even with the tide out, the sea would still reach the end and no one but a limbo dancer would be able to get under the pontoon.

'You won't be able to get round it, not unless you fancy getting very wet.'

Startled, Horton spun round to find a solidly built man scrutinizing him with curious and intelligent grey eyes in a bronzed weather-beaten face that sported a close-cropped greying beard. He was about six feet tall and wore shabby, soiled shorts and old leather sandals over bare feet that matched the sun tan on his face, arms and hands. He looked to be in his mid to late fifties but could be older.

'His Lordship likes his privacy,' the man added.

Horton thought he heard a hint of a Welsh accent. 'His Lordship?' He decided to play dumb.

'Lord Ames, landowner, property tycoon, yachtsman, businessman and lots more besides.'

'You know him?'

'Do I look as though I'd know someone like that?' the man answered with a smile, gesturing at his clothes. His lined faced crinkled up as his grey eyes studied Horton keenly.

Horton returned the smile. 'You never know.' He began to head back to the woods. The man fell into step beside him.

'And you don't look as though you belong here,' he said, eyeing Horton's motorcycle jacket, not with hostility or suspicion, but with interest.

'I took a wrong turning. I thought this was the way to the abbey.'

'That's the other side of Wootton Creek and the ferry terminal, about seven miles to the east,' the man answered, examining Horton disbelievingly.

He didn't blame him. It had been a pretty feeble excuse.

'If you fancied a spot of robbery, casing the joint and all that, my advice is don't. You'd be wasting your time. It's better protected than Fort Knox.'

'You've tried?' Horton teased.

'No, but a man who protects his privacy that fiercely has to have good security. Not that Lord Ames is a recluse when he's here — on the contrary, he entertains. I've seen his guests arrive.'

'Where do you live?' Horton tried not to sound like a policeman asking questions but to his ear he always did.

'Not far. I often come this way; you never know what you might find washed up on the beach. I look for flotsam and jetsam to turn it into art, or anyway, that's my excuse for bumming around beaches. It beats having a metal detector at the end of your arm and things clamped to your ears. I like the sound of the sea.'

Horton did too. 'And do you sell what you make?'

'When and where I can.'

'You have a studio?'

The man laughed. 'Nothing quite so grand.'

They had reached the edge of the woods. Horton halted. Clearly the man was reluctant to divulge where he lived and why should he to a complete stranger? No, he was wise to be cagey. 'And what name should I look out for if I'd like to buy any of your flotsam and jetsam?' Horton asked.

The man thrust a bronzed hand into the pocket of his shabby shorts and fetched out a grubby card. As Horton took it from the strong, suntanned hand he caught a glimpse of something deep in the man's eyes but couldn't place what. He glanced down at the card. It contained only a name: Wyndham Lomas. 'There's no address or contact number,' he said.

'I like my privacy too.'

Horton smiled and pocketed the card. Lomas made no attempt to move off. Perhaps he intended staying on the beach looking for his flotsam and jetsam. But it was time Horton was going. He had to call at the abbey. As he clambered over the fence into the woods Lomas called out, 'Don't let the dogs get you.' Horton hoped he was joking.

Twenty minutes later he was pulling into the abbey car park unmolested by any guard dogs. He headed for the café and gift shop where he found the café manager, Cliff Yately, a well-built man in his late forties with a round, friendly, open face, who greeted him warmly but with wariness in his wide, dark-brown eyes. Horton quickly reassured him that he was the bearer of good news and asked where he could find Brother Norman.

'With the vet and Jay in the piggery,' Yately replied.

It was just beyond the tea shop gardens. Horton saw the lean monk talking to a scruffily dressed man who was looking on with concern as another slender man beside them was examining a large golden red pig that Horton had been told was a Tamworth. Jay Ottley, the pig man, like Yately was not a monk, but unlike Yately, Ottley lived at the abbey. It had been Ottley who had discovered the robbery on his way to feed the pigs and had reported it to Brother Norman. As Horton drew level Brother Norman looked up and instantly appeared anxious. Ottley's attention for a moment was diverted from his beloved pigs. He scratched his shaggy greying beard with a worried frown on his careworn face. Horton understood why they looked concerned. Neither wanted to be called to give evidence in court, and now they'd be spared that.

Brother Norman said something to Ottley that Horton couldn't catch and stepped out of the piggery. 'Not bad news I hope, Inspector?' he said, folding his hands into the sleeves of his black habit, drawing Horton a short distance away. Horton found it as difficult to put an age to him now as he had the first time he'd met him in early July, when he'd informed the monk that the items stolen from the abbey had been recovered. Brother Norman's lined face peered out from the cowl, his pale blue eyes worried. He could be anything between mid-fifties and seventy. Since that initial meeting Horton had spoken with the monk several times, and over the last month leading up to the trial, he'd called here weekly, in his own time, to keep him abreast of developments in the hope of alleviating some of the anxiety. He needn't have come personally. He could have delegated it to DS Norris but he didn't trust the short, balding, overweight Isle of Wight detective to be reassuring. And besides, Horton liked coming here. He found it restful. But there had been another reason for his interest. Thea Carlsson.

He'd grown close to Thea during an investigation on the island in January. She had understood his anger and pain at his mother's desertion. She had claimed to be psychic and told him that his mother wanted to be found. He didn't know about that and he didn't really believe all that bollocks, but Thea had been the only person he had spoken to about Jennifer, apart from Cantelli. He'd barely said anything to Catherine, his ex-wife, sensing that she wouldn't really have been interested. And besides, their marriage had broken down before he'd discovered that his mother hadn't been the hard-bitten tart he'd been led to believe. Thea had stayed in the abbey guest house but had returned to her home country, Sweden, as soon as the investigation into her brother's death was over, making it clear to him that she needed space and time to herself. He'd never bothered to follow it up. Since Catherine had thrown him out, choosing to believe a false allegation of rape against him when he'd been working undercover, he'd been on his own. Just as he'd always been alone, he thought, since the age of ten. And lately he'd begun to feel his loneliness more keenly than ever.

He pushed aside his thoughts and gave Brother Norman what he hoped was a reassuring smile. 'For once it's not bad news,' he said, thinking it sad that most people associated the police as harbingers of doom. 'The men who robbed the abbey have changed their plea to guilty. So there's no need for you or anyone else here to appear in court. They'll be sentenced on Monday and your possessions can be returned to you after that.'

Brother Norman looked heartedly relieved. 'I'll tell Jay that; he will be pleased, as am I. Thank you, Inspector, for taking the time and trouble to come here personally to tell us.' He dashed a glance behind him and back to Horton. He seemed distracted. 'I must go. It's almost time for Sexts, a short service before dinner,' he explained to Horton's baffled look. 'I mustn't be late.'

Horton could see from the abbey clock that it was close on one. But despite his anxiety to get to his devotions, Brother Norman hesitated. 'I'm sorry I can't repay your diligence and success, Inspector, by giving you hopeful news of Thea Carlsson in return, but even if I knew where she was, I wouldn't be able to betray her confidence.'

'I know. Forget I asked,' Horton replied lightly, but he felt embarrassed that he'd even raised the subject. He didn't want Brother Norman to feel he owed him a favour.

'You'll come to see us again, won't you?' Brother Norman said. 'Even though the ordeal of the thefts is over.'

'Of course.' But Horton thought it might be best to put the abbey — and Thea — behind him once and for all. Maybe Brother Norman sensed his secret thought because before he hurried off to his prayers, he threw Horton a parting glance that held doubt and something akin to regret in the pale blue eyes and lined face.

Horton made the two o'clock sailing comfortably and grabbed a sandwich and a coffee on the ferry. Fifty minutes later he was heading along the corridor to CID. Bliss was in her office, on the phone, but before he'd gone a few steps she hailed him. He stifled a groan and turned back to see her skinny, upright figure in the doorway. She jerked her head to indicate she wanted him in her office. There in her customary slim black skirt and white shirt she eyed him as she always did, with distaste.

'I've just been phoning CID — where is everyone?' she snapped.

She made it sound as though he had half a dozen staff instead of two. 'I don't know, Ma'am. I've just come in.'

'Then you'll have to do.'

For what, he wondered. Clearly by her tone he was her last resort. Her disapproval of him was rooted in his method of policing, which went contrary to everything she stood for. Bliss was a strictly by-the-book copper, email, memo and meeting mad, while he was too hands-on, too maverick and allergic to anything that smacked of management speak, her favourite language. He eyed her narrow face and sharp green eyes. If he had expected her to ask about the court case then it looked as though he was in for a disappointment.

'We have a missing man,' she announced crisply.

Two it seemed, if you counted Cantelli and Walters.

'His name is Jasper Kenton. He's been missing since yesterday afternoon. He's a private investigator and the business partner of Eunice Swallows who owns the Swallows Investigation Agency. I want you to take the report.'

Horton didn't bother hiding his surprise. 'A uniformed officer can do that,' he replied, wondering why Bliss was keen to send someone of his rank out to it.

'I'm ordering you to do it, Inspector, and if you have a problem with taking orders then I suggest you change career.'

And wouldn't you like that, Horton said to himself.

'The office is in Albert Road, Southsea. Well, what are you waiting for?'

You to climb on your broomstick and fly away, Horton thought, with annoyance at her manner and the tone of her command. He got the address and headed out of the station. He'd never heard of the Swallows Investigation Agency or of Jasper Kenton or Eunice Swallows. But then he hadn't come across every private investigator in the city. What made this one so special, he wondered, that Bliss was prepared to sacrifice usual procedure? Perhaps there was more to Jasper Kenton's vanishing act than Bliss had told him. He'd find out soon enough. But as he drew up outside the office above a bohemian-styled café on the corner of a busy main thoroughfare, he couldn't help feeling this was a waste of his time — that Jasper Kenton had probably taken off for a long weekend and had simply forgotten to tell his partner.

CHAPTER TWO

'Of course he wouldn't have forgotten to inform me,' snapped the woman behind the large, pristine desk in the spacious office, viewing Horton over the top of her gold-rimmed spectacles as though he was an imbecile. Eunice Swallows was in her mid-forties, dressed plainly in shapeless black trousers and a black long-sleeved top. Her brown hair was short, sensible and tidy; she wore no make-up and the only jewellery he could see were small gold stud earrings. 'Jasper is most efficient.'

'Could he have gone to stay with friends or family?' persisted Horton.

'No. I've checked. Jasper only has a sister living in Marlborough but she hasn't seen him for years.'

'Friends then?'

'Jasper doesn't have any.'

How do you know, thought Horton, raising a sceptical eyebrow.

'He's a very private person,' she added, pursing her lips, clearly annoyed that her statement needed expanding. 'He left the office at four thirty on Thursday and should have been in today. I thought he might have overslept although that would be extremely unlikely. Jasper is always punctual. I

14

rang his mobile phone — he doesn't have a landline; says it's a waste of money — but I only got his voicemail. I have left several messages and I emailed him. When he didn't reply by lunch time, I grew more concerned. I thought he might be ill so I went to his flat.'

'Which is where?'

'Emsworth.'

A small village fronting on to Chichester Harbour, ten miles to the east of Portsmouth.

'We each have a key to the other's home in case of emergencies. Jasper wasn't there and there was no evidence that he had returned home last night. No unwashed crockery lying around or in the dishwasher and his bed was made up, but that's how I would expect to find the flat even if he had been home all night and left early this morning. Jasper is meticulously tidy.'

'Obsessively so?'

'No,' she snapped, moving a pen on her practically clear desk — apart from the computer, telephone and a buff-coloured folder — so that it lined up with her telephone.

'Have the neighbours or any of the other residents seen him or his car?'

'His flat isn't in a block of apartments. It's a converted sail loft with a garage below and there is only one other apartment next to him but that's a holiday let. It's empty at this time of year and yes, Inspector, I did check. There is a row of terraced cottages opposite, which face west whereas the sail loft faces south so there are no windows overlooking Jasper's apartment. However, I knocked on the property nearest to Jasper's and the woman who lives there said she didn't see him come home yesterday or leave this morning. I called DCI Bliss.'

'You know her?'

She looked as though she'd like to tell him that was none of his business. Her unplucked eyebrows puckered as she said curtly, 'Yes, from when she was stationed at Havant, before her promotion. Our offices were based there. We moved here a year ago.'

That explained the personal telephone call and why he'd not heard of Swallows before. It also explained why Bliss had sent him. He suspected that Eunice Swallows had called in a favour. He said, 'Mr Kenton has been missing just less than twenty-four hours; surely it's too early to get alarmed.'

She narrowed her eyes at him. 'It's totally out of character for Jasper to do this,' she crisply replied.

'What do *you* think might have happened to him?'

'He must have had an accident and before you ask, I have checked with the local hospital, and neither he, nor anyone fitting his description, has been admitted. There's nothing in his apartment to indicate where he was going either, but he could have been involved in a road accident elsewhere in the area or be lying injured somewhere. Here is a photograph of him.' She flicked open the folder on her desk and handed him a large photograph which she'd obviously printed off her computer. 'I've also emailed a couple of pictures to DCI Bliss and she can let you have them.'

Horton studied the slim, slight man with short thick dark hair, a thin face, solemn brown eyes and a serious expression, about mid-forties.

'I've printed off all Jasper's particulars including his address and vehicle license number.'

She gave him a sheet of paper, which he knew she must also have emailed to Bliss, as well as giving her the information she had relayed to him. It made a mockery of his visit here. Maybe by now Bliss had ordered Cantelli to run a check of the reported accidents and put out an alert. So why waste his time by sending him here? Perhaps Bliss was just trying to impress Eunice Swallows, or perhaps, as he'd thought earlier, she owed Swallows a favour. If that was the case then Bliss could have come herself, he thought with annoyance.

He consulted the sheet of paper Eunice Swallows had handed him. Jasper Kenton was forty-seven, single, five foot nine, weighed approximately ten and a half stone. He drove a new dark blue Vauxhall. The last time Eunice Swallows had seen him he'd been wearing a black two-piece suit and black slip-on shoes, a white shirt and maroon tie. He had no distinguishing marks or tattoos (how did she know, Horton wondered, unless Kenton himself had told her that) and he wore no jewellery.

'Was he carrying anything when he left the office?'

'His briefcase.'

'Containing what?'

'I don't know. I didn't search him,' she retorted. Then she added more evenly, 'It was his computer briefcase.'

'Any surveillance equipment in it?'

'I doubt it, but he has been issued with a camera, Dictaphone and video recorder. They're not at his apartment. They might be in the boot of his car.'

'So he could have been on surveillance.'

'No,' she answered with conviction.

'Why so sure?'

'Because we always discuss our cases and our actions so that we each know what the other is doing. It's best practice. He would have told me if he was undertaking a surveillance operation.'

'Perhaps something came up and he couldn't miss the chance of following it up.'

'Then he would have reported to me.'

'Maybe he couldn't and can't risk making contact. Perhaps his surveillance has taken him abroad or some distance away in the UK.'

But she was shaking her head. 'We always make it a rule to keep in touch. And he hasn't left the country because his passport is still here in the safe. We keep both our passports on the premises in case we need to go overseas in a hurry.' With that ruled out he asked, 'How did he seem?'

'Fine,' she answered crisply.

That was a fat lot of help. 'He wasn't anxious or excited?'

'I would have said if he was,' she said tartly. 'Jasper is rarely excited and never anxious.'

What is he, a machine? Horton was beginning to think this cool, tidy and organized individual was a figment of Eunice

Swallows's imagination. Either that or Kenton was exceptionally good at hiding his emotions, something Horton had once been expert at, but the recent events of his divorce and trying to get to the truth of his mother's disappearance had proved otherwise. He'd had momentary flashes of anger both with Catherine and with Lord Ames.

'Did Mr Kenton say anything to the staff about what he was doing last night?'

'No. We don't gossip and we don't have time to waste on idle chit chat.'

She was sounding more like Bliss with every minute. Perhaps Kenton had got fed up working for her and had taken off. Horton wouldn't blame him if he had.

'What is he currently working on?' Could it be something that might have caused someone to want him to disappear, he wondered. Was that why Bliss was concerned?

'Background checks on individuals, fraudulent insurance claims, suspected matrimonial infidelities, that sort of thing,' she said with an icy stare. Horton knew that expression of old. It said *don't ask me anymore because I'm not going to tell you.*

'Did he have any meetings scheduled for late yesterday afternoon or today?'

'No.'

'Have you contacted his clients to check if he's been in touch or called in to see them?'

'Of course not. I don't want them alarmed.'

No, mislaying one of your operatives didn't exactly instil confidence in a private investigation company. 'We could speak to them,' he said, anticipating the reaction he was going to get.

'No,' she said vehemently. 'This has nothing to do with any of them.'

'How can you be so sure?'

'I am. Look, put out the usual alerts. Surely even you can do that?' she added cuttingly.

Yes, and any police officer could have done that. Horton rose. He briefly thought about questioning the staff he'd seen when he'd been shown into Eunice Swallows's office — a very thin lady in her late fifties with a short severe haircut and two men stationed at computers, one in his mid-twenties, the other late thirties — but he'd already spent too much of his time here. He almost changed his mind though when Eunice Swallows whisked him out at the speed of light. None of the staff looked up from their desks. Probably too terrified of her to even blink.

He returned to the station, irritated with both Bliss and that Swallows woman, wondering if Bliss's strategy was to dump on him as many mundane and low-ranking jobs as she could as a way of making him so uncomfortable and angry that he'd apply for a transfer. *Just let her try*, he thought, marching into the CID operations room where he found both DC Walters and Sergeant Cantelli.

'How did it go?' Cantelli asked.

'My interview with Ms Swallows?' Horton tetchily replied.

'No,' Cantelli said, puzzled. 'The court case.'

He brought them both up to date with the outcome of that and the assignment Bliss had sent him on, which drew a surprised raising of dark eyebrows from Cantelli. 'They know one another,' Horton explained. Tossing the sheet of paper and the photograph Eunice Swallows had given him of Jasper Kenton onto Walters's desk, he added, 'Make out the missing persons report and put out the usual alerts, but it's low priority until Bliss tells us differently. So where were you two when your boss needed you before having to scrape the barrel by sending me?'

'In a Greek restaurant,' Cantelli answered.

'There's been another attack?' asked Horton, perching on one of several empty desks in the room.

Cantelli nodded. 'In the same road, and the same as the other two, racist slogans painted on the kitchen and passage-way walls.'

That made three in a fortnight. The other restaurants targeted had been Bangladeshi and Cantonese in a road in

Southsea just off the seafront, which seemed to boast more foreign restaurants than the United Nations had members.

'It's also the same MO, rear door forced, wouldn't have kept a nine-year-old out,' Cantelli relayed. 'And the security system was defunct. Nothing stolen or wrecked. Walters took some photos with his mobile phone.'

Walters tapped into his computer where he'd uploaded the photographs. Horton studied the pictures. The lettering was in large dark-blue paint scrawled across the wall of a passageway that led into the kitchen and on the available wall space in the kitchen. The slogans included 'Free UK of dirty immigrants' and 'Filth go home'.

Cantelli, looking over Horton's shoulder, said, 'It's polite as far as slogans go and no swastikas.'

Yes, and that was unusual. They'd had them carved on gravestones in the Jewish part of a local cemetery and on the walls of the four mosques in the city, but that had been some months ago and it didn't look to be the work of the same vandals.

'I'm organizing extra patrols in the area over the weekend,' Cantelli continued. 'And I've requested copies of all CCTV footage. Some of the other restaurants have their own and they're sending them over. We might catch sight of chummy.'

To Walters, Horton said, 'Have you got a list of the restaurant's suppliers?'

'Going back later to pick it up,' Walters answered, opening his desk drawer to reveal a mini larder and plucking out a bar of chocolate. 'I've got the list of employees though, and past employees. I was just going to check them with the staff lists from the other two restaurants. Most of the names sound foreign though so I can't see it being one of them.'

'Do it anyway. It might be a disgruntled employee who's been overlooked for a pay rise or promotion, or a former employee who's been sacked in favour of someone of a different nationality.' Horton addressed Cantelli. 'Fix up a meeting with DI Grimes and the STOP team.' It was one new initiative that Horton agreed with. The STOP team had been set up specifically to focus on hate crime and comprised officers from Special Branch and Counter Terrorism. It didn't mean that they were looking for a terrorist but someone holding strong views could end up taking action or being groomed by those who didn't care how they achieved their aims or who they maimed and killed in the process. 'You might also like to ask Tim Shearer if he could send one of his staff along. When we catch this bugger, I don't want him walking on a technicality.' He made for Bliss's office, knocked perfunctorily and entered.

'Well?' she said, looking up from her computer.

Tersely he relayed the outcome of his interview with Eunice Swallows, knowing that Bliss already had this information from Ms Swallows herself. She'd probably telephoned Bliss the moment he'd left. 'There's little we can do except the usual, unless Eunice Swallows is prepared to let us have a list of the clients Jasper Kenton is working for and those he is investigating, in case they have something to do with his disappearance. There is also the chance that's he's absconded with funds stolen from the firm or from one of his clients.'

'I doubt that,' she said primly.

How did she know?

Her phone rang. She nodded dismissal at him.

Glad to get away from her, he returned to his office. It was almost five and he had little to show for his day's work, but he was curious to know more about Swallows. He did an Internet search on her name, and within seconds he was reading how they had built up an enviable track record of success since being established four years ago. Before then both Eunice Swallows and Jasper Kenton had been working alone. Eunice Swallows came with vast experience in the field of retail fraud and employee theft. Jasper Kenton had worked with major corporations in London and was an expert in computer and Internet-based investigation, digital forensic examination and cyber security services. Something Eunice Swallows hadn't told him, though to be fair he hadn't asked. But it made him consider what he had just mentioned to Bliss. Could Kenton have stolen from a client or from the agency itself and absconded with the proceeds? If he was that much of a cyber expert then it was unlikely that anyone would notice for some time.

The website also mentioned that Kenton acted as an expert technical witness, providing case and trial consultancy in the field of cybercrime. Horton hadn't come across him but then he hadn't been involved in any complex cases that involved a high level of computer forensic data and Internet use. That would have been the remit of the Hi-Tech Crime Unit, the Serious Organized Crime Agency, or the Intelligence Directorate. Horton had dealt with pornography cases and investigations where computer evidence had been vital but the Hi-Tech Unit had assisted with those. Maybe he'd ask around internally to see if Kenton's name rang any bells. And perhaps Tim Shearer had heard of Kenton.

He made a mental note to ask him on Monday if Kenton hadn't shown up by then.

He saw Walters leave. Twenty minutes later Cantelli stuck his head round the door. 'The extra patrols are set up for after the restaurants close from one a.m. onwards. Let's hope it's a quiet night for fights otherwise they might get called away. And I've arranged a meeting with DI Grimes and his team for Monday morning, 9.30. Tim Shearer said he'd come himself. I'm off home now, unless there's anything . . .'

'There isn't,' Horton quickly broke in. He knew how important Cantelli's family was to him and they were deprived of the sergeant's presence enough times without him adding to it unnecessarily. Not that Charlotte ever complained and neither did Cantelli's five children, as far as Horton was aware. He wished Cantelli a good weekend with a silent longing that he could be with his own daughter, Emma. Maybe if he lived in a flat instead of on his boat Catherine would let Emma stay with him. Catherine thought the boat too cold and unsuitable for an eight-year-old. But he hated the idea of living in a poky apartment crammed in the middle of the city. At least with his boat he had the space of the marina and the sea beyond it, and he could satisfy his restlessness by sailing. Not tonight though, he thought, as he headed home in the dark and the rain. The wind was howling through the masts when he reached the marina. The rain was ricocheting off the deck like bullets and the sea was slapping against the hull of his yacht. Most days he enjoyed returning but tonight he felt a stab of envy at Cantelli in his warm, family house on the eastern edge of Portsmouth, surrounded by people who loved him and whom he loved.

He gazed around the chilly cabin, feeling its emptiness. His loneliness settled on him like a heavy weight. If he could just have someone. He had hoped that Harriet Ames, who he'd worked with a couple of times, might be that someone until he'd come to suspect that her father might be involved in his mother's disappearance. Perhaps he was destined to be alone, he thought, making a coffee and trying to shake off the clawing suffocating feeling of depression. Even Bliss had someone, he considered with bitterness, imagining her chatting with Eunice Swallows over a drink, discussing Jasper Kenton's disappearance. He didn't know that for a fact, but when had facts got in the way of depression?

Irritated with himself he slammed down his coffee cup and rose. Sitting here feeling bloody sorry for himself wasn't going to get him anywhere. There were only three antidotes for that: one was sailing, which was completely out of the question in this weather; another was work, which he'd had enough of for one day. So that left him with the third. He changed and went for a run.

CHAPTER THREE

Saturday

Horton was at his desk early the next morning. He had no need to be there and would have gone sailing if the weather forecast had been more optimistic, but rain and high winds had been forecast and it was better to occupy his time catching up with his backlog of paperwork than mooching about the boat. His run along the promenade last night had helped to lift the depression for a while, but the early hours of the morning had seen it return with a vengeance. After trying unsuccessfully for two hours to shake it off and return to sleep he'd given up and headed for work. He'd made good inroads into answering his emails and filling in forms — although the pile never seemed to diminish, only expand — and at 8.15 a.m. he thought he'd earned himself a canteen breakfast. He headed towards it, thinking he would treat himself to the full works — eggs, bacon, sausages, beans, tomatoes and anything else on offer — when Sergeant Warren intercepted him.

'Jasper Kenton's car's been found,' he said.

'Where?' Horton asked, half expecting Warren to say at the Continental Ferry Port or Southampton Airport car park, which would fit with his theory of Kenton doing a runner with a client's money. So he was surprised when Warren said it was parked in a resident's space at the Admiralty Towers car park on Queen Street. That was a modern seven-storey block of apartments close to The Hard and not far from the waterfront and marina at Oyster Quays. Had Kenton dumped his car there and taken a boat across to the continent or to the Channel Islands?

Warren continued. 'The resident whose space the car's parked in arrived there half an hour ago. He called the car park company to complain, but when he got no reply, he called us. He's the "I pay my rates and your wages so get someone down here now and move it" type.'

Horton knew them well.

'He says he has never seen the vehicle before and has no idea who its owner is. I've sent a unit over to pacify him but told the officers not to touch the car.'

Horton didn't have Jasper Kenton's car keys. They could force an entry and that would probably be quicker than asking Eunice Swallows to go to Kenton's house and return with a spare set of keys. Judging by what she had told him yesterday Kenton probably had them hanging in a special place, neatly labelled. But Horton had another idea.

'Call Nigel Bowman, give him the vehicle details and ask him to meet me there.'

Bowman was head mechanic at the police vehicle workshop. It would take Bowman about forty minutes to get a set of keys that would unlock the Vauxhall. There was the chance that Jasper Kenton was inside one of the apartments and had inadvertently parked his car in the wrong space. Horton could get a couple of officers knocking on doors but that was a lot of doors to knock on — and why hadn't Kenton called his business partner and told her he was there? Maybe because he was ill inside one of the flats, or perhaps even dead.

He instructed Warren to call Eunice Swallows and ask her if any of the clients Kenton was investigating lived at

Admiralty Towers or if Kenton knew anyone there. She'd claimed he had no friends but perhaps Kenton had a lover he didn't want Eunice Swallows to know about. He could understand that, having met the woman.

It was just after 8.30 a.m. when he swung into the ground level car park beneath the glass and steel apartment block. There were two parking areas: one for residents' parking, the other for public parking, the latter of which was used mainly by those visiting the nearby Historic Dockyard. As that didn't open until ten a.m. it was deserted. There were a few cars in the residents' spaces and a bad-tempered looking squat man in his late forties standing by a new high-performance sports car. Judging by his expression and his wild gesticulations he was haranguing PC Liz Jenkins, who remained stoically unmoved, maintaining only a look of polite interest on her attractive dark face. Horton knew the expression well. Jenkins would have experienced a lot worse.

The man's eyes flicked to Horton, registered the Harley and Horton's clothes and rapidly dismissed him. Horton was used to that. No one expected a police officer to be riding a motorbike unless he was a traffic cop in uniform. Horton crossed to PC Allen who was standing by Kenton's car.

'No keys in the ignition, sir,' Allen announced. 'It's locked. I tried the handle — with gloves on,' he added hastily, 'but Mr Roger Watling, that's the man with PC Jenkins, says he tried all the doors and the boot.'

Horton peered inside the dark-blue saloon. It was spotlessly clean and tidy with nothing visible on the seats and it clearly had not been broken into. The exterior and windscreen, however, were rain spattered and a little dirty. It had stopped raining at about three a.m. but that didn't mean the vehicle hadn't been parked here; he had no idea when it might last have been cleaned.

There was no ticket on the windscreen, which was no more than he had expected, not only because the vehicle was in a resident's space and therefore wouldn't have needed a ticket but also because this was the type of car park where you collected your ticket at the barrier and inserted it into the machine before leaving, paying only for the number of hours you'd been parked. The residents had their own entrance lane and barrier, which clearly Kenton must have entered by. There might be CCTV, he thought, glancing around, and with a bit of luck there might also be a system that had number-plate reading technology which could tell them when Kenton had parked here. However, the fact the car was in the residents' area and not the public car park meant that Kenton must either have been buzzed through by someone he knew living here, or he had a pass. There was every likelihood therefore that he was inside the building. Perhaps even now he was in one of these flats, perfectly safe and happy, wallowing in an excess of sexual bliss. But why park in Roger Watling's space and not the space of the person he knew? Perhaps he'd just got it wrong, but that didn't fit with the description Eunice Swallows had given him.

Horton crossed to Roger Watling and received a hostile glare from the short chubby man, dressed expensively but casually in chinos and a leather jacket over a T-shirt. His expression changed to one of shock when Horton introduced himself and showed his ID. 'You live here, Mr Watling?' he politely enquired.

'No. I live in London. I have an apartment here. I come down some weekends. Look, all I want you to do is move the bloody thing,' Watling declared, exasperated. His eyes were bloodshot and Horton could smell garlic and alcohol on his breath.

'Do you know a Mr Jasper Kenton?'

'No. Is that whose car it is?'

Horton retrieved his mobile phone where he'd uploaded a photograph of Jasper Kenton and showed it to Watling. 'Do you recognize this man?'

'Never set eyes on him. When are you going to get it shifted?' He ran his stubby fingers through his gelled hair.

'As soon as we can, sir. Have you any idea why Mr Kenton should park his car in your space?'

'None whatsoever. Now if—'

'How are residents permitted entry to the car park?'

'We have a fob.'

'May I see it?'

Watling huffed and puffed but thrust his fat fingers into the pocket of his trousers and pulled out his keys. 'That's it.' He indicated a small flat black pad on his key ring. 'I press it against the pad at the barrier and that gets me into the car park and into the apartment block.' He jerked his head at a door behind him. A sign above it read: 'Entrance to Apartments'.

'Were you here last night?'

'No. Look, I told this officer. I arrived this morning at about eight o'clock and found that car in my space.'

'Have you been up to your apartment?'

'No. I rang the car parking company and then you lot and was told to wait.'

Horton turned to PC Jenkins. 'Perhaps you'd like to go with Mr Watling to his apartment.'

'You don't think this man is inside it!' Watling cried, alarmed.

'We have to check, sir.'

'He bloody well better not be.'

But Horton wondered if Kenton had been investigating Roger Watling. If he had though, he'd hardly be likely to park in his space.

Watling marched off, leaving PC Jenkins to hurry after him. Horton didn't think Watling was going to be too pleased when they asked him for his prints and a statement. But maybe it wouldn't come to that if it transpired that Kenton was in the building.

Horton addressed PC Allen. 'Call in Watling's licence number and check it out.' His phone rang as a car pulled in and a long thin man with a hooked nose and cheery smile climbed out. He was brandishing a set of keys. It was Warren on the phone.

'Eunice Swallows is going to check if they have any clients who are resident at Admiralty Towers or if they are investigating anyone living there. She'll call you.'

Yeah, when? She'd told him yesterday that she and Kenton always discussed the cases fully.

So why the stalling tactics? The locks on the car gave a satisfying clunk as they sprang open. Pulling on latex gloves, Horton opened the passenger door and peered into the glove compartment. There were no driving gloves, as was usual these days, just the service history and car manual. He found a road atlas in the pouch behind the driver's door and nothing else. But there was an inbuilt satellite navigation system.

'Now for the boot,' he said to Bowman with a slight quickening of pulse. He'd looked into a few in his time and found some very nasty things. But there was no smell emanating from this one to warn them they might be in for a shock. Nevertheless, he tensed. Thankfully it was empty. There wasn't even a rug. And there was no sign of the surveillance equipment that Eunice Swallows said Jasper Kenton had been issued with and which she had suggested might be in his car. Allen came off the phone. 'Roger Watling's got two convictions for speeding. His main residence is registered as Battersea, London.'

PC Jenkins returned alone to say that there was no one in Roger Watling's apartment. 'I'm to let him know when the car is removed. He gave me the name and contact number of the managing agents.'

'Good, see if you can get a list of the residents.'

He was about to call Eunice Swallows, thinking he'd waited long enough for her to check her cases, when his phone rang and he saw that it was her.

'Have you found anything?' she asked. Did he detect a slight nervousness in her tone or was that just concern?

'No. Do you, or does Mr Kenton, know a Roger Watling?'

'No,' she answered promptly and firmly, which made Horton wonder if it was a lie.

'Is Mr Kenton investigating anyone who lives at Admiralty Towers?' he asked when she seemed reluctant to volunteer anything further.

There was a moment's silence, which gave Horton the answer, before she said, 'It's confidential.'

'Not if Mr Kenton is lying ill or injured inside an apartment here,' Horton said crisply, and clearly that wasn't Roger Watling's. That didn't mean Watling couldn't be involved in Kenton's disappearance though. They only had his word he'd arrived from London at about eight o'clock. 'I need the client's name and the number of the apartment.'

'The owner might not be there, and you can't break in.'

Oh, can't I, thought Horton, knowing he could if he suspected a crime had been committed inside the flat or if he had good reason to believe someone's life was in danger. A missing man and an abandoned car were good enough reason for him. Eunice Swallows must also know that.

'Do you want us to find Mr Kenton?' Horton asked tersely.

'Of course, but I can't let you trample over an investigation and put my client in a very difficult position, which is just what she wanted to avoid.'

Female then. 'Call her.' Or had Eunice Swallows already done that?

'I can't. We have an arrangement. You must understand how these things work.'

'All I understand is that you reported Jasper Kenton missing, you say you are concerned about his safety, and now you wish to obstruct us in our enquiries.'

'There is no need to be rude,' she snapped.

If that's rude, lady, you've led a sheltered life. Not bothering to hide his impatience he said, 'Does the apartment belong to your client?'

'It belongs to her husband.'

'A matrimonial investigation?' Horton said, quickly catching on.

'Yes.'

'This is Mr Kenton's investigation?' He thought it best to check.

'Yes.'

And Horton wondered if the errant husband had discovered Kenton watching him. Not through the concrete of the car park, but perhaps Kenton had followed this husband here. After parking his car, the husband had left the car park on foot and had gone outside to confront Kenton. But would he have invited Kenton in? Possibly, if he had decided he needed to tell Kenton about his affair. Kenton had gone up to the apartment where the two men had fought and where Jasper Kenton was lying injured or dead.

Eunice Swallows said, 'Jasper wasn't on surveillance though.'

'The name of the husband, Ms Swallows, and the number of his apartment, please.'

There was a moment's pause before she answered, 'Number twenty-five. It belongs to Brett Veerman, husband of Thelma Veerman. But you're not to mention the investigation or that his wife has hired us.'

'I won't,' he said, adding silently, *unless it's absolutely necessary*. He rang off after confirming he would call her back as soon as he could. Was Veerman up there now staring horrified at the bloodied corpse of the private investigator he'd attacked? Or had he killed him and absconded? Perhaps Veerman had killed Kenton in a mad moment of rage and had then killed himself, unable to live with the knowledge of what he'd done, or was that just Horton's imagination running wild? Probably. There was only one way to find out. To Allen he said, 'We'll knock politely. But better fetch the ram rod just in case.'

CHAPTER FOUR

The apartment was small, modern and minimalistic with bleached wooden flooring and horizontal slatted cream blinds covering the ceiling-to-floor windows. It was also tidy and spotlessly clean: no blood-spattered walls in the open plan living room, which gave onto a small kitchen, and no sign of Jasper Kenton, not even when Horton checked in the bathroom and double bedroom. And neither was there any sign of the owner, Brett Veerman.

If Jasper Kenton had been here then he'd left no trace, and Horton didn't think any of the residents would claim to have seen him. This was the sort of building where you didn't meet your neighbours — not because you were afraid of them, as might have been the case in the tower block where he'd lived with his mother, but because it was designed that way, little boxes behind closed doors. He doubted there was more than a handful of occupied flats on this floor anyway, which would be inhabited occasionally, used for weekends or a stepping-off place for the continent or the Isle of Wight. Nobody had emerged to see what was happening, even when Allen busted open the door.

He told Allen to call the locksmith and to stay outside the apartment. PC Jenkins was still with the car where she and Bowman were awaiting instructions. Horton crossed to the window and pulled back the blinds. He was looking down on the main road, which ran towards The Hard on his right, southwards, and to the centre of the city on his left, northwards. The apartment didn't have a sea view; instead, it overlooked the Royal Maritime Club on the corner of a road of council houses and maisonettes built during the 1950s when no property developer or councillor had envisaged the area becoming a tourist attraction. Then, the dockyard on his right hadn't been labelled 'historic' and neither had it housed attractions that now drew thousands of visitors from all around the world. It had been the city's major employer, with thousands of workers, and had attracted navies from around the globe.

He had a good view across the city to the east, including that of the giant tower blocks that graced the skyline. The nearest one had been his home until his mother had disappeared. He couldn't remember being afraid of any of his neighbours or any of the children who lived there. In fact, he'd played with the kids in the broken-down playground beneath their twenty-third-floor flat — the second they'd inhabited in that block of flats, he'd since learned, though he had no idea why they'd moved from the seventeenth floor to the top floor. Perhaps it was more spacious or there had been problems with the flat on the seventeenth floor.

There had been scuffles with the other kids but nothing any boy didn't usually get up to and nothing like the fights he'd endured after being moved from there to this area, or the battles that he'd fought at school. He'd learned the hard way to take care of himself. He'd come across a couple of those kids he'd fought with during his police career. Some had grown up to become violent criminals and he'd taken great pleasure in seeing them banged up.

He turned back to survey the room, wondering about the flat's owner. What sort of man was he? How old? What did he do for a living? Eunice Swallows had told him nothing about Brett Veerman, or her client, Thelma Veerman, and

Horton hadn't asked her about them; he'd been keen to see if Jasper Kenton had been here. He could get no firm impression of the apartment's owner from what he saw except that he was exceptionally neat. There were no pictures or photographs on the white painted walls. No magazines or newspapers lying around and there were no cabinets except for those in the kitchen. Aside from a sofa, which looked as though it had never been sat on, there was a small television set on a low table but no DVDs, no music system or CDs, and no books — all of which would have given him an idea of Veerman's tastes.

Horton crossed to the small kitchen and began to open the drawers, cupboards and the fridge. The latter was empty; the drawers contained only a few items of cutlery. In the cupboards were a packet of tea bags, a jar of coffee, two white mugs — both clean — and a white porcelain plate. There was no used crockery in the sink or in the dishwasher and no clothes in the washing machine. He touched the side of the kettle on the work surface — it was cold. Either Veerman had just purchased the flat or he rarely used it.

Did he entertain a lover here, as perhaps his wife suspected? If so, there was no sign of one, he thought, heading back into the bathroom. Again, his search of the cabinets yielded only a few male toiletries, including a toothbrush, toothpaste, aftershave (expensive), an electric razor and shower gel. The bed was made up, the sheets clean and there was no smell of perfume. There were also no women's clothes in the wardrobe and only a few men's clothes: two suits, both designer labels, good quality and expensive. He placed the trousers against him, and from the look of it, Veerman was about his height, six foot one. And the jacket? No, that wouldn't reach around his chest, so Veerman was leaner, with longer arms. There was a pair of casual trousers, the same size as the suit trousers, a couple of shirts, which by the collar size confirmed that Veerman was slender, and apart from some underwear only a couple of jumpers in the drawers, both bearing the labels of a prestigious London retailer. Of course, Horton had no confirmation that the clothes were Brett Veerman's; they could perhaps belong to a friend who was staying in the flat for a while.

He was curious to see Kenton's living accommodation, which would tell him more about the missing man than Eunice Swallows seemed inclined to divulge, unless it was as anonymous as this place, and the thought struck him that he only had Eunice Swallows's word that Kenton wasn't at his home. He considered this. Could the report of him missing be phoney? Perhaps Kenton and Swallows were lovers and she'd killed him and he was lying dead in his apartment. She was using delaying tactics to confuse the picture for when Kenton's body would eventually be discovered. She'd parked Kenton's car here to sidetrack them into making a connection with Brett Veerman. It sounded somewhat elaborate, but then people sometimes went to extreme lengths to hide a crime.

He called Eunice Swallows. She answered immediately.

'Well?' she demanded irritably, rather than with concern.

'Neither Mr Veerman nor Mr Kenton are here,' Horton replied evenly. He wasn't about to confide his thoughts to her.

'You entered forcibly.'

'Yes.' He heard her suck in her breath. 'It's OK; we'll make sure it's secure.'

'Then there's no need to pursue that line of enquiry any further.'

She seemed very keen to drop it, which made him keener to pursue it. Or perhaps that was her intention, to divert him from demanding to see Jasper Kenton's apartment. Not that he needed her permission. He could use the same reasoning to forcibly enter Kenton's home as he had at Veerman's.

He said, 'Mr Veerman *might* wonder why his front door lock has been changed.'

'You can say it was an attempted burglary.'

Oh, could he? Since when did she tell him how to do his job and when to lie?

35

When he didn't reply she said, 'I'm sure that Jasper's disappearance has nothing to do with the Veerman investigation.'

'Then why is his car here?'

'Maybe he was meeting someone.'

'Who? You said he didn't have any friends.' There was silence. He envisaged the disapproving scowl on her round, fleshy face. He continued, 'He must either have had a fob to get through the barrier system of the car park or someone buzzed him through.'

'It can't have been Brett Veerman. I can hardly see him letting Jasper in.'

Why not though? As he'd considered earlier, perhaps Veerman *had* invited Kenton in. Kenton had parked his car in one of the available spaces, which happened to belong to Roger Watling, and Kenton had left the car park in Brett Veerman's car. But to go where, and why? It could hardly be to discuss the matter with Mrs Veerman.

He said, 'I'd like to see Mr Kenton's apartment. And I need a list of his clients and those he was investigating in order to check them against the other residents here.'

'I really don't see that either is necessary.'

There was definitely something she was hiding. He was beginning to believe it was the death of Jasper Kenton and the fact that she might be involved in it. 'You can either meet us at his property or we'll force an entry.'

'I'll speak to DCI Bliss.'

'Do.' He rang off.

God, what a woman, he thought angrily. He was inclined to go ahead and order up a unit to accompany him to Emsworth but he thought sod it; Bliss for once could take responsibility for that, seeing as Ms Swallows was clearly her buddy. And Bliss could have her weekend disturbed. He wasn't even meant to be working. No doubt she'd soon be on the phone to him about it anyway and probably complaining that he'd been rude to Ms Swallows.

He gave instructions for Allen to wait until the lock was fixed and the door secure, and then with PC Jenkins to ask if anyone had seen Kenton. Horton emailed the photograph of Kenton to Allen's phone. He returned to the car park. There he asked Bowman to arrange for the car to be taken to the secure compound, where it would be held until they were instructed otherwise. PC Liz Jenkins went off to inform Roger Watling his space would soon be available.

Horton crossed to the barrier and studied the entry system. As well as the automatic fob entry there was a key pad. Perhaps someone had given Jasper Kenton the security code or he could have watched someone — Veerman perhaps — punch it in. Veerman would have had a fob though, unless he'd lost it. His lover then. And Kenton had simply copied it and gained entry.

Horton made a note of the company that had supplied the barrier entry system and headed for The Hard where he bought a coffee and a bacon sandwich for his delayed breakfast. Taking both, he walked back towards the Historic Dockyard and found a vacant seat overlooking the narrow harbour entrance. Despite the grey October morning and weather forecast there were several leisure craft making their way out into the Solent, along with an orange and black pilot boat and the Fast Cat ferry to the Isle of Wight. But, as he ate, his eyes were drawn to the little green and white ferry crossing to the town of Gosport opposite and his thoughts turned to the place where he believed Jennifer had been visiting the day she had disappeared.

He recalled his conversation with Dr Quentin Amos, who had been a lecturer at the London School of Economics in March 1967. Amos, a skeletal, balding, elderly man, with a terminal illness, living in a dirty urine-smelling flat in Woking, had told him that Jennifer had been involved with the Radical Student Alliance, which Horton had discovered had been formed in 1966 and, like the Vietnam Solidarity Campaign in America, had become a centre for the protest movement. The 1967 sit-in at the London School of Economics was considered to be the start of that protest movement. It went on to organize the mass anti-Vietnam War rally in Grosvenor

Square, leading to the Grosvenor Square riots in 1968, the year Zachary Benham had died in that fire. Amos's information about Jennifer put a completely different light on the woman Horton remembered and even those memories had been tainted by what he'd been told as a child after she'd abandoned him. But the words of his last and loving foster father, Bernard Litchfield, came back to him.

'Just because people tell you that, doesn't mean it's true. You have to find the truth for yourself. And even then, you must ask yourself whether it really is the truth, or what someone is persuading you into believing.'

Bernard's wise words applied both to Horton's professional and personal life. It was a shame he couldn't ask Bernard questions about Edward Ballard, because Bernard must have known Ballard, otherwise, why would he have given Bernard that Bluebird Toffee tin that had contained a photograph of Jennifer and Horton's birth certificate, both of which had been destroyed by a fire on his boat? He could get another birth certificate, but the only picture he'd had of Jennifer had gone. He remembered seeing Ballard hand the tin to Bernard one day when he'd bunked off school early. Bernard and Eileen Litchfield were dead, but perhaps their neighbours were still alive and maybe still living in the house next door. If so, would they remember much about the wayward boy the Litchfields had fostered? More importantly, had the Litchfields ever said anything to them about his background and his mother?

His thoughts returned to Amos, who had died in August, not from the cancer that had riddled his body, but of a heart attack. He'd bequeathed to Horton an envelope which had contained two blank sheets of paper. On the reverse of the envelope there had been a set of numbers — 01.07.05, 5.11.09 — which could, with some manipulation of the second set, correspond with the longitude and latitude of Haslar Marina in Gosport, which he could now see across the harbour. The marina location was 01.07.05 and 50.47.27. If he removed the zero, he got five, four plus seven gave him eleven and two plus seven added up to nine, giving the marina location. Except Haslar Marina hadn't existed in 1978. Then the area had been just sea and shore. Close to it though was the Royal Naval Hospital Haslar, now closed, and the heavily secured Fort Monkton, allegedly a communications training centre for MI5. Had Jennifer been heading there the day she had disappeared? Is that what Amos had wanted him to know?

Secrets and lies, Amos had told him. '*You might think the days of spies and the Cold War are over and that I'm an old man seeing shadows across every ripple of the sea, but they're not over; there is always evil below.*' What was the evil that Amos had alluded to?

But perhaps the numbers had no connection with the marina, the hospital or Fort Monkton, Horton thought, finishing off his sandwich. Maybe he was just so keen to find the meaning that he'd grasp at anything. They could be the combination to a safe or a safety deposit box code. A bank account number or dates. Without more information he was floundering. Why hadn't Amos given him more? A set of numbers was worse than useless without further reference and he had no idea where to look for that.

He tossed back a mouthful of coffee and turned his thoughts to Kenton's vanishing act. Just because Eunice Swallows was telling him that Kenton had disappeared didn't mean it was true. There had to be a reason why Kenton's car was parked at Admiralty Towers, and so far, Brett Veerman seemed the only link.

But maybe Kenton *had* absconded, and simply left his car there in the hope it wouldn't be discovered for some days. Being a computer expert perhaps he'd been able to access the security code from the car parking company's computers or had fitted a skimming device to capture the code when someone keyed it in. There was also the possibility that he owned an apartment there — but no, because if he did, he would have parked in his own allotted space and not Roger Watling's. Was Kenton really missing?

His phone rang. He expected it to be DCI Bliss but with surprise he saw the call was from Mike Danby, a former

DCI now running a private security company whose clients included Lord Ames. Horton answered it.

'Andy, you'd better get over here quick and bring the fat man with you.'

That, in Danby's code, meant Detective Superintendent Uckfield, head of the Major Crime Team, and there was only one reason why Danby wanted Uckfield.

'What is it?' he asked.

'Rather *who* is it,' Danby answered. 'It's Jasper Kenton. He's dead.'

Horton was momentarily dumbfounded. 'Where?' he asked, rising, tossing his paper coffee cup in the bin and hurrying towards his Harley.

'The Isle of Wight. But for Christ's sake, Andy, this has got to be handled carefully.'

'Why?' Horton asked, puzzled.

'Because Jasper Kenton is on Lord Ames's private beach.'

Horton froze. The very beach he'd stood on only yesterday. His heart was pumping fast. His pulse was racing. This couldn't be true. His head was teeming with questions and above them all was why there, why now, and for God's sake, why Jasper Kenton?

CHAPTER FIVE

Uckfield inserted a plump finger in his nose and began to pick it as he stared, frowning, across the shore from the police launch at a bundle covered by a cream cloth lying on the shingle beach some six yards to the west of the pontoon.

On the way across a choppy Solent, Horton had brought Uckfield up to speed about Kenton being reported missing, the finding of his vehicle and his forced entry into Veerman's apartment. Before leaving The Hard, Horton had also returned to Admiralty Towers and found PC Allen with the locksmith. He'd instructed Allen to take a note of all the vehicles parked at the Admiralty Towers car park. He knew the car park company could probably give them this information but he wasn't going to take any chances. They'd be checked against the list of residents, which he'd also told Allen to obtain, and that would be checked against a list of Swallows's clients and those they were investigating, which they would now need to insist upon.

Danby had explained to Horton on the phone that Swallows farmed out its close protection work to him. Horton hadn't called Eunice Swallows or DCI Bliss, and, surprisingly, Bliss hadn't rung him after his previous conversation with Ms Swallows. He wanted to make absolutely certain it was the body of Jasper Kenton, although he knew that Danby couldn't have made a mistake. And if truth be told, he didn't want Bliss on this trip. Uckfield hadn't insisted she accompany them either. It was Uckfield's remit anyway *if* Kenton had been murdered. And that was looking more than a strong possibility.

PC Ripley expertly brought the launch to a halt alongside Mike Danby's new motor cruiser at the end of the pontoon, despite the rising wind. Horton tied up and alighted onto the pontoon, glancing at the solid wooden door and wall bordering Lord Ames's property, thinking about his visit here yesterday. The questions that had sprung to mind at the shock of Danby's announcement were still there. Why here? Why now? And why Kenton? He didn't like the fact that a body had been discovered the day after he'd made a reconnaissance of the area. As a copper he didn't trust coincidences, and yet, he knew they happened far more often than acknowledged. Yet this one seemed personal. *If* Maidment and Foreland hadn't changed their plea to guilty, and *if* he hadn't taken his unexpected diversion, would Jasper Kenton have still ended up dead here? That was ridiculous though because he'd never seen or heard of Kenton before yesterday. But that jagged feeling between his shoulder blades made him wonder if he was being set up, although, why someone should kill Kenton in order to do so was not only puzzling but also incredible and ridiculous. There had to be a perfectly logical explanation for his body being here and the remoteness and privacy of the area were both pretty good reasons. The timing was just unfortunate.

He made to help Beth Tremaine, one of the Scene of Crime Officers, on to the pontoon, but she waved aside his assistance with a friendly gesture. Phil Taylor, the other SOCO, clambered off the boat and behind him, Jim Clarke, the lanky police photographer, followed suit. Uckfield eased his squat frame off with a grunt. At least they didn't need to worry about nosy passers-by, Horton thought, as they walked down the pontoon to where Danby was waiting for them on the shore, or securing the crime scene because nobody came this way. *But there had been that beachcomber, Wyndham Lomas.* A fact Horton had kept to himself because disclosing it would mean revealing that he had been here. He wasn't comfortable with that because he'd need to explain why. What could he say? *I wanted to see the countryside? I was on my way to the ferry?* Bloody funny way to get to the ferry, he could hear Uckfield saying cuttingly. But didn't he have a perfectly plausible explanation, the news that the weather vane donated by His Lordship would be returned to the abbey? OK, so it was a bit feeble and it didn't explain why he'd trekked through a small wood to reach the shore, but perhaps he could say he had wondered if he'd find someone at the rear of the property having drawn a blank at the front. He pushed the thought aside for now as they reached the broad-shouldered tall man in his late forties standing at the end of the pontoon. He'd deal with that later when he had more information.

Danby shook Uckfield's hand and nodded a greeting at Horton. 'Now do you see what I mean about unwrapping him?' Danby said, gesturing to the body as they headed towards it, repeating a remark he'd made to Horton on the phone. The tide was still on the rise and would reach the body in about two and a half hours. It wasn't far from where Horton had exchanged remarks with the beachcomber and he would certainly have seen a body if it had been here yesterday. Had the beachcomber put it here after Horton had left the area? Was that why he had been on the beach? And now Horton came to consider it, how had the beachcomber Lomas got here? Access to this area was extremely limited. Had he trudged through the woods after Horton? Even if he had, Horton couldn't see how he could have transported a body through it unless it had been conveyed in something like a wheelbarrow, and even then, it would have been extremely difficult.

Uckfield sniffed and retrieved a toothpick from the pocket of his waterproof jacket. To Danby he said, 'How come you're here?' It was a question that Horton had been about to ask, although he had guessed the answer, which was confirmed when Danby replied.

'I came over to check out the property and grounds while Richard's away. It's part of our security contract. I saw something lying on the shore as I approached by boat. At first I thought it was rubbish that had washed up, but when I got closer, I saw by its shape that it was a body. I went to investigate. I checked to see if the poor sod was alive, which was why I unwrapped part of it. I was gobsmacked when I saw who it was. I called you, Andy, and remained with the body to make sure it wasn't tampered with, but nobody comes along this stretch; there are no public footpaths and the land around here is private.'

But two people had been here yesterday: him and Wyndham Lomas. Horton said, 'When was the last time you saw Jasper Kenton?'

'Two weeks ago. He had a new client who wanted some close protection work.'

'Have you spoken to him since?'

But Danby shook his head. 'No. I emailed him though, to say I'd spoken to the potential client and had given him a quote, which incidentally he accepted yesterday. I was going to tell Jasper on Monday.' His words had taken them to the body.

Horton stared down at it. All he could see was a crop of black hair, a grey face and dark wide sightless eyes, but even with this limited view he recognized it was the man in the photograph that Eunice Swallows had given him. Jasper Kenton. There was no decomposition and no sea life feeding off the soft flesh of the lips and eyes. There was very little smell attached to the body, which meant that Kenton hadn't been dead for long.

The body was wrapped in what was clearly an old sailcloth, cream coloured and soiled, and was bound at the neck, chest, midriff and ankles by a thin white dirty rope of the type used on boats. Known to sailors as lines, these ropes are usually used to secure a boat to a pontoon or to attach it to an anchor or fender.

Horton confirmed Kenton's identity, thinking that this time it would be the duty of the Wiltshire police to inform the next of kin — the sister that Eunice Swallows had told him about who lived in Marlborough and who hadn't been in contact with her brother for some years. Perhaps she wouldn't be too upset.

Uckfield said, 'Well it's not suicide, because he couldn't have wrapped himself up like a mummy. And it can't be accidental death either, unless he was practising to be the next Houdini. Get some pictures, Clarke.'

They stepped away from the body as Clarke began to photograph and video it. There wasn't much that Taylor and Tremaine could do here, thought Horton, except take samples of the shingle and sand around the body in the hope that what they collected might show up on the killer's clothes or belongings.

Uckfield looked out to sea and then to his right. 'Where does that go?'

'To a creek,' Danby answered. 'There are woods either side of it. It thins out after about half a mile, giving onto a small field surrounded by trees. There's no slipway or public access to it. Lord Ames owns the woods on both sides and the land at the top of the creek. I can't see how anyone could have brought the body in that way. And at low tide it dries out to mud. You'd get well and truly stuck.'

'And the other side of the pontoon?' asked Horton, looking west.

'A tree-lined shore with no public footpaths or access by sea. There are dense woods and the land and shore are owned by Lord Ames right around the coast until you come to the private beach and land belonging to Osborne House, the royal seaside palace where Queen Victoria often stayed with Prince Albert and their nine children.'

'I don't need the guided tour or a history lesson,' grunted Uckfield.

But it was probably the reason why the Ames family had purchased adjoining land years ago. Horton said, 'Then it seems likely the body was brought in from the Solent by boat.'

With a worried frown Danby said, 'It could have been washed up on the high tide this morning just after or before two.'

Horton knew Danby didn't like the thought that Ames's pontoon had been used by the killer. He'd prefer the body to have been washed up accidentally because that meant keeping Ames out of the equation. Horton favoured that himself, given his appearance here yesterday, but he said, 'The body would have sunk.'

'There might have been an air bubble trapped inside the sailcloth that prevented it from sinking.'

That was possible. Horton said, 'Is there a connection between Kenton and Lord Ames?'

Uckfield eyed Horton shrewdly. No doubt it was a question he had been about to ask.

'No.'

'You asked him?'

'Yes, and I gave him a description of Kenton but he doesn't recognize him.'

'You called Lord Ames before you called me?'

'Of course.' Danby's penetrating green eyes studied Horton evenly.

'How did he take the news?'

'He was shocked, of course. He's given me full authority to assist all I can. None of the family are here, which is why I am. And the only connection between Jasper Kenton and Lord Ames is me. I know them both, but I didn't kill Kenton and I didn't bring his body here and call you.'

'Never thought you had for a moment, Mike,' Uckfield answered jovially, but judging by Danby's dubious glance he clearly wasn't convinced that Uckfield meant it.

Horton said, 'Was Kenton involved in any investigation for His Lordship?' Perhaps that was the reason why Eunice Swallows was guarding her client list so zealously. But what would Ames want Swallows to investigate when

46

Horton believed he had the British Intelligence services at his disposal? He had no proof that Lord Ames was connected with MI5 though. Maybe he'd got that wrong. He added, 'Could Kenton have been carrying out surveillance work on someone Ames employs, or checking an employee reference?' But that didn't explain why his car had been parked at the Admiralty Towers car park, unless that employee had an apartment there or had been visiting someone there and had killed Kenton and brought him over to the island. It seemed unlikely, because why place the body on Ames's land and draw attention to himself? Unless it was a former employee who'd been sacked as a result of something Kenton had discovered and the employee saw it as a way of getting even.

But Danby scotched that idea. 'I handle all the security checks on Lord Ames's staff right across his estate and all of his businesses.'

'It might have been something other than a security check,' Horton suggested.

'Like what?' asked Uckfield.

'Maybe he suspected two of his staff of stealing from him or thought his wife was running around with the gardener.'

'This isn't Lady Chatterley's bleeding lover,' quipped Uckfield.

'No, but it happens,' said Horton, and Uckfield would know more about illicit affairs than any of them. If it was female, attractive, preferably under the age of forty and up for it, so was Uckfield, despite being married with two daughters.

'I think he would have asked me to help if it was a delicate matter,' Danby replied a little stiffly.

Uckfield said, 'Have you been inside the house to make sure no one's stolen the family silver? Kenton could have been killed because he'd disturbed the burglars.'

'I doubt that,' Danby replied somewhat acidly. 'He wouldn't have got in. There are sophisticated security systems.'

'Better to be safe than sorry,' Uckfield added.

Danby eyed Uckfield suspiciously. As an ex-copper he knew what Uckfield was doing. It was a ploy to get rid of him. But he shrugged and headed back to the pontoon. Horton watched him jump up onto it with ease and make for the solid wooden door built into the wall. There Danby turned his back on them and tapped the security pad. Horton thought of the entrance barrier to the Admiralty Towers car park and again considered the possibility that Kenton might have watched someone key in the number and had then simply replicated it.

He turned back to the body. Clarke was checking the digital images he'd taken on his camera, while Taylor was grubbing around in the shingle and Tremaine was trying to lift fingerprints from the sailcloth. Horton didn't think she'd get anything even a quarter decent that the fingerprint bureau could work with.

He said, 'I'll ask Elkins to scout along the coast towards Osborne House in case there's a way onto the beach from that side. Clarke can take some photographs of that and of the entrance to the creek.'

'OK.' Uckfield reached for his phone. Over his shoulder he said, 'Call Dr Clayton, ask her to meet us at the mortuary on the island. No point in her coming here; there's nothing she can do except certify the poor bugger's dead and we can all see that. Tell Elkins after Clarke's got his photos to go back to Portsmouth and collect her. He can also pick up DI Dennings. I'll get him to set up an incident suite at Newport. You can come with me to the mortuary.'

Although the mortuary wasn't Horton's favourite place, he was glad that Uckfield had asked him to accompany him there. He'd wondered if the Super would send him back to Portsmouth with Taylor, Tremaine and Clarke, with this not being a CID matter. But Uckfield would pull in others from various departments to assist in the investigation, and clearly, he was going to be one of them. He was glad of that. He heard Uckfield say, 'DI Dennings, I hope you haven't got any plans for this weekend . . .' He moved away.

Horton rather hoped Uckfield had ruined Dennings' weekend. His views of Dennings, the great hulking oaf, were well known by Uckfield. It wasn't just sour grapes either, Horton told himself as he headed for Clarke. He'd worked with Dennings on vice and on covert operations with the Intelligence Directorate and Dennings simply didn't have the mental capacity to be a good or even a mediocre detective. However, that hadn't stopped Uckfield from appointing him to the Major Crime Team when the position had been promised to Horton. Uckfield claimed he was under orders from the then Chief Constable, his father-in-law, who hadn't wanted a cop who'd been on an eight-month suspension for rape allegations anywhere near it or the station, while Dennings who had been with Horton on that ill-fated operation had come out smelling of roses. Only because he'd sat on his fat arse and done nothing except stare through a telescopic camera. But he'd kept his nose clean and played it by the book. Since then, Uckfield had admitted secretly to Horton that he was keen to get Dennings out but claimed that his hands were tied. Even though they now had a new Chief Constable, Horton guessed he was still out of favour because of his unorthodox policing style. Horton wasn't sure how hard Uckfield was trying to ditch Dennings either. Even if Dennings did go, Horton doubted he'd be appointed in his place and certainly not if DCI Bliss was appointed Uckfield's second-in-command. CID looked much more attractive if that happened.

He wasn't improving his chances either, he thought, by withholding information. He'd missed the opportunity to tell Uckfield about the beachcomber, but he knew that even given the chance he would have remained silent. Every instinct was urging him to do so. But it disturbed him. Was he hindering a murder investigation? Wyndham Lomas had seemed pretty harmless. *Yeah, and so had Dr Crippen, Jack the Ripper and Frederick West*, he thought, relaying instructions to Clarke who nodded and went to join Elkins and Ripley on the police launch. Horton eased his conscience with the thought that he'd see what Dr Clayton had to report first. He could always return later and try to locate this Lomas. Surely he wouldn't be that difficult to find.

He returned to the corpse. Tremaine looked up and shook her head, which meant she could get little from the sailcloth. When Dr Clayton and the mortuary assistant unwrapped it from the body Horton hoped to be able to see what type of sail it was. Not that that meant much, because it wouldn't come with the boat's name stamped all over it, and even if it had some identifying feature that didn't mean it had come from the killer. It could have come from anywhere.

He was about to call Dr Clayton when his phone rang. It was Bliss. Horton knew she'd catch up with him eventually.

'Inspector, I have received a formal complaint about your attitude from Eunice Swallows. You entered the apartment belonging to the husband of one of her clients despite not having permission, on whose authority?' she snapped.

'My own. I had reason to believe Mr Kenton might be inside, possibly ill or injured. I was wrong.'

'I'd say you were. This does not—'

But he cut her short. 'Kenton's been found dead. On a beach on the Isle of Wight. I'm there now.'

There was a moment's stunned silence before she said, 'Why wasn't I informed?'

'I didn't realize you were on duty, Ma'am.'

'I—'

Again, he cut her off. 'Detective Superintendent Uckfield is with me at the scene. He *was* informed and it is now a Major Crime Team investigation.'

Again, a fragmentary pause. 'I'll call him.'

She rang off before Horton could utter another sound. Horton heard Uckfield's phone ring, the moment he came off the line to Dennings. Horton called Dr Gaye Clayton on her mobile, hoping she was available and not out sailing, although the weather wasn't exactly fair, he thought, looking up at the gathering dark clouds and at the high rolling waves topped with foaming white spray.

'Don't tell me,' she declared brightly, her West Country accent sounding stronger on the phone, 'you've interrupted the very important business of food shopping to say you've got a body.'

'Afraid so, and it means a trip to the island.' He told her that Sergeant Elkins would pick her up from the Commercial Ferry Port berth in ninety minutes.

'Good, that gives me time to go home and unload this lot.'

He knew that she lived alone. She'd once told him she was divorced but had never volunteered anything more about her personal circumstances, and he'd never asked. He'd seen her with male medical colleagues having a drink and didn't doubt she had admirers. Why shouldn't she? She was attractive, in a boyish kind of way.

Uckfield was still on his phone. Maybe he was still talking to Bliss or perhaps he was speaking to ACC Dean, his boss. Danby emerged from the rear of Lord Ames's property and Horton joined him on the pontoon.

'No sign of any intruder,' Danby reported, 'as I knew there wouldn't be. I'd like to stay until the body is removed.'

'Fine.' Horton called Newport police station and asked them to tell the undertakers to stand by at Newport Quay, which was a short distance from the hospital mortuary. He then rang the coastguard services and, after briefing the officer in charge, requested their assistance in removing the body and transporting it to Newport Quay, as the marine unit was tied up and he thought it would be extremely difficult to negotiate the body through the woods. They could have taken it via Lord Ames's back entrance but Danby hadn't volunteered that option and Horton didn't suggest it, although it would have given him the opportunity to see the property. The coastguard said they'd be across within twenty minutes.

Uckfield beckoned Horton over.

'Bliss is going to break the news of Kenton's death to Eunice Swallows. She'll get a full list of the cases Kenton was working on, along with names and addresses of the clients and those he was investigating.'

'Including details of the Veermans.'

'Yes.'

'We'll also need to check out this Roger Watling. I don't think he would have left Kenton's car in his space and then made such a fuss but he could have considered it a good diversionary tactic.'

'I'll get Trueman on to that. Wonder Boy's given permission for Bliss to work as the DCI in the incident suite, which Trueman's setting up now.'

Wonder Boy was one of Uckfield's kinder terms for ACC Dean, whom he often referred to more derogatorily as the gnome on account of his diminished height and beaky nose. Horton thought the news of Bliss's involvement wouldn't exactly thrill Trueman. He didn't need the hyperactive, over-critical DCI hovering over his shoulder and questioning his actions every other minute. But he'd bear it with the stoical silence that was his customary manner. Extra manpower would be drafted in and, depending on the outcome of the autopsy, it might mean that Cantelli and Walters's weekend could be disrupted. Horton had no conscience about disturbing DC Walters, but he did about taking Cantelli away from the bosom of his family.

They waited until the coastguard had zipped Kenton into a body bag, by which time it had started raining and the police launch had returned from its reconnaissance of the shore and creek entrance. Elkins said they'd gone as far as they could up the creek but not to the top. 'We'll need the RIB for that,' he reported. 'And there's no entrance we could see to the west of the pontoon.' Taylor had mapped the crime scene and he, Tremaine and Clarke left on the launch for Portsmouth. Danby offered Uckfield and Horton a lift on his boat to Newport Quay, which Uckfield accepted with alacrity. Horton wasn't complaining either. Despite it being a choppy journey, it was better than having to hack their way through the undergrowth.

Many times, as they headed up the River Medina to the island's capital town, Horton was tempted to tell Uckfield about his presence on that beach and about his chance meeting with the beachcomber, but he didn't. He didn't like the fact that he was withholding vital information. The thought made him tense. But he also didn't care for the coincidence. He didn't understand what was going on — *if* something was — and until he did, he was going to keep silent. Kenton might still have been alive on Friday at midday, but if he had been then Lomas could have been looking over the location with a view to taking Kenton's body there after killing him.

They took their leave of Danby, with Uckfield promising to keep him informed, and climbed into the waiting police car. As they were driven the short distance to the mortuary the beachcomber's words plagued Horton. '*You never know what you might find washed up on the beach.*' He did now.

CHAPTER SIX

'Looks interesting,' Gaye Clayton said. Dressed in her mortuary garb with a microphone headband placed under the cap covering her spiky auburn hair and a mouthpiece in front of her lips, which Horton knew was connected to a small recording machine in the pocket of her mortuary plastic gown, she eyed the corpse on the slab with a gleam in her green eyes. Looking up, she addressed them. 'Are you staying for the autopsy?'

Uckfield replied. 'No, only until you unwrap him. We want to know how he was killed because I don't think he crept in there and zipped himself up.'

'Can't see any zip,' she replied, her freckled face peering at the body, 'unless it's last year's model and it's up the back.'

Uckfield smiled facetiously.

She nodded at the mortuary attendant, a sturdy, solemn man in his late fifties, who stepped forward with a digital camera and video. Uckfield tutted impatiently and shifted his bulk as the corpse was again photographed and videoed. Gaye Clayton was good, the best forensic pathologist Horton had come across, and she wouldn't be hurried by Uckfield or anyone else.

He studied Jasper Kenton's lifeless, pale face that was now visible through the opening of the sailcloth, peering out like a man behind a curtain not wanting to be seen. It must have given Mike Danby quite a jolt finding the body of someone he knew on the land of one of his most prestigious clients. Not that he had displayed that when they'd met, though he'd sounded shaken enough on the phone. Danby was ex-job and would have been used to seeing bodies in worse states than this; he would have quickly engaged one of the techniques for coping with witnessing a violent death — they each perfected their own. After the initial shock the adrenalin of the investigation would kick in. Horton felt it now, but this time it was tinged with anxiety and apprehension which he couldn't shake off. The forehead was visible, the brown eyes were still open, and the nose and fleshy lips with the cleft in the chin were showing beneath it.

'Do you have an ID?' Gaye asked.

Horton told her who it was and relayed the circumstances behind the finding of the body and its location. She listened attentively without comment. By the time he'd finished, the mortuary attendant indicated with a nod that he had got the pictures he wanted.

'Shall we turn him over? Perhaps you'd give us a hand, Inspector?'

It was the first time Horton had viewed the rear of the corpse and his interest was immediately heightened when he saw that the sail had been doubled up around the body with the ends joining at the back and the knots in the lines securing it tied expertly. His eyes flicked to Gaye, who had clearly read his thoughts.

'They're bowline knots,' Horton said. Even though Uckfield owned a boat it was of the motor cruiser variety and Horton wasn't sure he knew all things nautical — in fact he doubted it. 'They're perfect for when you need a strong loop of line around something to secure it. This killer knew what he was doing.'

He thought back to where Kenton's car had been found. Both Oyster Quays Marina and the Camber were within walking distance of the Admiralty Towers car park. Had Kenton met someone on a boat in either of those places? But if so, why park in Roger Watling's space? Maybe Kenton knew it would be vacant until Saturday morning and was expecting to be back long before then.

Horton watched with bated breath as the mortuary attendant began to untie the knots. After a few moments he peeled back the double thickness of the sail to reveal that Jasper Kenton was naked.

'No immediate evidence of cause of death,' Gaye said, studying the neck, buttocks and back of the legs. 'No sign of strangulation or stabbing and no blunt force trauma to the skull. Inspector, if we could call on your assistance again, we'll lift him and get him unwrapped, as Superintendent Uckfield put it. Perhaps you'd like to help me extract the sail, Superintendent.'

Uckfield looked as though he didn't like to but had to grudgingly oblige.

Horton took a breath and steeled himself for the unpleasant task of lifting the body with the help of the burly mortuary attendant. Gaye first drew the lines away and put them in an evidence bag and then with Uckfield's assistance began to pull away the sail from the body. Horton could see that although sizeable it wasn't from a big yacht. He and the mortuary attendant replaced the naked body of Jasper Kenton onto the mortuary slab while Uckfield and Gaye stuffed the sail into a very large evidence bag and heaved it onto the trolley.

Red faced from the exertion, Uckfield said, 'The killer must have had a hell of a job wrapping him up in that.'

'Which suggests he is strong and fit,' answered Horton, thinking of the beachcomber, recalling those strong suntanned hands as he'd given Horton the tatty business card. He'd certainly looked fit even though he must have been in his fifties.

But Gaye contradicted him. 'The victim could have fallen dead or unconscious on the sailcloth, which had already been folded over in preparation to receive the body. It would only be a case of undressing him, unless he was already naked, and then easing the body one way and then the other to tie the knots. It would have been easier if there were two of them. Let's turn him over and see if we can find out how he died.'

This time Horton's services weren't required. The mortuary attendant and Gaye turned the body on to its back and immediately Horton saw what must have been the cause of death. 'He was shot,' he declared, staring at the round-shaped hole in the upper thorax of the hairless chest before exchanging a swift glance with Uckfield who was looking worried, and rightly so.

Gaye frowned as she studied it. 'It looks that way but I can't say for certain until I open him up, or even if it was the cause of death. He could have been alive when he was put in that shroud and placed in the water and therefore drowned.'

Horton suppressed a shudder at the thought. And judging by Uckfield's glowering countenance he didn't like what they were seeing any more than Horton did. What on earth had Kenton been doing to get himself shot, stripped, bundled up in a sailcloth and dumped on the shore?

'Whoever shot him aimed well,' he said.

'Yes. Right at the heart,' Gaye answered almost abstractedly, which wasn't like her, thought Horton, wondering what she was thinking.

He said, 'His clothes have been removed to try and hide forensic evidence.'

'Probably. And just to make it more difficult,' she added, 'your killer decides to wrap him up in a sail to further confuse any traces of forensic evidence and leave the sea to eradicate even more.'

Uckfield sniffed. 'A clever-dick killer. Let's hope he made some mistakes along the way. They usually do.'

Gaye looked up. 'We might get something on where the body was prior to being found on the shore from an analysis of hair and skin. But there's more.' She paused. Horton could see her mind racing with thoughts. 'The body is wet.'

'Yeah, well it has been in the sea,' Uckfield sneered sarcastically.

Gaye rolled her eyes at him while Horton rapidly thought.

'Wet all over?' he asked sharply.

'Yes.' She waited for him to say it.

'Which means he must have been immersed in the sea before being wrapped in the sailcloth.'

'The sailcloth is laminated, which means it's waterproof and from what I could see there didn't appear to be any tears or holes in it, but we've only shoved it into a bag, not examined it. You'll need to have it tested to see if it has lost its waterproof capability. And if he was shot and fell on to it then there might be traces of blood. But he might not necessarily have been in the sea. I'll test skin samples for saline content, but he could have been shot in the bath or the shower, hence his nakedness, and the killer could then have wrapped him in the shroud and put him in the sea. He could even have been shot in a shower on board a boat.'

'I thought you were meant to be giving us something to help our investigation, not make it more complicated,' grumbled Uckfield. 'Time of death?'

And this, thought Horton, was a critical point.

She considered this while scanning the corpse. 'As you know, a body usually sinks because the specific gravity of it is very close to that of water. As putrefactive gas formation decreases, so does the gravity of the body, which creates enough buoyancy to allow it to rise to the surface. The length of time this takes depends on whether the body is dressed in heavy clothing, which this victim wasn't, although I would say that sail was heavy enough to make him sink. Normally, at this time of the year, his body would have risen to the surface between three and five days but the victim hasn't been dead that long. Even despite being cocooned there would have been much clearer signs of decomposition than there are. Post-mortem lividity looks well established, as you can see by the purple colouring of the skin, and rigor mortis is also well established, but the temperature of the sea might have slowed it down. I'd say time of death was likely twenty-four hours ago, but that is very approximate. You could be looking at less or possibly more.'

Uckfield raised his eyebrows as though to say *thanks a bunch.*

'I might be able to be more precise when I open him up, and when we examine stomach contents.'

Horton's own stomach churned as though in sympathy, reminding him he hadn't eaten since that bacon sandwich on The Hard, which seemed a lifetime ago, not that he felt much like food now. He quickly assimilated Dr Clayton's information.

'That puts the time of death to sometime late Friday afternoon, but he was last seen leaving Swallows at 4.30 p.m. on Thursday. Are there signs that suggest he was restrained?'

'Difficult to tell because of the lividity but I'll certainly take a closer look.'

Horton addressed Uckfield. 'We need to know what time he entered the Admiralty Towers car park.'

'Get Trueman on to that. Any ideas on the shroud, apart from it being a sail?' Uckfield asked Gaye.

'It looked old, considerably worn. I couldn't see a number on it, could you?' she asked Horton. A sail number might help to identify the boat it had once belonged to, although that wouldn't necessarily give them the killer. The sail could have been abandoned or sold on long ago, or the boat itself could have been sold. They might get a manufacturer's mark or name on the sail, Horton thought, which could give them the name of the person who had bought it, *if* the manufacturer had kept records, but that didn't mean he was the killer. In fact, Horton doubted he was because he couldn't see this killer giving them such a nice big signpost saying 'killer this way'. It could have been purchased second or third hand years ago. He said he hadn't seen any number on it and Uckfield shook his head to indicate he hadn't seen anything either, but they hadn't unfolded it.

Gaye glanced at the mortuary clock. 'I'll hopefully have more for you by 7.30.'

Horton took the evidence bags containing the sail and the lines, thanked her and addressed Uckfield after they had disrobed and were heading out of the mortuary.

'It could have been an accident, the gun went off, the killer panicked, undressed the body and wrapped him up like that, thinking he might sink when thrown overboard.'

'It looks to me as though someone aimed right at his heart. And that means either an ace shot, or someone he knew well enough to get that close to him. Someone he didn't expect to shoot him or he thought wasn't capable of doing so.'

'Unless he was bound and gagged and unable to move.'

Uckfield grunted an acknowledgement. 'Bliss should have that list of Swallows's clients by now. If not, find out what's keeping her. I'll get Kenton's flat sealed off. Marsden can go in there tomorrow. Dennings will instigate a search of the beach where Kenton was found and those woods to see if we can find the weapon, but I can't see this killer going to all that trouble with the corpse and then tossing his gun aside. We've got about a good hour and a half of daylight left.'

'Not in those woods you haven't, Steve; they're really dense.' For a moment Horton thought he'd given away the fact that he'd been there but Uckfield didn't pick up on it.

'OK, we'll go in as soon as it's light tomorrow.'

'Better inform Danby. It's private land.'

'Yeah, wouldn't want His Lordship's nose put out of joint. He might complain to Wonder Boy,' Uckfield sneered, climbing into the waiting police car. He gave the driver instructions to take them to Newport station, adding to Horton that he'd stay on the island until he had further information from Dr Clayton. 'Call Elkins, get him to collect you and get that stuff over to the lab and examined pronto.' But as they drew up outside the police station Uckfield's phone rang. 'Bliss,' he mouthed to Horton and indicated for him to remain in the car.

Horton watched Uckfield, wondering what Bliss had discovered. Uckfield made no comment except to grunt and sniff. Then he said, 'OK, Inspector Horton will deal with that.' He rang off. 'Eunice Swallows says the only client they have on the Isle of Wight is the wife of the man whose apartment you forcibly entered this morning.'

Horton raised his eyebrows. It sounded promising. And it fitted with his theory that Brett Veerman could have seen Kenton following him and approached him. 'Where do they live?'

'Just outside Fishbourne. Gulls End, Northwood Lane.'

Not far from the abbey, and if Horton remembered correctly the lane backed on to the Solent. His interest heightened.

'Interview them both. I'll get those evidence bags shipped back to the mainland labs.'

Horton handed them over.

Climbing out, Uckfield added, 'The car will drop you off there, but tread carefully for now. You'll be revealing to Mr Veerman that his wife thinks he's got a bit on the side and to Mrs Veerman that we suspect her husband of being involved in murder. Tell them as little as possible. Go easy until we've got more evidence.'

'And if Brett Veerman confesses to killing Kenton?' Horton said with a hint of sarcasm.

'We wouldn't be so lucky.' No, Horton didn't think they would.

CHAPTER SEVEN

Horton eyed the large contemporary house at the end of a long gravel driveway and thought that whatever Brett Veerman did for a living it paid extremely well. The place must be worth a couple of million pounds at least. Or perhaps it was Mrs Veerman who had the money and she was getting fed up sharing it with her husband's lover.

He climbed out of the police car, pleased that the rain had abated for a while, and turned his gaze from the timber and glass three-storey house to the triple garage block on his right. In front of it was parked an expensive silver Volvo. The grounds were expansive and well cared for but a little bland, just grass and a few shrubs and trees. The house itself was the last along a private wooded lane and Horton had been correct: it backed onto the Solent. He set off towards the left of the house where he caught sight of the gunmetal grey sea beyond a long stretch of grass, at the bottom of which was a tall, slim man hosing down a dinghy. Beside him to his left was a sizeable timber boat shed.

Horton made to head in that direction when the front door of the house opened and two liver and white Springer Spaniels charged out, careering around him without barking. They were followed by a slim woman in her early fifties wearing stout shoes, khaki trousers and a dark green fleece jacket along with a scowl, which she directed at the police car. She was carrying a dog lead.

'You've come to see me,' she said crisply in a slightly husky voice that had an edge of condescension about it rather than sexiness. Eunice Swallows had obviously called Thelma Veerman. He made to show his warrant card but she waved it aside.

'Can we walk.' It wasn't a question. She set off after her dogs at a brisk pace, leaving him little option but to join her. He didn't mind though. It was better to get her on her own. But he would need to talk to her husband later.

He stopped only to tell the police officer he could go. There was no need for an officer to accompany him to take notes during the interview, which was meant to be low-key and informal according to Uckfield's instructions. And from here, when he'd finished, he could walk either to the car ferry terminal to the west at Fishbourne or to the hovercraft and Fast Cat passenger ferry to the east.

Thelma Veerman looked relieved when the police car passed her in the driveway. It turned left as they turned right onto a footpath that led to the abbey and the car ferry terminal beyond it.

'You know why I'm here?' he began. How much had Eunice Swallows told her?

'It's because Mr Kenton is dead.'

'Yes.' He'd have preferred to break the news himself, to gauge her reaction, but he guessed that Ms Swallows was trying to do a damage limitation exercise by forewarning her client. Thelma Veerman seemed tense and anxious, understandably so thought Horton. He waited for her to ask the usual questions. How did he die? Where was he found? But she made no further comment. 'Was Jasper Kenton your contact at the Swallows Agency?' he asked when it seemed clear she wasn't going to speak. The dogs raced ahead of them along the deserted gravel footpath, sniffing the ground in a zigzag pattern as they went.

'Yes.' She brushed her shoulder-length fine fair hair off of her face, which he noted wore a perpetual frown. Her grey-blue eyes, though sharp, also held suspicion, which wasn't unexpected given his arrival and the subject matter, but there was also an air of superiority about her that might have been to disguise her unease or possibly even shyness. She seemed reluctant to expand — was that out of embarrassment, he wondered, rather than a deliberate ploy to be uncooperative because she was ashamed of having called in a private investigator to spy on her husband?

'How long had you known Mr Kenton?'

She flashed him a startled look. 'I didn't know him.'

'But he was helping you with regards to your enquiry. You must have had contact with him.'

'Of course I did, but that's not the same as knowing someone.'

OK, so he'd rephrase the question. 'What were your impressions of Mr Kenton?'

'He seemed very professional. A quiet man. Thoughtful rather than forceful.' She eyed him keenly. 'Do you think his death was suspicious?'

'I'm afraid so.'

She pushed a slender hand through her hair again and her frown deepened, but she remained silent.

Horton said, 'Why do you think your husband's having an affair?' He watched for her reaction and waited for her to demand what that had to do with him or Kenton's death, but she didn't. She stared straight ahead but her brisk footsteps never faltered.

'The usual thing,' she said after a moment. 'His mobile phone ringing and him going out of the room to answer it. And although Brett's always worked irregular and long hours, there seems to be an even greater reluctance to come home, and when he does, he often goes out very soon afterwards or up to his study. He avoids being with me as much as possible. It's been like that for months and I've just got to the stage where I have to know.'

He was slightly surprised by her forthrightness. After her initial remarks he had expected reticence.

She continued. 'We've been married for twenty-five years, Inspector. Our son, John, is a nursing officer in the Royal Navy. Brett would have liked him to be a doctor, but John didn't want that. He has a first-class honours degree in adult nursing.'

She said it proudly and a little defiantly as though she dared him to say it wasn't enough. Was that what her husband said?

'I thought that if Brett no longer wants me then I don't see why I should hang around wasting my life waiting for someone who doesn't care for me.' She threw him a glance. He couldn't read her expression. He heard no bitterness in her voice. She simply stated it as fact.

'I engaged the Swallows Agency at the end of September following a meeting with Eunice Swallows at a café on the seafront in Portsmouth. There she introduced me to Mr Kenton who said he would be investigating my husband. I knew that if I confronted Brett without any evidence, he'd just say I was being stupid. Brett is a thorough man who likes to deal in facts.'

'He sounds like a lawyer,' Horton said, fishing.

'He's an ophthalmic consultant surgeon.'

No wonder he could afford such a prestigious property backing onto the Solent. And perhaps that explained her defensiveness when she'd spoken of her son's career. No doubt Brett Veerman had expectations of his son becoming a doctor instead of a nurse.

The trees suddenly gave way to open fields either side of them and on their right Horton could see the ruins of the original abbey, which Brother Norman had told him had been established in the early 1100s until Henry VIII had dismantled it. Thelma Veerman showed no inclination to turn back as they headed towards the modern abbey, built at the turn of the last century.

'Had Mr Kenton discovered anything?' asked Horton.

'Only that Brett had bought an apartment in Portsmouth three months ago without telling me and in his name alone. But Mr Kenton said he couldn't find any evidence of there being another woman.' She threw him a glance. 'Have *you* found evidence of an affair?'

He thought of that bland minimalistic flat. 'No. But then we're not looking for it.'

'Of course.'

She seemed worried, understandably so given that she not only suspected her husband of marital infidelity but that he was soon to discover he had been spied upon. He wondered what his reaction would be. Was she afraid of her husband? Was he abusive, either physically or mentally, or both? Would he walk out on her or give her the silent treatment? Maybe he'd be able to answer some of those questions after speaking with him.

'When did you last see or speak to Mr Kenton?'

'Thursday at midday.'

Four and a half hours before he had left the office.

'The arrangement was that I call him at a pre-set time every Thursday from a payphone.'

'What did he say?'

'That he had nothing further to report except that my husband wasn't in debt so he wasn't lavishing money on this other woman, and so far, he couldn't trace any other assets belonging to Brett or any other bank accounts here or abroad, but he was still working on that. And he was also tracking Internet sites for conferences and seminars Brett attended to see if any particular woman cropped up frequently at the same places as him.'

'An affair with a colleague?'

'It's the most logical explanation. I can't see Brett risking his career and reputation by having an affair with a patient.'

Horton could see that there was something else bothering her, but whether that was about Kenton's death and her husband's alleged infidelity or something completely different he didn't know and she didn't seem inclined to tell him.

He said, 'Were you and your husband at home last night?'

'I was. Brett was working late, or so he said,' she added now with a hint of nervousness.

'What time did he get in?'

'Two a.m.'

'That's very late to be working.'

'Brett often has operations until very late. Last night could have been one such case. He might have been called to undertake an emergency operation. Or that's what he'd say if I questioned him. For all I know he could have been meeting this woman in this apartment of his.'

And had Jasper Kenton been onto that? Again, he wondered if Brett Veerman had discovered Kenton keeping surveillance on him and confronted him about it. Even if he had done, it didn't mean he'd killed him. And how would Veerman have got the body here? He couldn't have sailed that small dinghy Horton had just seen in the garden from Portsmouth to the island in the dark and rain. Perhaps there was a bigger boat in the boathouse or down on the shore out of sight.

He said, 'How do you know it was two a.m.?

'I looked at the clock when I heard him come in.'

'Did you speak to him?'

'There was no point.' She fell silent as they walked on. Horton let it stretch for a while in case she wanted to add something. She didn't.

They had reached the abbey grounds and Thelma Veerman halted. Ahead the path led to the café and gift shop. It would be closed now; it was well after 4.30 p.m. and if they didn't head back soon they'd be walking in the dark.

The chapel bell sounded. 'That's Vespers,' Thelma Veerman said, looking up at the abbey clock. 'Evening prayer. Saint Benedict said it should be done before the lamps are lit. "Be ye angry, and sin not: let not the sun go down upon your wrath." Ephesians: chapter four, verse twenty six. It's about forgiveness.'

She turned back towards the house leaving him to ponder what she meant. Forgiveness for her when her husband discovered she'd engaged a private detective, or forgiveness for her husband for killing Jasper Kenton? Or perhaps she should forgive her husband for having a lover. Maybe she'd already done that many times in their married life.

Horton fell into step beside her, feeling her sadness. She called the dogs to heel. They came instantly. After a while Horton broke the silence. 'Has your husband been out this morning?'

'Only on the dinghy at 9.30 a.m. And again this afternoon.'

'Is it usual for him to go sailing twice in one day?'

'Occasionally, yes. With the winter coming on he probably thinks he won't get much more chance to do so. He says sailing helps him to relax. Maybe the operation last night wasn't a success. He doesn't talk about his work.'

Horton wondered what they did talk about, but as she'd already explained, they had stopped communicating, it seemed, a long time ago. He thought Veerman must be a highly experienced sailor to have gone out in this afternoon's weather. He'd know all about sails, bowline knots, the Solent, its coasts and marinas.

'Do you have another boat as well as the dinghy?'

'Not now. We used to own a Jeanneau Sun Odyssey thirty-two-foot yacht. We sold it when John left home seven years ago.'

Perhaps Kenton had found evidence of Brett Veerman owning another boat. And maybe he'd followed him to it.

'What made you choose the Swallows Agency?'

'I'd been thinking about engaging a private investigation agency for some time. I couldn't research them on the Internet at home in case Brett checked my viewing history on the computer or on my phone so I used the library in Ryde to look some up. It had to be a Portsmouth agency because that is where Brett is primarily based, although he has a clinic at the private hospital at Havant and treats patients at the Moorfields Eye Hospital in London, as well as giving lectures all over the world. I liked the idea of Swallows because it's run by a woman and I thought she would understand.'

'Were you disappointed when she allocated the work to Mr Kenton?'

'Not after meeting him, no. Eunice Swallows convinced me that Mr Kenton was the best person for the job. I'm sorry he's dead.' She eyed him curiously and again with that frown of concern. 'Do you think his death has anything to do with his job?'

Horton gave his stock answer of it being too early to say but added, 'I need to speak to your husband, Mrs Veerman.'

'I know.'

'Have you told him about the private investigation agent?'

'No.' She tensed and pulled herself up. 'I guess this will finally force things into the open.'

Horton rather thought it would.

CHAPTER EIGHT

She asked him to wait in the hall while she fetched her husband, who was still in the garden, even though it was growing dark. Horton guessed it was to give her time to break the news to him.

He studied the spacious modern hallway with wide tall windows that stretched to the height of the house. It was gloomy, empty and cold. It was also spotlessly clean, but there were no paintings on the plain cream-coloured walls, no furniture and all the doors giving off into the rooms both to his left and right and further down the hallway to the rear of the house were closed. The light grey tiled floor made it feel cold and bleak, reflecting the Veermans's marriage, he thought.

He headed for the rear of the house where he pushed open a door and stepped into a white modern kitchen that echoed the cold, unwelcoming feeling of the hall. It and the house seemed at odds with Thelma Veerman and the dogs. She should have been in a country house traditionally furnished, he thought, gazing out of the wide patio windows that gave onto the lawns. Standing by the water's edge, Horton could see in the lights attached to the boathouse that Thelma Veerman was talking to her husband. Brett Veerman was still beside the dinghy, but no longer hosing it down. Horton wondered what he'd been doing while they'd been taking their walk. Maybe he had only just finished giving the boat a thorough clean. And why would he take so long doing that? Was it more than salt water he was trying to wash off?

Horton couldn't see Thelma's face but he could tell by the set of her shoulders that she was telling her husband about Swallows. Brett Veerman was eyeing her with a frown on his dark-featured face, which even from here Horton could see had strength and intelligence. Thelma gestured towards the house and Veerman glanced towards where Horton was standing. Could he see him in the gloom?

Veerman addressed his wife, who glanced over her shoulder at Horton before turning back. Brett Veerman said something more, then strode past his wife towards the house. Thelma Veerman turned and watched him, looking puzzled rather than upset before looking back to sea. Horton heard her calling to the dogs. Was she crying, he wondered. He wished Cantelli was with him, because he had the feeling that Thelma would have opened up to the sergeant; women often did.

The kitchen glass door slid open. Veerman kicked off his shoes and stretched a hand out to Horton who took it and wasn't surprised to find the grip firm and dry. Veerman seemed curious rather than concerned or angry. His blue eyes assessed Horton coolly. He looked younger than Horton had originally estimated and possibly younger than his wife by a few years. Or perhaps he'd just worn better. His short dark hair was peppered with grey but in a way that made him appear distinguished. His face was craggily good looking, lined and lightly tanned. Yes, Horton could see both patients and nurses falling for this man.

'My wife has just informed me that the private detective she engaged to discover if I was having an affair has been killed, so you'll forgive me if I seem a little dazed.' He pulled off his sailing jacket and placed it on the back of one of the tall chairs at the kitchen breakfast bar, revealing a round-necked pale blue jumper bearing a designer label over a checked shirt. His clothes, like those Horton had seen in the apartment that morning, were all of excellent quality. And the height and build of Veerman confirmed to Horton that they had been his. He wondered how Veerman was going to take the additional news that they'd forcibly entered his apartment earlier.

'We'll go up to my study,' Veerman said, leading the way into the hall and up the stairs to the second floor, pushing on the lights as they went, which to Horton made the hall look even more stark and unwelcoming. The doors on this floor, like those below, were closed. Horton's phone vibrated in his jacket pocket, but he didn't look to see who the caller was. Veerman gestured him into a room, which like the kitchen below ran along the breadth of the rear of the house. And just like the kitchen it had glass doors on one side which gave on to a balcony with views across the Solent to Gosport, Portsmouth and beyond. The darkening day was punctuated with the lights of passing boats and ferries and the glimmer of those on the mainland. Horton couldn't see Thelma Veerman in the garden and he hadn't heard her enter the house — but then from here he probably wouldn't have done.

His eyes swept the room, taking in the telescope and a pair of binoculars on top of the cupboard sandwiched between the built-in floor-to-ceiling bookshelves before noting that the room, much like Veerman's Portsmouth apartment, was contemporarily furnished, clean and extremely neat. The books gave it some character, but even so, it still lacked warmth, just like the hall and kitchen.

Veerman invited him to sit, not at the modern table in front of the windows, but at the easy chairs and coffee table set some distance behind it. As he did, Horton noted a neat pile of papers, the top one showing diagrams and photographs of eyes.

Veerman sat opposite. 'My wife might have told you that I'm an ophthalmic consultant surgeon,' he said, noting

Horton's gaze. 'I'm not sure how I can help you with your enquiries, considering I was unaware I was being investigated.' His voice was deep and carried a quiet air of authority about it.

Horton handed across his mobile phone showing Kenton's photograph. 'His name is Jasper Kenton.'

'No. I've never seen him before.'

'His car was found parked at the Admiralty Towers car park.'

He hadn't given that information to Thelma.

Veerman eyed Horton closely and took a moment before answering. 'I see.'

Horton thought he did. If Veerman had shot Kenton in that apartment, then he must have scrubbed it from ceiling to floor to get rid of the blood and Horton couldn't see the man in front of him doing that.

'Do you have your fob to enter the car park, sir?'

'I do. It hasn't been stolen.' Veerman reached into his trouser pocket and pulled out a set of keys. Amongst them was the black key fob similar to the one that Roger Watling had shown him.

'Where were you last night, Mr Veerman?'

Veerman crossed his legs, but his eye contact never wavered.

Horton saw a cool, intelligent, self-assured man.

'At my apartment at Admiralty Towers.'

'All night?' pressed Horton, knowing from Thelma Veerman that he hadn't been.

'From 9.30 p.m. until I left to catch the last sailing of the night, the 11.59 p.m. Wightlink car ferry.'

'You went to Admiralty Towers direct from work?'

'From Queen Alexandra Hospital, Portsmouth, yes.'

Veerman would know better than to lie about something they could so easily check. But Horton was curious as to why Brett Veerman found it necessary to have a flat so close to where he lived. He asked.

'As you are aware, Inspector, living on an island can be inconvenient at times. I can be on call, operating late at night, or all night if it is an emergency, and I have late-night private clinics. Sometimes there are no sailings to the island when I finish work or I am too tired, so I stay in the apartment.'

It was good, but it didn't fool Horton. 'I understand that you've only had the apartment for three months; what did you do before then?'

Was that a flicker of annoyance in Veerman's eyes?

'I stayed at the hospital, that is in the nurses' quarters close by. There are some rooms assigned for the doctors' use. Occasionally I'd stay with a colleague,' Veerman answered smoothly.

'So why the change of heart now?'

'Why not?'

'Your wife was unaware that you'd bought the apartment.'

'Do you tell your wife everything?'

'I don't have one.'

Veerman merely inclined his head. Horton had wondered if Veerman's instinctive response would have been *lucky you*. 'Were you alone at your apartment?'

'Of course. Despite what my wife thinks, I am not having an affair.'

Veerman didn't look as though he was lying, but then he was probably an expert at hiding the truth, having had years of practice cushioning bad news for his patients and avoiding answering direct questions.

Horton said, 'Did you see a blue Vauxhall parked in the residents' car parking area when you left Admiralty Towers last night?'

'No.'

'Do you know a Roger Watling, who also lives at Admiralty Towers?'

'I don't know anyone there. I'm not interested in chatting with the neighbours. The apartment is just somewhere to rest or stay over when I need to.'

And it had certainly looked that way to Horton. 'What time did you arrive home?'

'About 12.45 a.m.'

Horton hid his surprise. That wasn't what Thelma Veerman had told him. She'd claimed that her husband had got home at two a.m. So, who was telling the truth? If Thelma Veerman was correct then that gave her husband seventy-five minutes — to do what? Put Kenton's body in the dinghy? And if that was the case then had Veerman shot Kenton in the car park in Portsmouth, bundled his body into the boot of his car and brought it over? Or had he enticed Kenton onto a boat he kept close by, killed him and brought him to the island to dump there? But there would be time for theorizing later.

'Is that your Volvo on the drive, sir?'

'Yes.'

And Volvo estates meant no boot, but the body could easily have been covered by a rug. Horton hadn't seen any blood in the car park, but then he hadn't been looking for it and Kenton could have been shot some distance away from where his car was parked.

'Did your wife ask why you were so late?'

'No.' Veerman rose and in a firmer tone said, 'I'm sorry I can't help you, but this man's death has nothing to do with me.'

Horton also rose. He thought it time to tell Veerman about entering his flat. 'In the course of our inquiries this morning, sir, it was necessary for us to make a forced entry into your apartment.'

'You did what?' Veerman cried with genuine surprise. Then he added stiffly, 'You had no right.'

'I think you'll find we had every right, sir,' Horton answered evenly, 'if we believe it might help save an individual's life or is connected with a crime.'

'You actually thought that I'd attacked this man!' Veerman cried incredulously. He appeared angry but Horton was getting a gut feeling that this was simply an act. Maybe he was seeing what he wanted to see. He tried to think impartially as Veerman said crisply, 'I shall make an official complaint.' He swept past Horton and wrenched open the door.

Horton remained where he was for a moment, keeping his steady gaze on Veerman who held it without flinching.

Horton reached the door before saying conversationally, 'Do much sailing, Mr Veerman?' If he was hoping to wrong-foot Veerman then he was disappointed.

'As much as I can,' Veerman answered stiffly, shutting the door to his study firmly behind Horton and heading down the stairs.

'Been out in your dinghy today?'

'Yes.'

'Where did you go?'

'Just out in the Solent, not far. Not that I can see it is any of your business,' Veerman tossed over his shoulder as they reached the hall.

Oh, isn't it, thought Horton. Veerman had the front door open but again Horton paused on the threshold. 'Do you own another boat apart from the dinghy?'

'No. Now I have—'

'Do you know Lord Richard Ames?'

Veerman looked taken aback by the question, then puzzled. 'Yes. Why do you want to know?'

But Horton wasn't going to answer that yet. 'Thank you for your assistance, sir.' He would like to have asked how Veerman knew Ames but he'd save that for another time. Although perhaps he could hazard a guess. They could belong to the same yacht club and that would be easy enough to check.

The door closed behind Horton with a solid clunk. There was no sign of Thelma Veerman or the dogs, but she could have been anywhere inside the house or in the grounds to the rear of the property. Maybe she'd gone for another walk before plucking up the courage to face her husband, although it was dark now.

Horton considered what he'd learned and what he'd seen. There certainly didn't appear to be any love between the Veermans. And if there wasn't, would Brett Veerman have been angry enough to strike out at a private investigator spying on him? Horton doubted it, unless that PI had discovered something Veerman didn't want revealed. Was he capable of killing though? Maybe. If the stakes were very high.

He peered inside the Volvo. There was a rug in the back but nothing visible to the eye that could confirm it had been used to hide Jasper Kenton's body. He noted the vehicle registration number and when he was in the lane outside, out of sight of the house, he retrieved his mobile phone. The call he'd missed had been from Uckfield. Horton played the message.

'I've been called back to Portsmouth for a meeting with the ACC. When you've finished with the Veermans get over to the mortuary. Dr Clayton must have something more for us even if she hasn't finished dissecting the poor sod.'

Horton turned left and headed eastwards towards civilization, calling Newport station as he went. He requested a car to meet him and take him to the mortuary. Uckfield had sounded terse; that was normal. But the ACC working on a Saturday was not.

Horton rang Trueman. 'What's this about Uckfield being summoned back?'

'Dennings is also on his way back. The Super and DCI Bliss are in with the ACC. And the Chief Constable's just arrived.'

So the big guns had been called in and Horton thought he knew why. Lord Ames. It had to be. And he was betting that Ames was keen to keep the news that a body had been found on his property out of the press, but was there more? Had Jasper Kenton been working for Ames, as Horton had posited earlier, a suggestion that Danby had denied and Uckfield had poured scorn on? Had Kenton discovered something that Ames didn't want coming out?

He rang off, suspicious and curious. He was, he also realized, hungry. He'd been planning on grabbing something to eat before getting the ferry or Hovercraft across to Portsmouth, but both food and the ferry would have to wait. Eating before a trip to the mortuary was never a very good idea. He didn't know what kind of information Dr Clayton was about to throw at him. He only hoped she'd finished the autopsy by the time he arrived.

CHAPTER NINE

'Kenton *was* shot, but not with a gun, with a crossbow,' Gaye Clayton announced while disrobing to reveal her trim figure clad in faded jeans and a T-shirt.

Horton couldn't have hidden his surprise at this news if he tried. He didn't think he'd ever have a homicide by a crossbow. It was even rare in suicides and accidental deaths. He didn't insult her expertise by asking if she was sure. He knew she was. His brain raced to assimilate this new information. He thought of Brett Veerman, but the idea of him killing Kenton with a crossbow seemed ludicrous. But it didn't seem so peculiar when he thought of the beachcomber. God, Uckfield was going to love this!

'Or to be more accurate,' Gaye added, 'he died of his injuries from a pistol crossbow wound. To put it bluntly he bled to death.'

She threw her gown in the bin and began to wash her hands, glancing at him over her shoulder. 'The penetration measurements are similar to those inflicted by a knife or other sharp instruments, but because the wound shape was round, I first thought it might be caused by a bullet. But there was no exit wound and no bullet or fragments of bullets internally. So I looked a little closer.' She wiped her hands on the paper towel, tossed it in the bin and turned to face him. 'To be precise he was shot with a conical-shaped bolt from a pistol crossbow. It penetrated three inches into the body, severing the main artery and causing massive internal bleeding. The depth of the penetration means he was shot at close range.'

'How close?'

She stepped towards him until she was standing about eighteen inches away. He gazed down at her, his heart suddenly racing. 'Sorry about the perfume,' she said softly and smiled.

'What perfume?' he answered quietly. The clatter of a mortuary instrument in the room outside sliced through the air and startled them both.

'That's very close,' Horton said, drawing himself up and postponing any analysis of his reactions to her. 'I'd say intimate. A woman?' he asked evenly.

Gaye moved away. Horton took a breath.

'Whoever it was, it doesn't appear that the victim lashed out in retaliation. There's no evidence of skin under his fingernails and no marks or scratches on his body to indicate he tried to defend himself.'

'Would he have been capable of doing so?'

'There's clinical data that confirms a victim might have the ability to act and survive for a period of time after being shot. He can even remove the bolt from his body — not a good idea, because he won't know what internal damage has been caused and he could make matters worse. Your victim might have done this after the killer fled, or the killer himself might have retrieved the bolt after the victim fell.' She headed into the small office behind the mortuary. Horton followed her, finding his pulse unwilling to settle back to normal.

'But someone removed the bolt because as you and Superintendent Uckfield saw, it wasn't in the body. A removed bolt alters the wound patterns, so too does rapid decomposition, which thankfully in the case of this victim doesn't apply, but if he hadn't been found when he had then it would have been impossible to determine what had killed him.'

'Unlucky for the killer that the body washed up on the shore.' Or was it?

She began to gather together her laptop computer and belongings. 'Maybe, but if the killer's gone to so much trouble, i.e. stripping the body and then wrapping it up, you'd have thought he or she would have made sure to dump it far out to sea, or on a rising tide so that it would sink.'

'So he either wanted the body to be found or got careless.'

'Or was disturbed and had to act in a hurry.'

But why on Lord Ames's property? Because it was remote? Because the killer knew that a rendezvous there would be totally private? Had the killer, possibly the beach-comber, Lomas, drawn Kenton there and killed him with a pistol crossbow? My God he hoped not, because that meant he'd withheld critical information. Or had Brett Veerman moored up on the pontoon in a boat other than his dinghy and left the body there? It was also possible that he could have taken the body there that morning in the dinghy, having transported it from the rear of his car. But where could he have shot him?

Gaye broke into his thoughts. 'Are you going back to Portsmouth?'

Horton said he was. There didn't seem much point in staying on here. He couldn't revisit where Kenton's body had been found in the dark. Besides, Uckfield needed this new information as soon as possible. And the whole team were already in Portsmouth.

'Good, I'll head back with you.'

They turned out of the mortuary and into the corridor. Horton offered to carry her computer bag and she gave it over willingly with a smile.

She continued. 'I've taken photographs of the wound and of the internal injuries. The radiology images might show the path of the wound. I'll examine those more closely on Monday.'

Horton didn't know much about pistol crossbows but he soon would. 'Could it have been fired accidentally and whoever did it decided to try and confuse the picture when they saw that Kenton was going to die, by stripping him, wrapping him up and depositing the body some distance from where the accident occurred?'

'It's possible.'

'Who would own a pistol crossbow?' he said as though to himself.

'Legally anyone over the age of eighteen,' Gaye answered.

But Horton knew that wouldn't stop anyone of any age acquiring one.

Gaye echoed his thoughts. 'It's illegal to use a crossbow for hunting but people do. And it can be used for target practice or competitive sport. It's also the choice of weapon in military units in some countries because it kills silently.'

Horton groaned. Had a former soldier returned with it as a keepsake? Was the beachcomber ex-services?

'I know that doesn't help much,' she said cheerfully, mis-interpreting his groan. 'And just to make it more complex the benefits of pistol crossbows as opposed to other crossbows is that they're small and light—'

'Which a woman can handle.'

'They can handle all types of crossbows, Andy.'

'Sorry. Of course they can.' He smiled. 'I was just con-sidering that alongside the fact that Kenton was shot at close range.'

'But you're right: it could easily have been a woman and it doesn't necessarily have to be an experienced shot either,' Gaye added. 'Pistol crossbows take little practice or skill to shoot.'

'Could he have been restrained before being shot and while being shot?'

'There's no evidence of that or that he was gagged. But his body has been moved. The pattern of lividity bears that out and there are abrasions on the ankles and back indicat-ing he was naked when this occurred. But he was already dead when he was immersed in water and it is saline. Of course, as I said before, you need to check the waterproof

81

capability of the sailcloth. His body could have lain on the shore already covered and the sea washed over it and seeped through the sail. Or he could have been dragged from the sea, then stripped and wrapped in the sail and my money's on the latter.'

'Time of death?' Horton asked, pausing outside the hospital entrance.

'That's the tricky one. The actual time of death is probably as I said, sometime late Friday afternoon, or early Saturday morning, but it could be earlier than that. The rate of internal haemorrhaging can depend on the age of the person and if there were any pre-existing medical problems. Very young and very old people would be at greater risk of dying quickly, and as your victim was at neither end of the age spectrum and he was in very good health, it would have taken him longer to die. He could have been shot up to eighteen or twenty hours before he actually died.'

And that put it back to late Thursday night or the early hours of Friday morning, matching more closely with the last sighting of Kenton by Eunice Swallows at the office.

They postponed talking shop as the taxi driver made for the Hovercraft terminal at Ryde. Horton let his mind roam across the facts of the case that he'd gathered so far, but his thoughts kept getting hijacked by the proximity of the woman beside him and the way his body had reacted when she had come so close to him. He'd always found her attractive but not in a sexual way, or so he'd thought. The strength and method of his reaction had surprised him though. Perhaps it was his need for female company and not specifically Gaye Clayton that had made him respond so strongly. Had she been teasing him or had there really been something that had passed between them? If so, she showed no signs of it as she sat beside him on the Hovercraft. He wondered what she was thinking.

They didn't speak during the ten-minute crossing. The noise of the Hovercraft made it difficult for them to converse anyway and impossible to talk about the case as they'd have to raise their voices and the other passengers would hear them. Through the windows of the Hovercraft, he caught the glimpse of the security lights of Fort Monckton as they sped past. His suspicion that Lord Ames was connected with MI5 made him again wonder if Jennifer had been meeting him there. Had she got too close to the truth about something he was connected with; something that was too dangerous to be revealed? And perhaps that was why Jasper Kenton was dead — because he, like Jennifer, had got too close to the truth about something highly damaging to His Lordship. But what? And why leave evidence on your own doorstep? No, if it was connected with Ames, he'd have gotten rid of the body. There would have been no trail.

They took a taxi to the station, where fifteen minutes later, in the incident suite, Gaye was repeating to Uckfield, Bliss, Dennings, Trueman and Marsden what she'd told him earlier. Horton hadn't already broken the news to Uckfield because there had been no chance of doing so before their arrival. As he had predicted, Uckfield had looked shocked and then irritated. The others too had shown their surprise, except for Trueman who had quickly turned to his computer and had begun tapping away at the keyboard.

Before Gaye had finished Trueman was printing off pages and handing them to Horton, who pinned them on the crime board.

'Is this the type of weapon used?' Horton asked.

She glanced at them and nodded.

Horton studied them, as did the others. The first pistol crossbow was a basic model. It looked exactly like a pistol with a bow mounted on top of it. It was twelve and three quarter inches long and sixteen and a half inches wide. Too big to fit in your pocket, thought Horton, but small enough to carry in a large shoulder bag or rucksack, or perhaps to retrieve from behind a rock or mound of earth. The compact version was only slightly longer at seventeen inches and the same width. Even the more deluxe models weren't much different in size, just over seventeen inches long and nineteen inches wide, but there was a difference in weight and the speed at which they could fire bolts.

Trueman informed them that there was no register of people who bought or owned crossbows, so tracing the murder weapon that way was impossible.

'Great,' cried Uckfield, frustrated.

Trueman added, 'And even trekking around all the archery clubs might not reveal who it is. Anyone can buy one of those things on the Internet.'

Uckfield exhaled and plonked himself down on one of the chairs, which squeaked in protest. Horton thought the Super looked troubled but then Uckfield's expression was often one of bad temper.

Gaye relayed the information about the time of death being a lot later than when the victim had actually been shot. She concluded by saying that she'd let Uckfield have her full report on Monday after she'd viewed the radiology images. Horton offered her a car to take her to the port to collect her Mini but she declined. 'It's only a five-minute walk under the subway.'

When she had left, Horton gave a succinct account of his interview with the Veermans, including the discrepancy in the time that Thelma Veerman claimed her husband had arrived home and when he said he had.

Uckfield said, 'She could have mistaken the time — and besides, if Kenton was shot on Thursday night, then it doesn't matter what time Veerman arrived home in the early hours of Saturday morning.'

Uckfield had a point. It was Veerman's movements for Thursday night that they needed to check. Horton addressed Trueman. 'When did Kenton arrive at the car park?'

'We're still waiting for the information and for the CCTV images.'

'They're taking their time.'

'It's the weekend and the staff who can help won't be in until Monday.'

Annoying, thought Horton. Uckfield made no comment though, which surprised Horton, as usually Uckfield would have been bellowing at Trueman that, weekend or not, he needed that information now!

Horton said, 'Well at least we can conduct a search of the area where Kenton's body was found and there's his car to examine for forensic evidence. I'd like to follow up Veerman's movements for Thursday evening.' But even that might be difficult at the weekend. He doubted if the same staff would be on duty, and certainly not the administration or the out-patient clinic staff.

Uckfield rubbed his neck and shifted his bulky figure in the chair. Horton saw him throw Bliss a glance and quickly tried to interpret it. What was going on here? Uckfield sniffed and said, 'Veerman's not the only client Kenton was investigating.'

'Are there any others with an apartment in Admiralty Towers?'

Bliss answered. 'No.'

'What about this Roger Watling? Does he feature on Kenton's list? Have we checked out his alibi?'

Again Bliss replied, 'Eunice Swallows claims he's not connected with any of Kenton's investigations.'

'Can we trust her evidence?'

'Of course we can,' Bliss snapped.

Why? *Because you say so*? Horton was about to voice his opinions when Uckfield jumped in. 'In case you don't believe that, Inspector, DCI Bliss is to go into Swallows on Monday morning, undercover, and with Eunice Swallows's full permission.'

That gave Eunice Swallows two nights and one day to sanitize her records. Horton said nothing. He'd only be wasting his breath. The decision had already been made and he could tell by Uckfield's steely gaze that nothing was going to change it.

Uckfield hauled himself up. 'DCI Bliss is to start employment there as a freelance private investigator engaged by Eunice Swallows to take over Jasper Kenton's cases. This will give her access to all the agency's files and reports and especially to those that Kenton was working on. She'll have complete access to his office computer and will liaise with the Hi-Tech Unit as and when needed. This way we can preserve Swallows's client confidentiality and keep the investigation low-key. It's a pity you interviewed the Veermans.' Uckfield put his baleful eye on Horton, who had to choke back the reply that he'd been ordered to do so by Uckfield himself. Uckfield was backtracking with the speed of a landslide off the coast of Dorset.

'You didn't tell them how Kenton was found?' Uckfield queried.

That wasn't even worthy of answering so Horton said nothing, just pressed his lips together. What the hell was going on here? Trueman's expression was inscrutable as usual. Marsden looked baffled, but then he was too young and too junior to have been involved in any high-level discussion that had obviously taken place before Horton's arrival. DI Dennings, the fifteen stone of muscles that Gaye Clayton called Neanderthal man, was looking smug and Bliss looked confident and cocky.

Uckfield said, 'Did the Veermans strike you as the blabbing kind?'

'No,' Horton tersely replied. 'I don't think they've got a lot to blab about. Their marital breakdown is hardly front-page gossip, but Brett Veerman said he'll be complaining about the forcible entry.'

'Shame you barged in like that before having all the facts.'

So that was the way it was going to be. He was being made scapegoat.

Uckfield continued. 'DCI Bliss will report directly to me. The ACC and I will make the decision on who needs closer investigation. From the media point of view, and for those outside of this room, the investigation is to be kept low-key.'

'How low?' Horton asked tetchily. So bloody low that it was going to be buried in the basement? And if the orders came from on high then Uckfield or Bliss would follow them slavishly; both valued their promotion prospects too much to do otherwise.

Uckfield eyed him steadily. 'As far as anyone outside this room is concerned, Kenton's death looks to be accidental.'

'Strange bloody accident,' muttered Horton, earning a black look from Bliss. 'How did he end up dead on the Isle of Wight in a sailcloth?'

Uckfield ignored him. 'Sergeant Elkins and PC Ripley will also be told not to speak to the media about the incident.'

'And the search for the murder weapon?' Horton asked.

'It's unlikely to be in the woods or on the beach,' Uckfield answered in a dismissive tone that said *don't contradict me.* 'But a search will be conducted *if* our enquiries establish it is necessary.'

Yes, and if the Chief Constable approves it with Lord Ames's blessings, thought Horton angrily.

Uckfield continued. 'If the media or anyone else outside the inquiry discovers that Kenton was wrapped in a sailcloth then we'll think again. But for now, the official line is that Kenton's body was found on the shore on the north of the island with all the hallmarks of it being a tragic accident.'

'Is that what we tell his sister?' Horton asked tersely.

Bliss answered. 'It's what she has been told and she didn't question it.'

'She wouldn't if she hasn't been given the full facts,' snapped Horton.

Bliss said, 'The Wiltshire police say she showed no emotion at the news of her brother's death. She told them that she'd lost touch with him years ago. She doesn't want to identify the body but she said she'll make funeral arrangements once the body is released. Eunice Swallows will make the formal identification on Monday at the Portsmouth mortuary.'

Uckfield added, 'The coroner has been informed and more time has been granted before a formal inquest takes place to allow DCI Bliss to work undercover.'

'It's amazing what being a peer of the realm can do,' Horton muttered.

Uckfield scowled at him and Bliss pursed her lips together. But it was Uckfield who answered. 'It's not the fact that the body was discovered on Lord Ames's property—'

Horton scoffed, drawing another dark look and a deep frown of disapproval from Bliss.

'But that he is currently undertaking some especially delicate trade negotiations in Russia and this could jeopardize them. The media would have a field day. They'd imply he was involved and that would wreck his credibility or at least question it and delay the negotiations, maybe even halt them. It's taken Lord Ames, the Department of Trade and Industry and the Foreign Office four years to get this far.'

So Ames *was* pulling the strings to get it hushed up. He must have been very annoyed when Mike Danby told him about the corpse. And Ames would know that Danby, an ex-copper, wouldn't move the body just to please His Lordship. Horton wondered if Ames had asked him to. Ames would also know that Danby would tow the party line and keep quiet over the circumstances of Kenton's death. He had too much to lose by not doing so. And what if Horton was to mention his beachcomber, Wyndham Lomas? What would Lord Ames do then? But Horton thought he knew the answer to that. He said nothing. He could tell that Bliss was delighted with her high-profile assignment. Had she been chosen because of her connection with Eunice Swallows? *You bet*, thought Horton. But it made sense.

He said, 'So we sit around until Monday.'

Uckfield glared at him. 'On Monday there will be a full forensic examination of Jasper Kenton's car.'

'And his apartment?'

'It's locked and we have the only key to it. It's not going anywhere tomorrow and it will only raise curiosity if we seal it off with crime scene tape and post an officer outside. Write up your reports and let Sergeant Trueman have them.'

'And that's it?'

Bliss said crisply, 'I understand that Sergeant Cantelli has a meeting with DI Grimes on Monday morning to discuss the racist attacks on restaurants. I'm hoping that you and your team will get a quick result.' So it was *his* team now, not *hers*? She really had wangled her way into the Major Crime Team and Uckfield didn't appear to be protesting. Well, he was welcome to the ice maiden. He was being squeezed out. Was that at Lord Ames's request, he wondered, heading back to his office. At least he didn't have to disturb Cantelli's weekend.

At his desk he checked his messages. There was nothing of any great importance and there had been no further attacks on restaurants last night. He hoped it would stay that way tonight. His reports could wait until Monday. No one else seemed in a hurry to do much so why should he? But he settled himself at his desk and called up the databases. First, he turned his attention to the beachcomber. As he'd expected there was no record of a Wyndham Lomas that fitted the profile of the beachcomber. The name was false. He was curious as to why Lomas, or whatever his real name was, had gone to the trouble of having cards printed. Was Lomas a con merchant who Kenton had been after, the cards part of his guise to fool people into thinking he was pukka?

He extracted it from his wallet and studied it carefully. There was only the name on it, hardly worth having it printed, but he could see that it had been run off on a computer printer rather than being produced by a professional printing company. Perhaps Lomas added a phone number or email address depending on his scam. He placed the card in an evidence bag and sent it by internal post to Jane Astley in the fingerprint bureau, asking her to let him know if she could get any prints from it that weren't his.

Next, he looked up Brett Veerman, recalling the intelligent, self-assured, calm man with an air of arrogance about him. Veerman had threatened to make a complaint regarding the forcible entry of his apartment, but on reflection, Horton wondered if he would. His protest struck Horton as being an act, almost as though he had been going through the motions expected of him. Maybe he was being fanciful but the more he considered it the less he could dismiss it.

Brett Veerman had no convictions, not even for speeding. Horton wasn't surprised. He typed Veerman's name into an Internet search engine and was soon reading about his career. It was pretty impressive stuff. Not that Horton understood it all, but clearly Veerman was a well-respected expert in his field with a string of initials after his name. Horton had no idea what they stood for. He read that Veerman had trained at Southampton Hospital where he had qualified with a distinction in surgery. He was an expert in cataract surgery, the treatment of glaucoma, as well as corneal grafts and laser eye surgery. He was a Fellow of the Royal College of Ophthalmologists, and saw private patients in clinics in London and Portsmouth, and at both locations he also treated NHS patients. He'd pioneered a number of innovative microsurgical instruments, which, Horton thought, must have brought him in a bob or two, and he was much in demand as a guest lecturer around the world. Veerman obviously had a very big reputation to protect and if Kenton had got something dirty on him then perhaps Veerman would go to extreme lengths to protect it.

He switched off his computer, picked up his helmet and jacket and, turning off the light, headed through CID. Then there was Thelma Veerman. An embittered woman. No, not embittered, but cold inside like the house he had seen. As though all emotion had been frozen inside her. He flicked off the light in CID. His mobile phone rang. It was Mike Danby. Horton smiled wryly to himself. He'd been expecting it.

'Fancy a drink and something to eat?' Danby asked.

Danby was not one of Horton's regular drinking partners — in fact no one was except occasionally Uckfield, and that was usually connected with work. Horton no longer drank alcohol anyway, but he was hungry. There was a reason why Danby had invited him for a drink and Horton knew it wasn't for the pleasure of his company.

CHAPTER TEN

'I guess you know why I rang you,' Danby said, supping at a pint of beer. They had found a table that overlooked the entrance to Portsmouth Harbour. The pub wasn't at the modern waterfront development of Oyster Quays but in nearby Old Portsmouth — which had sprung up after the Norman Conquest, flourished during the twelfth century, been granted a charter in 1194 by Richard I, had been heavily bombed in the Second World War and developed after the 1960s, and yet still retained many of its ancient buildings and fortifications and its unique view, Horton thought, staring across the harbour entrance at the lights of Gosport opposite. He could see a small motor boat ploughing its way into the harbour through the waves and the rain and behind it the lights on the decks of the Isle of Wight car ferry. He'd ordered home-made steak and ale pie, vegetables and chips. Danby had done the same. The bar in the room behind them was crowded.

Horton said, 'Maybe you want to offer me a job again, Mike?'

'Maybe I do. I'd still like you on board.'

'You don't sound as certain as you used to,' Horton answered, watching him carefully over his large Diet Coke.

'Worried about this murder investigation and that I might have something to do with it?'

'Of course not.'

'I'm a cop, remember,' Horton said lightly. 'I can read people.'

'Then you're reading me wrong,' Danby said with conviction.

But was he? 'You're wondering if I killed and dumped Jasper Kenton's body on Lord Ames's property.'

'I'm not, Andy.'

But maybe someone was. Lord Ames. 'But you are curious as to what I was doing there yesterday.'

Danby looked surprised, but Horton knew it was phoney. 'Oh, come on, Mike, you know I was there. Did you see me on the CCTV footage which you told Uckfield wasn't running because there was no one to view it?' And did Uckfield know he had been at the scene? Horton wondered. But if so then Horton was sure he would have seen it in Uckfield's expression. Perhaps Uckfield was getting cleverer at hiding his thoughts or perhaps, Horton thought, he was losing his touch.

Danby took a sip of his beer and studied Horton steadily over the rim of his glass. He seemed to be making up his mind about something. After a moment he put down his beer. 'Richard Ames uses a remote security system. For his estates in Wiltshire and Scotland, and his house in London, he employs a national UK company who have a full control room facility and are able to respond immediately to any intruder alert by not only summoning the police but also by sending security personnel to deal with it.'

'Costly.'

'He considers it worth it.'

'Why?'

'Oh, come on, Andy, you know he's worth a fortune. He has some extremely valuable race horses in his stables in Wiltshire, not to mention art, antiques and jewellery in his properties. Then there is always the chance of kidnap and ransom demands.'

'Agent Harriet Ames seems to have avoided them.'

Suddenly Horton saw something that hadn't occurred to him before. Harriet Ames at a desk in Europol was fine. On an investigation not so fine. She hadn't exactly been keeping a low profile recently with her involvement in three investigations, all involving him, with the last one in August. Perhaps that was why she had hinted at a discord between her and her father. Daddy didn't like her being at the sharp end. Not that she'd said as much but he'd seen it in her eyes. Now she was firmly back in The Hague, analysing criminal activity, and maybe she'd been told to keep her head down, or her father had exerted his influence to make sure she did.

From what Danby was saying the amount of security that Lord Ames commanded was serious high-level stuff. Perhaps it was more than property he was concerned about. Perhaps it was his role as an agent for British Intelligence that troubled him the most. And who was protecting him now, Horton wondered, as Danby was here? Who protected the rest of the family, Harriet Ames included? Was she at risk? He felt an uncomfortable stir in his gut. He shelved the thoughts and concentrated on what Danby was saying.

'For the Isle of Wight property, which is only used for Cowes Week and other major sailing races in and around the Solent, Richard has a system that can be monitored remotely and viewed from his laptop or mobile phone.'

'But he's not glued to the screen waiting for an intruder.'

'No. Sensors pick up anyone approaching the property from all its boundaries, and of course entering it, and send an alert to Richard's mobile phone and computer.'

'And he calls you out.' Horton recalled what Danby had told them this morning. Horton thought it likely then that Ames had seen him outside his house and on the beach on Friday.

'Yes, and I can send one or more of my operatives to check it out.'

'And did you send someone on Friday?' Horton asked. Was the beachcomber part of Danby's security team? He seemed too old for that, and too dishevelled, but perhaps that was how he was supposed to appear.

'No. I only learned you'd been there three hours ago.'

Horton rapidly calculated. After Ames had spoken to the Chief Constable and slowed down the investigation. 'Why?'

'Isn't that what I'm supposed to ask you? Hoping to catch a glimpse of Harriet, were you?' Danby said, jokingly.

But Horton didn't respond to the smile.

Solemnly he said, 'Is that what Lord Ames told you to suggest?'

Danby looked annoyed before a broad smile lit up his face and touched the penetrating green eyes, which had terrified many a suspect in the interview room. With real warmth he said, 'I'd definitely like to have you working with me, Andy.' This time Horton returned the smile.

'Why *were* you there?'

Ames was obviously keen to find out and Danby had been primed to ask. And that meant Ames had said nothing to the Chief Constable about Horton's trip.

'A valuable wrought-iron weather vane donated by Lord Ames to Northwood Abbey was stolen in June. The culprits were apprehended and appeared in court this week, initially pleading not guilty but yesterday they changed their minds and copped to it. I thought someone at the house might like to tell Lord Ames the good news.'

Danby eyed him disbelievingly.

'I was on my way to the abbey to inform them and thought I'd just drop by to see if anyone was at home. I wasn't sure if Ames employed a housekeeper.'

'He doesn't, not there.'

'I gathered that.'

Did Danby know he hadn't tried the intercom? If he did his expression didn't betray it. But Ames would know it was a lie when Danby relayed this to him. That didn't bother Horton one bit. He also wondered if Ames had told Danby that he had trekked through the wood and landed up on the beach by the pontoon.

He said, 'What made Ames ask you to check out the property this morning?'

Danby took a draft of beer before answering. 'He received another alert at 1.33 a.m. from the rear of the property, but when he viewed the area from his computer, he couldn't see anything and there was no other alert or anything suspicious. He let it go but on waking thought it best for me to take a look. That's when I found Kenton.'

Had Ames really received an alert at 1.33 a.m.? If so, then the timing could fit with Brett Veerman, except for the fact that it would be very difficult sailing a small dinghy in the dark and rain onto that shore, not to mention also returning home for two a.m. In fact, Horton thought it highly improbable. But a boat with an engine might be a different matter. And perhaps Veerman had an outboard engine on that dinghy. Had Lord Ames seen and recognized Brett Veerman? Horton made a mental note to check with the Castle Hill Yacht Club in Cowes tomorrow to see if the two men knew each other from there, and how well acquainted they were.

He continued. 'So this morning you arrived by boat, saw the bundle on the beach and went to investigate and found Jasper Kenton. So far everything tallies with what you told me and Steve Uckfield earlier. But after this it doesn't. Instead of calling me, you called Richard Ames, understandably, as he is your client. You tell him who the victim is and how you found him. He says he received the alert but had dismissed it as irrelevant—'

'Richard feels bad about that.'

I bet.

'I . . .'

'No, let me go on,' said Horton, but couldn't because their meal had arrived. There was a hiatus while the waitress served it, checked everything was OK and then left them.

Horton sprinkled salt on his chips and continued. 'Richard Ames denies knowing Jasper Kenton — maybe that's the truth, maybe not. You ask him what he wants you to do, he says report it to the police of course, but he suggests you call me as we know one another.'

Horton stabbed a few chips and conveyed them to his mouth. 'I bring Uckfield, as you suggested and knew by default that I would have to anyway. When Uckfield sends you back inside to check over the house you take the opportunity to call Ames and report back to him. He tells you to keep him informed, which is why we're here enjoying pie and chips together.' And in between times Ames has made one or two top-level calls giving his instructions. Uckfield is summoned back to the mainland, told to pull out Dennings and tread softly. Who gave the order for Bliss to go undercover at Swallows? Was that simply a delaying tactic until Ames and his cronies could be sure nothing would backfire on them, or to spin out the investigation until after the trade delegation to Russia? Or was there another reason?

'So how is it going?' asked Danby.

'Slowly,' answered Horton, then smiled. 'You don't expect me to tell you, do you?'

'No harm in asking.' Danby pushed back his plate with half his meal untouched. Maybe he wasn't hungry or maybe he was troubled by something.

Taking another mouthful, Horton said, 'Tell me about Jasper Kenton.'

Danby drained his glass. 'After I've got us a refill.'

He made for the bar while Horton finished his meal wondering if Danby had used the excuse of getting more drinks to buy himself time to consider his response. There were several people waiting to be served. Horton scanned the crowded bar. Amongst the couples and foursomes there were two solitary males, one in his mid-forties, the other about ten years younger. One was drinking a lager and reading a newspaper; the other, younger man, was doing something with his phone and had what looked like a large glass of Coke in front of him. Neither looked interested in them and neither looked as though they worked for the police or the intelligence services but Horton would reserve judgement on that.

He turned away to look at the harbour. Did Danby know that Lord Ames worked for the intelligence services? Or was he completely wrong on that score? God, he wished he had more facts but they were as hard to come by as a virgin in a brothel.

Danby returned with their refills. He set them down and Horton returned his attention to the man in front of him, noting that one of the two men drinking alone, the one with the phone, had left, his large glass of Coke half finished. Perhaps he was in the Gents. Or perhaps he wasn't thirsty.

Danby said, 'Kenton and I met at a security conference. He and Eunice had been running their agency for two years and mine had been going for six years. I was looking to expand. Jasper and Eunice agreed to sub-contract their close protection work to me. It's worked very well.' His expression clouded over. 'It's strange he's dead. And strange how he died. It makes me think it must be someone he was investigating on behalf of a client because his private life was hardly controversial. In fact, it was so quiet as to be boring. And, if truth be told, Kenton was a little boring himself. No, that's probably not fair,' Danby added as though he'd had a stab of conscience about speaking ill of the dead. 'He had the perfect qualities for what he did and he did it well.'

'Which were?'

'He was very thorough. I used to give him reference checks, which some of my clients asked me to undertake — not Lord Ames's staff though,' he hastily added, repeating what he had told them earlier. 'I gave Kenton the job of vetting all my staff. He'd leave no stone unturned. He made Sergeant Trueman look sloppy.'

Horton raised his eyebrows. 'I don't believe anyone is capable of that.'

'No, maybe not,' Danby answered with a smile. 'But Kenton had that same ability as Trueman to ferret away at something and collate the evidence in a logical and understandable manner, and to get it from places you thought inaccessible. His computer forensic skills were superb.'

'So he wasn't really a surveillance operative?' Horton asked, thinking of the Veermans.

Danby considered his reply for a moment. 'Not in the sense that you and I understand, staking out a house or business premises and trailing suspects. His expertise was in setting up a surveillance system, and no he didn't do Richard Ames's security. He'd do phone taps, place listening devices, record the information, trace and analyse social networking and Internet profiles, interrogate hard drives and retrieve emails and other information that people thought they'd erased — but as to sitting in a car and watching someone or following them, that wasn't his forte.'

'Why not?' Horton asked, interested.

Danby ran his hand through his cropped, receding dark hair peppered with grey. 'I can't put my finger on it, Andy. Just gut feeling. Yes, he could fade into a crowd. He wasn't too big or too tall. He didn't have any distinguishing features that would make him stand out. He was neither good-looking nor ugly, perfect for the job, but there was something about him that would make me hesitate.'

'You'd be worried he couldn't handle himself if discovered?' posed Horton.

Danby frowned as he considered this. 'He wouldn't bottle out. On the contrary, he'd face up to it. But he had a slightly superior manner that might get up some people's noses, especially if he thought he was right.'

And had that resulted in his death? Had he been spotted and then goaded his killer into firing that pistol crossbow? The weapon of choice didn't fit with it being a spur of the moment killing though.

Danby said, 'You know what it's like, Andy, there's that copper's instinct that warns you not to go there or do or say something, and it was like that with Jasper. I just wouldn't have felt comfortable with him as an operative. As a desk man yes, totally at ease with that.'

Horton knew all too well what Danby meant. He should have listened to his instinct twenty months ago when Lucy Richardson had set him a trap. He'd been working undercover trying to find out what was going on at an all-male health club in Oyster Quays, suspected of importing and distributing hardcore pornography. He'd gotten close to Lucy, who worked there, and, eager to get a result, he'd taken his eye off the ball. Before he knew it, she was crying rape. The operation was jeopardized, his marriage destroyed and his career stalled. That was history. This was now.

'Did Kenton have a girlfriend?'

'Not that I know of, though I guess there must have been some relationships in the past. And before you ask, he wasn't homosexual either, or at least I don't think he was.'

'Anything between him and Eunice?'

Danby looked surprised. 'No, they were just business partners.'

'You're sure?

'Positive,' Danby answered with a conviction that made Horton wonder. Danby hesitated for a moment before continuing. 'You asked me earlier when I last saw Jasper and I said two weeks ago when he referred a potential client to me, but I've remembered that I saw him last week, although he didn't see me. I was just coming off the car ferry and he was waiting to board it.'

So Kenton had travelled to the Isle of Wight a week before his death. No reason why he shouldn't, apart from the fact his body had been found on the island. So where had he gone and who had he seen? Thelma Veerman? But she'd said she hadn't seen him since that first meeting in Portsmouth. She could be lying but he didn't see why she should. Had Kenton been checking up on someone connected with Ames? Was it the beachcomber? Had Kenton's killer been right there in front of him? God, he hoped not. Maybe Kenton had just fancied a day on the island, but Horton knew that didn't feel right.

'What time was this?'

'About 1.40 p.m.'

Kenton would have been on the two o'clock sailing then. Horton tossed back the remainder of his drink, noting that the man who had been reading the newspaper had left the bar and the man with the phone had never returned.

'Did Richard Ames and Kenton know one another?'

'No'.

'Did they ever meet?'

'No. I was the interface between them. How was he killed?'

'I can't say.'

Danby nodded knowingly. After a moment he said, 'It must be chance he was left where he was.'

'What else did Ames ask you to do apart from pumping me to see what I knew?'

Danby smiled. 'Just to keep the family out of it if possible.'

'Uckfield's handling that, courtesy of the Chief Constable.'

Danby drained his glass and glanced at his watch signalling the meeting was over. As they made their way out, Horton said, 'Do you know or have you heard of Brett and Thelma Veerman?'

'No.'

'Have you heard any of the Ames family mention them?'

'No.'

'He's an ophthalmic surgeon. Have any of them had any problems with their eyes?'

Danby looked bemused at the question. 'They might have done. But it's not something I'm aware of.'

Danby would surmise that the Veermans featured in the investigation somewhere, probably connected to Swallows, and no doubt that information would be fed back to His Lordship. They stood for a moment looking out across the harbour. Horton asked Danby about his boat.

'I keep it at Hamble Marina.'

Expensive, thought Horton, but then Danby could afford it.

'I bought it six months ago for work. It's quicker than hanging about waiting for the ferry and unlike you I don't have the police launch at my disposal.'

'But you didn't take it the day you saw Kenton at the ferry terminal.'

'No. I had to see another client in Yarmouth. I do have more than one client on the Isle of Wight,' Danby said pleasantly.

They fell into step heading back along the old High Street to where Danby had parked his Range Rover and Horton his Harley. There were few people about and those that were seemed keen to get to their destination. The rain was light now but the wind was restless and blustering around them as though it wasn't quite sure which direction to settle itself in. Horton knew that feeling.

Danby climbed into his car and drove off with a toot and a wave. He hadn't asked to be kept informed of Kenton's murder investigation because he knew Horton couldn't make promises like that. But as Horton headed for his marina, he wondered what Danby would tell Ames or rather what Ames would make of what Horton had said. Had Ames been fishing for information about the beachcomber or had he wanted to discover why Horton had visited the house and beach? Perhaps both, because that was the only reason why he would have asked Danby to sound him out. Any other information Ames would be able to get via his intelligence contacts and from the Chief Constable, Paul Meredew. Not that Horton had given away much, he thought, if anything.

On his boat he lay on his bunk mulling over what Danby had told him about Jasper Kenton and what he'd heard at the briefing. Several things stuck in his mind, and niggled away at him. Had Kenton been working on surveillance despite Eunice Swallows denying it and Danby saying he was unsuited to it? Where had Kenton been going on the Friday before his death? Was it significant? Did Brett Veerman have anything to do with the murder? Could he own another boat, which he'd motored into the Camber or Oyster Quay, and

Kenton had discovered this and hadn't reported it to Thelma Veerman? Or perhaps he had and Thelma had deliberately not mentioned it to him when he'd interviewed her earlier. He could feed all his questions to the Major Crime Team, but as Uckfield seemed reluctant to move on the investigation, and certainly to do nothing until Monday, Horton thought that tomorrow he'd make some inquiries of his own. He'd start with checking if Veerman and Kenton had been seen at Oyster Quays or the Camber.

CHAPTER ELEVEN

Sunday

He drew a blank at both. And there was no record at either Oyster Quays Marina or the Camber of Brett Veerman keeping a boat there. Horton called the marine unit. Sergeant Elkins wasn't on duty but Horton asked PC Debbie Hoskins to make inquiries at the various boatyards and marinas around the coast and on the Isle of Wight to find out if Brett Veerman kept a boat elsewhere, and to check if Jasper Kenton had been seen at any of them.

He then doubled back to the ferry terminal close by and within minutes was speaking to the ticket office supervisor. She confirmed that Brett Veerman had indeed caught the 11.59 p.m. sailing to Fishbourne on Friday night as he claimed. It had reached its Fishbourne terminal at 12.35 a.m. From there Horton calculated that it would take Veerman only ten or fifteen minutes to drive to his home, which fitted with his testimony, but if Thelma Veerman was correct then where had her husband gone and what had he been doing for seventy-five minutes? Did it matter? Yes, if he had Kenton's body stashed somewhere.

He asked if Veerman had been on a sailing on Thursday evening. The answer was no. But the supervisor confirmed that Jasper Kenton had been on the two o'clock sailing on the previous Friday, as Danby had claimed. Horton wondered if the satellite navigation device in Kenton's car would show his destination. He made a mental note to ask but he thought that if Kenton's visit to the island had been connected with a clandestine meeting, then he'd hardly record it on the satnav system — or if he did, he'd make sure to erase it.

He bought a day-return ticket and half an hour later he was on the ferry heading across the Solent in search of someone he'd told no one about. Maybe tomorrow he would have to reveal the fact that he'd been at the scene and that he'd had company. But as he ate his sandwich lunch, he knew he'd say nothing because he was keen to see if Lord Ames revealed that information, and if he didn't, he wondered what that signified.

It was another question to add to his growing list, which rumbled around in his mind, along with those connected with his mother. He again considered if it was worth trying to trace anyone who had known his foster parents in case they had spoken about Jennifer. The easiest place to begin would be checking out the neighbours. Something he would make time for soon. It was unlikely they would come up with any fresh information, or even still be living in the same house, but as he'd drawn a blank on trying to locate the remaining two men in the photograph — Antony Dormand and Rory Mortimer — or their relatives, the only avenue open to him was to try and track down anyone who had worked with Jennifer in London, or at the casino in Portsmouth and he wasn't confident that would give him any answers. It would also take considerable time.

His thoughts occupied him across the Solent, but he put them on hold as he disembarked and made for the Castle Hill Yacht Club in Cowes. There was no chance of bumping into Lord Ames with him being in Russia. After showing his ID, Horton asked the secretary, a man whose backbone had apparently been replaced with a poker, and who was troubled by a permanent nasty smell under his long sensitive nose, if Brett Veerman was a member. Peering at Horton disdainfully over the rim of his spectacles, the secretary looked as though he was about to refuse to give Horton that information, but as other members entered the yacht club and looked warily and disapprovingly at Horton in his leather biker's clothes, the secretary ushered Horton outside saying that Mr Veerman was indeed a member. In fact, he had been for the last fifteen years, and was a most respectable man.

'I hope nothing untoward has happened to Mr Veerman.'

Horton simply replied, 'Thank you. You've been most helpful,' leaving Poker Man with a corrugated forehead and apprehension in his eyes.

As Horton made his way to Ames's property he surmised that Veerman and Lord Ames knew one another from their membership at the yacht club. But how deep that connection went he'd leave to probe for another time. It was also possible that Veerman had been a guest at one of Ames's parties and that meant Veerman would know the location was isolated and private.

He drew into the lane and pulled up by the field containing the small group of stone buildings that he'd seen on his first visit. Silencing the Harley, he kicked down the stand and crossed to a small gate displaying a 'Keep Out' sign. He climbed it and made for the buildings. They didn't look as though they were inhabited and the grass leading towards them was wild and overgrown, not trampled down. He wondered if Ames's security sensors reached this far. If so, would Lomas suddenly appear or would someone else show up — one of Danby's operatives perhaps?

Two of the buildings were adjoined in the shape of an L, with the furnace building detached from them. That was clearly uninhabitable. There were no windows or doors and it was little more than a shell with several tiles missing from the roof, exposing the timber rafters. Horton stepped inside anyway and gazed around. Just earth and dirt, no farming implements, no debris.

The other two buildings boasted a complete roof but only the smallest of them had windows and a door. Horton walked around the outside, studying the ground as he went. There was nothing to see except gravel.

He peered through the grimy windows but the inside was too dark for him to penetrate. The door was strong, a weathered oak, and secured with a stout padlock. It looked new but Horton thought it could be easily forced. He was tempted to try but held back. He gazed up and around it. Why bother to padlock the door if there was nothing inside? Was it to stop tramps from getting in and sleeping rough? Or perhaps there were farm implements inside, though there was no farm here or farmhouse. That was a few miles back, close to the main road.

Perhaps Lomas had padlocked it because inside were his flotsam and jetsam that he made artworks from. Yet if he lived here surely there would have been some evidence of that, a seat outside perhaps, some plants or remains of plants, boots or shoes, a clothes line, an old bicycle, tools, rubbish.

He turned and surveyed the field where his Harley was parked. Yes, he could see the track leading to Ames's house quite clearly from here. If the beachcomber lived here then he would certainly have seen cars arriving in the past and his Harley on Friday. But if this was where Lomas lived then he was the neatest and most minimalistic beachcomber artist Horton had ever come across. And it would have been impossible for him to have taken Kenton's body from here to the shore. Horton supposed that Lomas could have frogmarched a living Kenton there and then shot him with a pistol crossbow but the distance was considerable — across the field, back along the lane, then a right turn down toward the woods, through the woods and onto the shore — and surely Kenton would have got the better of the older man long before then.

He returned to the Harley and made for the woods where once again he alighted. It was a dull and damp October day and the wood seemed menacingly dark as Horton traipsed through it. He came out onto the shore and retraced his steps from Friday. Ames's security sensors would be going overtime now, he guessed, smiling wryly. He didn't care. He stood in exactly the same spot as he had on Friday when the beachcomber had hailed him. He was at the rear of Ames's land, facing the long and sturdily constructed pontoon. Then it had been almost high tide with the sea lapping under and against it. Now it was just over two hours to high tide but there was still no way around the pontoon unless he climbed on and over it or around it, in which case he'd get his feet wet.

Horton eyed the rear door that led into the grounds of Ames's house. There couldn't be sensors on the shore — on the pontoon, yes, but he wasn't on the pontoon and he hadn't been on Friday. But perhaps whatever system Ames had installed could pick up a fly alighting on a pebble sixty yards away, and if that was so, then Ames must also have seen the beachcomber. And yet Danby hadn't mentioned him. Was that because he had been told not to or because Ames hadn't mentioned the beachcomber to Danby? If so, why not?

He turned and headed back in the direction he'd seen the beachcomber take until he came to the creek. There was no way across it except by boat and opposite he could see a band of trees that abutted directly onto the shore, making it impossible to launch a boat from there. The creek culminated in another band of dense woods, as Danby had said, and again there was no place to launch a boat. The shore to his right curved round and adjoined the woods he had trekked through. At high tide, the sea would wash up against the roots of the oaks that bordered it. There was no access for a boat. But perhaps Lomas had motored into the creek earlier and had left his boat half in, half out of the water and walked to where Horton had met him. He recalled Lomas had been wearing sandals but he couldn't remember if his feet had been wet. Or perhaps he had come through the same woods as Horton had done but earlier, at low tide, and walked along the shore out of sight of Horton, looking for his flotsam and jetsam until he'd returned to where he'd found Horton.

Could Kenton's body have been in a small boat hidden from view in this creek? It was possible. And once Horton had left the area, Lomas had returned to his boat, motored it into the Solent close to Ames's pontoon, jumped out of it, and tipped it over, along with Kenton's body, so that it landed face down on the shingle. Then all he had to do was right the boat and body and sail away. The same could be said for Brett Veerman, who could have motored here in his dinghy on Saturday morning.

Horton returned to his Harley. At the field he again stopped and stared at the stone buildings. There were still no signs of life in or around them. He revved up and headed for the ferry, wondering if Ames had viewed his reconnaissance of the area from his computer screen somewhere in Russia and if so, what he'd do next. Send Danby to pump him for information again? Or send someone else?

He did neither. Horton spent an undisturbed night, but not an untroubled one. His dreams had been a strange mixture of Kenton and Jennifer, and along with them came Thelma Veerman who metamorphosed into Richard Ames. That had shaken him awake and had kept him awake for some time, until he had finally drifted into a dreamless sleep, which lasted until just after 7.30 a.m. After a run along the seafront to clear his muggy head, a shower and breakfast, he stopped off at the sailmakers at the marina. Not for his own purposes but to pick Chris Howgate's brains about the sail that had gift-wrapped Jasper Kenton. Without the sail though there was little Chris Howgate could tell him. Horton had suspected as much.

'It looks old,' Howgate said, peering at the photograph of the sail in the evidence bag that Horton had copied to his phone. 'And filthy. Doesn't look as though it's ever been laundered.' Horton thought that might be to their advantage because there would be an accumulation of crystallized salt, dirt and mildew on it, which might help them match where it had come from. Horton was still wondering if that could be Veerman's boathouse.

At the station he diverted to the incident suite and took a seat opposite the burly dark-haired Trueman with the permanent nine o'clock shadow on his strong jaw. Trueman told him that Uckfield was in a meeting and Dennings had gone with Marsden to Kenton's apartment. Horton asked Trueman what he had been able to unearth on Kenton.

'He worked for two international pharmaceutical companies at their UK headquarters in London, before he joined Eunice Swallows,' Trueman relayed. 'Started as a computer analyst with Finecare Corporation in 1989 and worked his way up to become their head of IT security after eight years. He was then headhunted by Wimco where he was Global Head of IT Security.'

'Must have been earning a fortune.'

'He chucked it all in four years ago to join Eunice Swallows.'

Just as Danby had told him. 'Any reason why?'

Trueman shrugged his broad shoulders. 'Maybe he got sick of the pressure or fancied being his own boss. I'm applying for access to his bank account and his phone records.'

'Could Kenton have come into contact with Brett Veerman when he was working for one of those pharmaceutical companies?'

'I can't see how, although there could be a link between the drugs they manufacture and those that Veerman might prescribe.'

'Can you check if any of them are specifically for eye care?'

Trueman nodded.

'The Swallows website says Kenton acted as an expert technical witness. I'd like to know which trials he gave evidence at.'

'Bliss might discover that at Swallows, but I'll get on to it.'

Trueman didn't need to ask why. He'd know that Horton was wondering if Kenton's expertise had helped to put away someone who had wanted to get even.

Horton rose and crossed to the crime board. 'Unusual murder weapon,' he said thoughtfully, studying the pictures of the pistol crossbows. 'Any other homicides around the UK that match this MO?'

'There have been crossbow murders but a different type of crossbow, and nothing where the body has been wrapped up in an old sailcloth or anything else come to that. We're going to do the usual rounds of all the archery clubs but . . .'

'You're not hopeful.' Horton thought, like Trueman, it was unlikely that they'd get a lead that way.

He made for his office but met Cantelli and Tim Shearer in the corridor. The STOP meeting was over and Cantelli reported that there had been no racist slogans painted on restaurant walls over the weekend. Horton asked Shearer if he'd ever come across Jasper Kenton when in London.

'The name doesn't ring a bell. Crook or victim?'

'Victim.' Horton swiftly relayed the outline of the case and Kenton's background to them both, adding, 'He might have acted as an expert witness in cybercrime investigations.' Shearer said he'd make some inquiries and let him know.

Heading for CID, Cantelli said, 'Is there a link between Jasper Kenton and Agent Harriet Ames? Could Kenton have discovered some information about a crook wanted by Europol and the killer dumped the body on Ames's property as a warning that the same could happen to his daughter, Harriet, unless she lays off investigating?'

They halted by the vending machine. Cantelli's words brought back some of Horton's conversation with Mike Danby about Ames's protection measures.

'I can't see Europol, or Harriet Ames, giving into threats like that, but her father can pull strings.' And he had, judging by the pace of the investigation. Pushing a button for a black coffee Horton rapidly considered this new take on Kenton's death. Reaching for his plastic cup he said, 'Kenton was a computer forensic expert so it could be linked to a major international fraud or scam. It would explain Bliss going undercover. She's working at Swallows so that she can have access to Kenton's files, with Eunice Swallows's permission. And it would also explain Uckfield putting a lid on the media coverage.'

If it was the case then the Major Crime Team would be working with the Serious Organized Crime Agency and the Intelligence Directorate, and Harriet Ames had probably already been questioned about Jasper Kenton. She and her bosses could be trawling through their investigations to find a link to whomever it was Kenton had been about to expose.

'I wish I knew which cases Kenton had been working on,' Horton said with feeling, as Cantelli retrieved his plastic cup of tea from the machine. 'The only one I do know about is Thelma Veerman's husband's suspected infidelity and I don't see him as an international crook. Unless . . .' He recalled what Trueman had just told him and what he'd read on the Internet about Veerman.

'Unless?' prompted Cantelli.

'There's a drug connection. Perhaps Veerman was involved in drug trials at one of the companies Kenton worked for, and suppressed or covered up vital information about their side effects. Or he's obtaining drugs from the hospital and selling them on. He's a cool customer, aloof and mocking underneath that superior manner.' He turned into the CID office, where DC Walters was tucking into a packet of crisps and staring at a computer screen.

'Or maybe he *is* just having an affair.'

And that meant it couldn't have anything to do with the beachcomber. Only the uncomfortable feeling in Horton's gut told him it might. He said nothing to Cantelli about that or his trip to the Isle of Wight yesterday, or that he'd been on the beach the day before Kenton had been found there. Not because he didn't trust Cantelli — he did — but it might put the sergeant in a tight spot if it later transpired that the beachcomber was relevant, or even critical, to the crime and Cantelli had known and kept quiet about it. He didn't want to get the sergeant into trouble.

Horton addressed Walters. 'So which of the restaurants gave you a free meal over the weekend, or have you managed to wrangle two free meals and you're leaving the third until tonight?'

Walters looked sheepish. 'Only doing a spot of surveillance and not being paid for it. All in my own time, guv.'

'Are you sure you're not our graffiti artist, working your way through every foreign restaurant along that stretch of road so that you can get free meals?'

'Course not,' Walters declared indignantly.

Horton eyed him sceptically. But in his heart, he knew that Walters didn't have the brains to work that one out. He might capitalize on it though, which he'd obviously done, but he wasn't crooked.

'So what did you get, apart from chicken Vindaloo and gut rot?'

'Nothing except a verbal onslaught on how useless the police are and that we'll never catch the bugger who's doing it, and even if we do, we'll probably tell him not to be a naughty boy and send him home with a lollipop.'

Cantelli grinned. 'Sounds about right. DI Grimes is giving us some assistance. PC Tina Collins from the STOP team will work with us to help identify our culprit. She's twenty-eight, single and very attractive.'

Walters leered.

Cantelli added, 'She's also very intelligent.'

'So you've got no chance there, Walters,' Horton added.

Cantelli grinned. 'She's got a lot of information on extremist groups and individuals operating in the area. She'll be here in a few minutes.'

Horton said, 'Go through the file with her, Walters; she might be able to throw some new light on the case. Cross check her list of names with ours. If you find any possible suspects, interview them.'

Horton's phone was ringing. He entered his office and picked up the receiver. It was Sergeant Elkins.

'We can't find any boat in any of the marinas belonging to Brett Veerman, Andy,' Elkins announced, but Horton caught the edge of excitement in his voice. 'But we have found one belonging to Jasper Kenton.'

'Where?' Horton asked eagerly and with surprise. No one had mentioned Kenton had a boat or that he even liked sailing.

'Hamble Marina.'

Where Danby had said he kept his boat.

'We're there now.'

'I'm on my way.' He rang off and hurried back into CID. 'Get your coat, Barney. We're going on board a boat.'

CHAPTER TWELVE

'He purchased it from Jacinda Boat Sales on the fifteenth of September,' Elkins explained, as they fell into step beside his sturdy figure and headed for a pontoon at the far end of the large marina. 'It's a 1997 motor cruiser, twenty-eight foot, with a twin diesel one hundred and seventy horsepower engine.'

Powerful enough to take Kenton across to Jersey or Guernsey — France even — and certainly to the Isle of Wight in a very short amount of time, thought Horton. On their way he'd discussed with Cantelli the fact that neither Mike Danby nor Eunice Swallows had mentioned Kenton having a boat. Cantelli had ventured that perhaps Kenton had only recently acquired it, or perhaps he hadn't mentioned it to his business partner in case she nagged him to take her out on it. Cantelli could be right and perhaps Danby didn't know about it either, even though it was at the marina where he kept his boat. Still, it was a pretty big marina with over three hundred berths.

Horton also wondered why, when there were several marinas close to where Kenton had lived, that he'd chosen to keep his boat twenty-two miles away to the west of Portsmouth. Was that significant? He didn't know. What he *did* know was that there was now a possibility that Kenton's boat could have been used to transport him, alive or dead, across to the island on Thursday night.

Elkins continued, 'It came with the berth.'

Which probably explained why Kenton had left it here. 'Did he say why he wanted to buy a boat?' Horton hadn't discovered anything so far to indicate that Kenton was a sailor, but then he knew precious little about the man. He might have owned boats since boyhood. And Dennings and Marsden might already have discovered paperwork and photographs in Kenton's flat confirming this.

'The salesman said Kenton was very chatty. He—'

'Chatty?' Horton interjected sharply. That was a new take on the former PI.

'Yes,' Elkins answered. 'He said Kenton told him he'd never owned a boat, but thought it was about time he gave it a go, living so close to the sea. He wanted something relatively small and easy to handle, but not too small in case he wanted to take guests with him. It's a four berth with a double bunk in one cabin and the divan in the main cabin makes up into another double berth.'

Horton frowned, perplexed.

'What is it?' Cantelli asked.

'This doesn't sound like Jasper Kenton. Eunice Swallows said he was a private person and had no friends. And Mike Danby claimed Kenton was quiet and reserved.'

'Well Kenton is definitely the owner,' Elkins confirmed. 'I showed a photograph of him to the salesman and the marina manager and both gave a positive ID.'

Cantelli said, 'Maybe Kenton put on a front for the salesman. Some people do.'

Maybe. But just who did Kenton intend taking out to sea with him? Had that person done just that and killed him? Was there someone in Jasper Kenton's life that Eunice Swallows didn't know about? Or wasn't saying?

'It's down here.' Elkins indicated the long pontoon with a mixture of large motor cruisers and sailing yachts. The wind was rising and whistling softly through the masts. There was a slight ripple on the water and Cantelli gave it a wary look as they stepped on to the pontoon. He reached for his chewing gum as Horton asked Elkins how much Kenton had paid for the boat. 'Forty-seven thousand pounds.'

Cantelli almost swallowed his gum. 'Maybe we should become private investigators.'

Elkins smiled. 'Yeah, but where's the job satisfaction?'

'Who needs job satisfaction with that kind of money in the bank?' Cantelli answered, but Horton knew he didn't mean it. He couldn't see Cantelli doing anything other than being a cop, just as his grandfather on his mother's side had been one.

'Was there a marine mortgage on it?' Horton knew Elkins would have asked.

'No. He paid cash, or to be precise it was paid via bank transfer. But he had the funds to cover it.'

Cantelli gave a soft whistle and looked sad, probably at the thought of what that kind of money could buy for him and his family. And it wouldn't be anything to do with boats or for his personal pleasure.

Perhaps forty-seven thousand pounds was a drop in the ocean for Kenton. He had no dependants and his salary at those two pharmaceutical companies must have been generous. He could probably have afforded a newer, more expensive boat. But perhaps he had been careful with his money and had sunk much of his savings into the business. He wondered how financially sound Swallows was.

They'd reached the boat where PC Phil Ripley was waiting for them.

'It's a nice motor cruiser,' Elkins said, running his eyes over the sleek white boat with a green canvas cover over the cockpit. It was if you liked that sort of thing, thought Horton. He didn't. He preferred one with sails. Kenton's boat was dwarfed by larger, shinier and newer motor cruisers either side of it and opposite. There didn't appear to be anyone on board any of the boats surrounding Kenton's and neither had they seen anyone on the pontoon on their way here.

Horton pulled on his latex gloves and unzipped the cover, noting that it and the boat were in very good condition and were spotlessly clean. Elkins rolled back the covering as Horton stepped on board. Cantelli looked dubious for a moment before following. The vinyl cockpit seats looked as though they'd been renewed or otherwise rarely used. The teak laid decking was clean and unmarked. There was an electronic navigational chart plotter at the helm, which might give them information on where Kenton had taken the boat.

The hatch down to the cabins was padlocked but there was no security alarm on it, which Horton thought unusual for a private investigator, especially one, according to Danby and Eunice Swallows, who could set up fairly sophisticated surveillance systems. Perhaps, like Ames, Kenton had pressure sensors and there were discreet monitoring cameras hidden around the cockpit or inside the boat. Horton couldn't see them. And if there were cameras then Kenton wasn't around to view them, but someone must have in their possession Kenton's computer, phone, camera and other surveillance equipment. And perhaps that someone was aware that they were here now.

Horton nodded at Elkins who removed a small set of bolt cutters from his pocket. Within seconds the padlock was unlocked and the hatch removed. Horton peered into the main cabin from the open hatch. Everything looked neat and tidy. There was nothing on the table and only a couple of cushions on the cream and blue upholstery. He descended and Cantelli followed him. There wasn't a lot of room for the three of them so Horton asked Elkins to see if he could get anything from the navigational system at the helm, which was unlikely because they didn't have the boat keys to switch on the engine. Maybe Dennings would find them in Kenton's apartment, unless they had been on Kenton when he'd been killed, in which case the killer had them. Elkins would also check the lockers in the cockpit.

While Cantelli searched the main cabin and galley, Horton entered the only other cabin, a double berth, as Elkins had said. In the wardrobe he found a waterproof sailing jacket and navy blue sailing cap. There was also a holdall on the floor, which he lifted on to the bed and unzipped. Inside were two pairs of casual trousers, three polo shirts, of which two were pale blue and one was white, two beige jumpers, a couple of pairs of pants, socks and trainers. There was also a toiletries bag containing a shaver, shaving foam, toothbrush, toothpaste and shower gel. All were neatly and expertly packed. Horton carried the holdall into the main cabin where Cantelli had placed a folder on the table containing the documents of sale and other details about the boat.

'Nothing else,' Cantelli said. 'Just a few pieces of crockery and cutlery. No food or drink.'

Horton asked Cantelli to bring the file with him. He grabbed the holdall and returning to the deck, asked Elkins if he'd found anything of note in the lockers. The answer was no. 'I'll get hold of a set of keys for the helm and see if Kenton used the navigational aid recently,' Elkins added. 'And I'll get a new padlock for the hatch.'

Horton asked Ripley to stay with the boat until they could get the scene of crime team there. He took some photographs with his mobile phone and noted the name: *Bright Girl*. To Elkins he said, 'Contact the Border Agency and ask them if they've seen the boat anywhere in the Solent recently or if it's been stopped. Also check with the marina managers at Ryde, Bembridge, Cowes, Ventnor Haven and Yarmouth on the Isle of Wight, to see if Kenton's been into any of them.'

Horton asked Cantelli to interview the salesman while he made for the marina office. On his way he called Trueman and relayed the news about the discovery of the boat.

'Dennings is still at Kenton's apartment. I'll ask if he's found anything relating to Kenton owning a boat and I'll get Taylor and Tremaine down there.'

Horton emailed over the pictures he had taken.

At the marina office Horton introduced himself and asked to speak to the manager. A few minutes later he was talking to an auburn-haired man in his early thirties with a tanned face and bright friendly eyes.

'Yes, that's Mr Kenton,' Paul Campbell confirmed when Horton showed him the photograph.

'When did you last see him?'

'Sunday before last. He came in to ask where he could buy some fuel. I told him it was on B pontoon, which is at the opposite end from where he's berthed. I showed him the location on the marina plan and asked if he would like a member of staff to help him, because he was new to the marina and new to boating.'

'He told you that?'

'Yes. When he took over the berth. I asked if he had done any courses and he said he didn't think it was that necessary; it was much like driving a car.'

Horton eyed Campbell incredulously.

Campbell grimaced. 'I know. I warned him that the sea was very dangerous and unpredictable, but he smiled and said he wasn't going far. Far or not, I told him the Solent is treacherous at any time of the year. But he was confident he would be all right.' Campbell shook his head sorrowfully. 'You see them all the time, people who buy boats and have absolutely no idea how to handle them or read charts. Just because the boats have the latest electronic gadgetry, they think they'll be all right, but they don't understand the tides or the weather.'

Horton knew that all too well, and Elkins and his marine unit knew it even more so.

Campbell continued. 'Mr Kenton said he wouldn't mind someone showing him where the fuel was so I sent Rob down to help him. Rob said he had to show Mr Kenton how to manoeuvre the boat off his pontoon and guide him down to the fuel pontoon. Mr Kenton is very inexperienced.' Then it clicked. Campbell looked concerned. 'Has anything happened to him? Only his boat's still in the marina, or it was the last time I looked.'

'Which was when?'

The marina manager rubbed the back of his neck, his forehead screwed up in thought. 'Saturday, I think. Yes, I'm sure it was.'

But Horton heard the edge of doubt in Campbell's voice. He didn't blame him for that. It was a big marina and there was no lock so it was easy to slip in and out without being noticed. Horton broke the news that Jasper Kenton was dead, but didn't say how he'd died or where, and quickly added, 'We're trying to trace his movements for Thursday and Friday. You have CCTV in the car park and on the pontoons — would they show Mr Kenton's car arriving?'

'Not if he came here then. We only keep it for forty-eight hours unless there's a reason to keep it longer, like a theft or disturbance, not that we have many of them,' he hastily added. 'I wiped it clean this morning at nine o'clock. So we've only got CCTV from then.'

Pity. Horton gave Paul Campbell his card and asked him to contact him if any of his staff recalled seeing Kenton's car in the car park on Thursday evening or Friday, or if anyone had seen Kenton on his boat or on the pontoon. There was one other place he could ask. Horton called in at the marina bar and restaurant and showed Kenton's photograph to the manager and two of the staff, but none of them recalled seeing Kenton and denied knowing him. He joined Cantelli outside the brokerage and they headed back to the car.

'It's just as Dai said,' Cantelli reported. 'The salesman claims Kenton was very friendly. He saw the boat, made up his mind almost instantly and didn't haggle over the price. The salesman said he wished all his customers were so easy to please. All Kenton stipulated was that it had to come with a berth here. He also told the salesman that it was the first boat he'd owned.'

Now Horton was really troubled. 'This doesn't sound like Kenton at all. It doesn't match with what Eunice Swallows and Mike Danby have told me about him. According to them it's unlikely that Kenton would make a decision on the spur of the moment. He'd be much more likely to make a thorough study of the type of boat to buy, test some out and certainly go on a few courses before buying one.'

'Maybe he did and he lied to the salesman and the marina manager.'

'Why?'

Cantelli shrugged. 'To make him look big.'

And that didn't sound like Kenton either. Danby had said Kenton could have a slightly superior manner but not in a cocky or flash way, or perhaps he had misinterpreted what Danby had said. Or Danby was wrong. He glanced at his watch.

'Head for the mortuary, Barney. Eunice Swallows should have made the formal identification of her partner by now. I'd like to know how she reacted. I'll talk to Dr Clayton. Visit the eye clinic and see what you can sniff out about Brett Veerman. But keep it low key. Make no mention of the investigation.'

Cantelli nodded. Horton knew he could trust him to do that and still find a way to get information. 'See if you can find out where Veerman was Thursday night and his movements for Friday. Use your charm on the nurses.'

'Well it worked once,' Cantelli said grinning, referring to his wife Charlotte. 'Never know your luck, it might work again.'

And meanwhile, Horton thought, recalling that close encounter with Dr Clayton in the mortuary at Newport, he might try his luck with her.

CHAPTER THIRTEEN

'You've missed Eunice Swallows by about an hour,' Gaye said, waving Horton into a seat across her untidy desk and pushing down the lid of her laptop. He was pleased to find her immersed in paperwork rather than human entrails.

He eyed her steadily hoping that his expression didn't betray the stirring in his loins.

'I thought she'd have been here earlier,' he said.

'She was due at eleven but business matters prevented her. So she slipped out in her lunch hour.'

Business matters must have been DCI Bliss's arrival working undercover. 'Slipped out?' he queried. 'Makes it sound as if she thought she'd pop in while buying a sandwich.'

'It's what she said. In fact, I quote her exact words.'

Horton raised his eyebrows.

'Yes, not the caring kind, or I should say maybe not someone who shows her emotions. Perhaps she's just clumsy with words. She was business-like and quick. It was a simple case of "yes that's Jasper Kenton". There were no tears and she didn't seem shocked.'

'Who was with her?'

'PC Seaton.'

Horton wondered if Seaton had got more from her. He was a good young officer and keen to get into CID, but knowing how tight-lipped and fierce Eunice Swallows was he doubted it. 'Did she say anything else or ask any questions about his death?'

'No, she was remarkably lacking in curiosity as well as emotion.'

So she either knew all there was to know because someone on the team had told her — Bliss — or she hadn't cared enough about Kenton to inquire. Perhaps, as Gaye Clayton said, it was just her way, because if she had killed her business partner, then surely she would have faked some kind of emotion.

'Is there anything more you can tell me about Kenton?'

'Looking at the radiology images, which I was doing before you arrived, I think it likely he was dead by late Friday afternoon or early evening but was shot, as I said, sometime late Thursday night or early Friday morning. He wasn't drugged. How's the investigation going?'

'Slowly.'

'Like the way the victim died,' she quipped with black humour. Horton understood that.

'Do you know Brett Veerman? He's an ophthalmic consultant surgeon.'

'Dealing with corpses as I do, I wouldn't have much cause to come across him in my line of work,' she said pleasantly. 'Even if the person who has died has donated his or her corneas the body will be quickly taken to surgery and I wouldn't have any involvement in it or any need to discuss it with Mr Veerman. I know the name though and that's about it. Do you want to know if he conducts corneal transplants?'

'Only if he was doing that or any other eye operation Thursday night and what he did after it.'

'You think he might be the killer.'

'Let's say I can't rule him out but it's just a theory, and at the moment one which Uckfield doesn't seem to be buying into. We've got no evidence to back it up except that Kenton was investigating Veerman for suspected infidelity and there is a discrepancy of times between when his wife says he arrived home in the early hours of Saturday morning and when he says he did. I know that doesn't tie in with Kenton being shot on Thursday night but it could still be significant. Cantelli's sniffing around to see what he can find out.'

'And you'd also like me to make some discreet enquiries.'

'Not if it will compromise your professionalism.'

'It will cost you. And more than a couple of drinks.' She eyed him coquettishly.

'I'll buy you dinner,' he promptly replied, thinking how nice it would be to spend the evening in her company and wondering if she'd accept. She didn't look horrified at the prospect.

'At a place of my choosing?'

'Yes.'

'Even if it costs a fortune?'

'It'll be worth it.'

'You're on.'

He returned her smile. Rising reluctantly, but with pleasure at the thought of spending more time with her and away from the stench of the mortuary, he said, 'I'd better rescue Barney before they mistake him for a patient and whip out his appendix.' He left feeling more cheerful than he had for some time. But Cantelli was looking frazzled around the edges.

'You'd think I was asking for an on-demand liver transplant,' he said with frustration outside the bustling hospital, which looked more like a shopping mall entrance than a place of healing. Even the wheelchairs were chained liked shopping trolleys, Horton thought sadly, and required a coin deposit refunded on return to their base, no doubt to save them from being stolen or ending up ditched in a side street or the creek that surrounded the city. 'I know everyone is busy,' Cantelli continued as they headed to the car, 'and the National Health Service is stretched to breaking point—'

'Gone well beyond that.'

'Yeah. But I've been passed around more times than a hat at a busker's night in the pub. Good job I wasn't dying of anything contagious.'

'Probably wouldn't have noticed.'

'No. Eventually though I ran across one of Charlotte's nursing friends. It's a miracle I found one in that maze of a place and Charlotte having left nursing so long ago. I thought all her friends would have jacked it in by now. But Brenda, bless her heart, is going to get me a list of the consultants operating on Thursday night and Friday. I couldn't just ask for Veerman's list because I didn't want to draw attention to him. She'll email it over as soon as she can but it might not be for some time. Sorry, Andy, but that's the best I could do in the circumstances and without making it official. Except for the fact that those I did speak to in the eye clinic said Mr Veerman was wonderful. I said I was checking out how good he was for my mum's cataract operations.'

They had reached the car. 'Don't worry, your nurse contact might come up with something and I've got Gaye working on it.'

'I wish her luck,' Cantelli said with feeling.

And perhaps they would make the request official if he could persuade Uckfield to do so. Heading back to the station he asked Cantelli to contact the powerboat training companies in the area. 'Find out if any of them provided training to Jasper Kenton over the last few months. I find it hard to believe that he'd buy a boat and take it out without doing a course.'

As Cantelli made for CID, Horton headed up the stairs to the major incident suite where he found a small team of officers and civilians installed at computer terminals. He placed Kenton's holdall, containing his clothes, and the file detailing the purchase of the boat, on the desk beside Trueman. There was no sign of Dennings and Marsden. Uckfield was in his office. Seeing Horton, Uckfield rose and joined him and Trueman.

'So Kenton owns a boat, what of it?' Uckfield declared after Horton had relayed the morning's discovery. But Trueman had already printed off the photographs that Horton had emailed earlier and had pinned them on the crime board, so Uckfield must have seen them.

'It could have been used to take him, alive or dead, to the Isle of Wight,' Horton replied, wondering why Uckfield looked so doubtful about that. Horton told him about the conflicting descriptions of Kenton's personality. Uckfield dismissed it as being of no account.

'Thelma Veerman would describe him as being quiet,' Uckfield said. 'He's hardly likely to go around grinning, making jokes and slapping her on the back. It doesn't exactly instil confidence in the client if the private detective she's engaged is all "hail fellow well met".'

'Then why didn't Eunice Swallows and Danby describe Kenton as being like that?'

'So he's got a bit of a split personality.' Uckfield shrugged. 'He *is* the victim not the killer and I can't see him being killed because his mood changes depending on who he's with. If that was the case, I'd have murdered the ACC long before now,' he joked. But Horton wasn't prepared to share it.

'Why not?' he quipped, annoyed that Uckfield seemed so uninterested. 'Perhaps whoever Kenton was involved with finally got fed up with having to deal with this dual personality. Kenton pushed him too far, the killer picked up the pistol crossbow and shot him on the spur of the moment and then left him to bleed to death.'

'But that—'

'Doesn't explain why he was wrapped in a sail and ended up on the shore on the Island,' Horton added wearily and tetchily. 'I don't think a woman alone could have manhandled the body unless she's built like a Russian shot putter. Has Bliss reported in?'

'Give her a chance, she's only just started. I'm meeting her later for a debriefing.'

'What about Dennings then? Has he got anything from Kenton's apartment?' Horton saw Uckfield look beyond him to the door.

'Let's ask him.'

Trueman's phone rang and Horton and Uckfield crossed to Dennings who had just entered with Marsden.

'Neat as nine pence,' Dennings said in answer to Uckfield's question. 'Everything in its place and clean enough to eat your dinner off the floor. Touch of the OCDs if you ask me.'

And a person suffering from obsessive-compulsive disorder didn't sound like the impulsive man Kenton had been described as at the marina, but it did fit with what he'd seen of the motor boat.

'Anything in the flat relating to him owning a boat?' asked Horton.

'Couldn't find any oars or old bits of sail if that's what you mean,' Dennings answered flippantly.

It wasn't. 'Any keys?' snapped Horton.

'Only this one and it's the spare set to his car.'

Horton glanced down at the evidence bag that Dennings placed on the table. In it was a key, tagged with a label, and written on the label in small, round, neat handwriting in ink was the registration number of Kenton's car.

'Kenton must have had his boat keys on him when he was killed,' Horton declared, 'which means he must have been intending to go to the boat. Boat keys are usually attached to a cork float in case they're accidentally dropped overboard,' he explained for the benefit of the non-sailors, Dennings and Marsden. Uckfield would know this. 'So they're hardly the sort of keys you carry around with you every day.' Horton saw Trueman come off the phone. He didn't join them but turned his attention to his computer.

Dennings shrugged as if to say *please yourself*. Addressing Uckfield, Dennings continued, 'He's got a bicycle, rowing machine and a running machine in the garage, but no shooting targets or pistol crossbows.'

Horton hadn't expected there to be anything like that. The latter belonged to the killer.

Dennings continued, 'The apartment is above the garage and opens into a lounge that gives onto a small room that Kenton obviously used as an office, but there's no computer and no phone, just a desk with only a few bits of stationery in it and a couple of files containing guarantees, equipment instructions, security conference notes. Nothing from his bank or of a personal nature like his birth certificate.'

Horton guessed Kenton must have kept that off-site in a safe somewhere along with any other personal items that could possibly be stolen and used for identity fraud. Eunice Swallows had told him that Kenton had kept his passport in the office so it was possible his birth certificate was also there, and if so, Bliss would have it.

Dennings confirmed this by saying, 'No utility bills either. Must have destroyed them after paying them, or perhaps he paid them all online. No evidence of him having a girlfriend and no family photos or personal correspondence. Couldn't find any back-up memory sticks or hard drive and no safe.'

Uckfield said, 'According to Eunice Swallows they use a secure online back-up company where all their confidential files are sent each night but Kenton hadn't filed anything for Thursday.'

So Bliss had reported something back, thought Horton. Uckfield clearly wasn't telling him everything, but then *he* wasn't confiding everything in Uckfield. It wasn't a good way to conduct an investigation but for now it would have to suffice. He again considered Cantelli's suggestion that Kenton could have been on to something connected with an investigation being conducted by Agent Harriet Ames in Europol. But if that were the case then why hadn't Detective Chief Superintendent Sawyer of the Intelligence Directorate stuck his beaky nose in?

Marsden, standing beside Dennings, chipped in eagerly. Consulting his notebook he said, 'The bedroom was also tidy and clean, even under the bed. Good quality clothes and neatly folded, a couple of pale blue shirts, several white ones, all freshly laundered and ironed immaculately. Half a dozen black and grey T-shirts in neat piles and colour coded, socks rolled up into matching pairs, again laid out by colour, as are his underpants.'

Uckfield said, 'Bloody hell, talk about anal.'

Marsden gave a dutiful smile and, again consulting his notebook, continued, 'In the wardrobe there were also two suits, one dark and the other light grey, and four pairs of black trousers. Two pairs of black polished shoes along with a couple of pairs of expensive trainers, but no casual clothes.'

'There are some in the holdall,' Horton said, looking behind him at where he'd placed it on the desk next to Trueman, who at that moment caught his eye.

'That was a call from the car park company,' Trueman said, addressing them. 'They've sent over the information we requested and I've just checked through it. The number plate recognition software shows Kenton's car entering the Admiralty Towers car park.'

'When?' asked Horton eagerly.

'4.41 a.m. on Saturday morning.'

'Are you sure?' Horton asked, his brain racing. He threw Uckfield a glance. The big man was also looking puzzled.

'You know what this means,' said Horton to Uckfield.

'Yeah, a dead man can't drive.'

No. And neither could someone who had been on the Isle of Wight, tucked up in bed with his wife. And that, Horton thought with disappointment, meant the killer couldn't be Brett Veerman.

CHAPTER FOURTEEN

'They could be lying,' Horton ventured. 'They could be in this together.' Dennings was eyeing him as if he'd just declared he'd found a way to hold back the tide and Uckfield just as incredulously.

'Why should they?' Uckfield answered. 'And why would they put Kenton's car in the Admiralty Towers car park if they killed him?'

'Perhaps Thelma Veerman drove the car there to get even with her husband for having affairs, or to get him out of her life. If he got convicted and sent to prison, she'd be free of him. I know she'd also be implicating herself but perhaps she'd deny it, or claim he coerced her, or that she was driven to do it.'

Uckfield peered at him as though poised to lift the phone and call the men in white coats. OK, so it was unlikely, but not impossible.

He addressed Trueman. 'Does Kenton enter the car park at any time on Thursday after 4.30 p.m. or during Friday?'

'No. That's the first time his car shows up there, and I've gone back to the Monday before. I've also checked Roger Watling's vehicle. He doesn't show until Saturday morning just before eight, as he said, and London have confirmed his alibi for Friday night.

'I'm asking them to check him out for Thursday night.'

'Also if he owns a boat.'

Trueman nodded. 'Brett Veerman's vehicle entered the car park at 9.25 on Friday evening and left at 11.30 p.m. which tallies with the time he caught the ferry.'

'Is it there on Thursday night?'

Trueman scrolled back down the list. 'No.'

Uckfield sniffed and eyed Horton keenly. 'You're still favouring him despite the fact he wouldn't have parked the victim's car in his own car park and he was probably in bed at the time?'

Rapidly Horton tried to pull together his thoughts. Again he addressed Trueman. 'Can we see who is driving Kenton's car?'

'No. I'm sending the image over to the lab to get it enhanced, but whoever's driving is wearing dark clothes and has a dark cap pulled low over his face.'

'Or *her* face,' added Horton.

Trueman nodded. 'And the CCTV cameras don't pick up the driver walking away.'

Dennings chipped in. 'And there won't be any footage of Veerman confronting Kenton, or escorting him out of the building to his car, because neither of them were in that car park on Thursday evening.'

Horton had worked that out himself but he didn't bother saying so. It had been his original theory. That had changed now he knew Kenton had a powerful motor boat and his boat keys appeared to be missing.

Trueman added, 'I'll get hold of CCTV footage from Queen Street and the Historic Dockyard to see if we can spot Kenton's car in the area.'

The high brick walls of the dockyard faced onto the entrance to the Admiralty Towers car park. Cameras might have been pointing that way. They might have picked up something, but Horton wasn't banking on it.

He said, 'There is the possibility that Brett Veerman met Kenton on his boat at the Hamble on Thursday night. They went out on it across the Solent and put in somewhere.' But not at the end of Lord Ames's pontoon because Ames would have picked that up on his computer. Unless he had done, spotted Brett Veerman, recognized him and was protecting a yacht club friend. He didn't voice the latter thought to Uckfield.

'Why?' demanded Uckfield.

'Because Kenton had something on Veerman,' Horton continued. 'Something so damaging that Veerman had to prevent it from coming out no matter what the cost. And maybe Kenton was going to blackmail him. Perhaps Kenton's done a bit of freelance investigating on the side before.'

'OK,' Uckfield grunted and sat down heavily. 'Seeing as you're still determined to put Veerman in the frame, let's hear it all.'

But Horton hesitated. Did he put forward his idea that Veerman could be involved in an international drugs crime that connected him to Europol and Harriet, as he and Cantelli had discussed earlier? No, he decided to keep quiet on that for now, but he could still run through another possible scenario.

'Brett Veerman meets Kenton on his boat at Hamble Marina on Thursday night. Veerman has come prepared with a pistol crossbow to kill Kenton, but Kenton is obviously oblivious to this. They take the boat across the Solent to Veerman's house. High tide on Thursday night was just after midnight so they could have got close to the shore where Veerman lives and where he's already placed his dinghy.'

Marsden said, 'Why would Kenton go voluntarily?'

'Perhaps Veerman has promised to pay him off in return for his silence, and claims he has to get the money from his house.'

Uckfield sniffed to indicate he thought that was weak. Horton did too but again it *was* possible.

'Once close to Veerman's house, or on the shore, Veerman shoots Kenton. He knows that the method of death will cause little blood spatter, if any, and that it is also a silent weapon, in case anyone is around to hear it, which is unlikely. There's only Thelma and she's inside the house. It is isolated and it's dark. Veerman manhandles Kenton to his boathouse. Kenton is still alive but in no position to put up a fight with a bolt in his heart. Veerman leaves him in the boathouse and waits until he slips into unconsciousness, then he returns Kenton's boat to the Hamble and stays on it, making sure everything is clean before leaving for work on Friday morning in his own car as though nothing has happened.'

Dennings heaved himself onto a chair, which creaked at the impact. 'So how does he get Kenton's car from the Hamble to Admiralty Towers for 4.41 a.m. on Saturday, when he's asleep on the Isle of Wight?'

'*If* he's asleep on the Isle of Wight.' Horton addressed Trueman. 'What time are the ferry sailings on Saturday morning from Fishbourne?'

'One a.m.'

Horton said, 'He couldn't have been on that because he was on the ferry heading to Fishbourne.'

'And the next sailing after that is at four a.m.'

And it would take about thirty-five minutes to cross to Portsmouth, another thirty minutes to drive to the Hamble, collect Kenton's car and then drive it back to Portsmouth. It wasn't possible unless . . .

'He had an accomplice,' Horton said, his mind racing. 'Thelma Veerman could be lying and she caught the one a.m. sailing.'

But Trueman shook his head. 'No one could have done — it was cancelled.'

Horton rapidly rethought. 'OK then, Veerman pops out of the hospital on Friday and drives to the Hamble. His accomplice or lover follows him. Veerman switches to Kenton's car and drives it back to Portsmouth where he leaves it parked in a side street. His accomplice drives him back to the Hamble where Veerman gets into his own car and returns to work. But the accomplice moves the car into the Admiralty Towers car park in the early hours of Saturday morning.'

But Uckfield wasn't buying it. 'Why, when it will implicate Veerman in Kenton's death?'

'And why wait until Saturday morning?' interjected Dennings.

Horton felt like saying *how the hell do I know*. He thought swiftly. 'Because the lover wants to force their affair into the open.'

'And risk being caught!' exclaimed Uckfield incredulously.

And Uckfield knew more about lovers than any of them, considering the number of affairs he'd had. Horton recalled his conversation with Danby about Kenton not being very good at surveillance operations. He'd already previously considered that Veerman could have spotted Kenton following him and that now seemed even more likely. And Veerman and his lover had carefully planned this murder.

Undeterred by Uckfield's lack of enthusiasm for his theory, Horton continued, 'After helping Veerman to move the car, Veerman tells his lover that they'd better cool off for a while until the heat of the investigation dies down. But the lover suspects she's getting the bums rush and thinks sod it, he's not going to get rid of me like that, after all I've done for him.'

'You should write TV soap scripts,' muttered Uckfield.

Horton ignored the jibe and Dennings's sneer. 'She moves the car into her boyfriend's car park, maybe not even knowing we'd make the connection, perhaps she thinks we're thick, but Veerman will understand the implication of it.'

'There's no forensics on the car,' Trueman interjected. 'No blood and no recognizable fingerprints except for a few on the inside of the boot hatch that match Kenton's. They've got a few hair samples, the colour of which match with Kenton, but we won't get a DNA confirmation for a while yet. They're hoping to get some prints from the foot pedals. But the car is so clean inside that it looks as though it's been valeted.'

'And outside?'

'Salt on the bodywork, windscreen and windows and some traces of salt underneath and on the tyres.'

'As if it was driven into the sea?'

'No, parked close to it. They're working on trying to get traces of grit and gravel from the tyres.'

'A clean-up job then before being dumped in the car park.' Uckfield scratched his neck and studied Horton dubiously. 'First Thelma Veerman is in league with her husband and now it's a lover — make up your mind.'

'The lover is more plausible given what Thelma Veerman told me about her husband and the fact she'd hired a private investigator. Brett Veerman might not even have driven the car to that area. He could have given Kenton's keys to his lover on Friday with instructions to collect it from the Hamble and take it somewhere and dump it. Maybe she did and then changed her mind in the early hours of the morning after Veerman had told her they had to cool the relationship. When I told Veerman where the car had been found and questioned him about whether he still had his key fob on him, he was remarkably cool. Perhaps too cool. There was no distress, bewilderment or anger.' Horton recalled the intelligent, self-assured man. 'Perhaps he'd had time to prepare his reaction because his lover had already told him what she'd done.'

Dennings piped up. 'Hang on, why did Brett Veerman wrap Kenton up in sailcloth and dump him on the shore?'

'To hide forensic evidence, which could lead back to him, and because he thought the weight of the sail would drag the body down. He didn't count on it being washed up on the shore.'

But even as Horton said that he didn't feel entirely comfortable. He was sure the body had been placed and that a clever man and a medical one such as Veerman wouldn't make such a mistake. But then killers did make mistakes, thank God.

Uckfield was still looking unconvinced. 'But having a bit on the side wouldn't necessarily damage his career.'

'It would if she were a patient.'

'He's an eye surgeon, not a gynaecologist,' Uckfield exclaimed.

'Doesn't make any difference, he's still breaching ethical guidelines. If he tries to implicate her, she'll say she didn't know that Veerman had killed Kenton. She was just asked to move Kenton's car, but when she discovered on Friday night that her lover had killed Kenton, she was horrified. She'll claim she was afraid and was forced into helping him. A good lawyer will make her story sound convincing. It's his word against hers. And there's no evidence to connect her with Veerman because before parking Kenton's car at Admiralty Towers, she's taken all Kenton's surveillance equipment, his laptop and mobile phone and stashed it in her car. Perhaps Veerman told her to do that. But now she has something on Veerman that she can use to force him to divorce his wife, or so she thinks.'

'Then he'll kill her.'

'Probably.' Solemnly Horton added, 'She'll end up with a bolt in her heart. So *if* there is a woman involved, we need to find her quickly, and that means we need a warrant to get information from the hospital about Veerman's movements on Thursday night and Friday. They won't give it to us without it. Cantelli's tried.' He didn't mention they were using their own private resources to try and obtain it.

Uckfield hauled himself up. 'I'll talk to the ACC in the morning.'

Why not now, Horton thought, impatiently. But Uckfield was looking at his watch as though he was late for his meeting with Bliss. Horton wondered what the ACC would say, or rather what Ames would say after Dean or the Chief Constable reported back. Horton still thought the lover angle the strongest but he wasn't ruling out the drugs scam or that the beachcomber could somehow be involved.

Returning to CID he found Cantelli on the phone and Walters at his desk. Walters announced that he and PC Tina Collins had identified three possible suspects for the racist restaurant attacks, all with extreme right-wing views, all male and all Caucasian.

'One's in his twenties, the other two are in their mid to late forties,' Walters said. 'I've been trawling the Internet for comments they've made on forums and social networks. The idiots often like to brag about what they've done. PC Collins is checking on their whereabouts, social security and employment backgrounds.

'We'll talk to them tomorrow.' Horton nodded agreement.

Walters added, 'There's nothing linking the restaurants with regards to employees, current or past, or suppliers.'

Cantelli came off the phone. 'None of the companies I've spoken to so far have given powerboat training to Jasper Kenton.'

'Widen the area of search tomorrow. Check out those along the coast to Southampton and to Chichester.'

Cantelli said he would write up the report from their visit to the marina and the hospital. Horton didn't see any need to include one about his conversation with Gaye Clayton. In his office he rang Phil Taylor of SOCO to see if he'd got anything from the boat.

'No evidence of blood,' Taylor intoned in his usual mournful manner. 'We've managed to lift a few clear prints.' Which, Horton thought, would probably match Kenton's. They would also need to get the prints of the man who had sold the boat to Kenton, and those of Rob Tuckerton who had helped Kenton refuel the boat. Horton asked Taylor to do that and send them over to the fingerprint bureau.

'Sergeant Elkins is here and would like a word.'

Horton waited while Taylor handed over his mobile phone.

'The Border Agency hasn't seen or stopped *Bright Girl*,' Elkins reported. 'Ripley's spoken to a couple of boat owners in the marina but neither of them know or recognize Kenton or remember seeing his boat go out. The locksmith has managed to unlock the helm and I've checked the navigational charts. There are no journeys entered on it for the last three months, so if he took the boat out he didn't use that. The last trip that was logged was to the Channel Islands and that was before Kenton purchased the boat on the nineteenth of September.'

'How much fuel is in the tank?'

'It's half full. I'll get on to the marinas on the island tomorrow.'

Horton sat and contemplated the case. Was he wrong about Brett Veerman? Why was he so convinced he was their killer? He sighed and pushed thoughts of Veerman aside and turned to clearing his messages. He wondered if Tim Shearer would come back to him with information on Kenton. Trueman hadn't mentioned that he had news from the legal fraternity or police in London of Kenton having appeared as an expert witness and he would have done if he'd got something. He was just impatient. And he was uncomfortable with this softly, softly approach of Uckfield's. He was also uneasy about his own part in stifling progress in the investigation by his continuing silence about being at the scene the day before. He tried to console himself with the fact that it was still early in the investigation but the clock on this case was running extra slow and no one seemed keen to speed it up. He was almost tempted to suggest that they have someone tail Brett Veerman, but he knew what the response to that would be. They didn't have the manpower and ACC Dean would never sanction it. Perhaps they should hire a private detective, thought Horton wryly. Bliss?

He rose and peered out of the window. There was no sign of Uckfield's BMW so he must be with her now. Cantelli knocked and entered to say he was off home. Walters had already left. Horton rang Trueman and relayed what SOCO and Sergeant Elkins had said. Trueman would get their reports in due course.

Replacing his phone, Horton wondered if he should call Mike Danby and ask him to meet for a drink. He had some questions to put to him about Kenton's boat. Or perhaps he should call Gaye and ask her if she'd like that drink and meal tonight? It would be good to have company and especially hers, he thought, with that same sense of excited anticipation he'd experienced before. But despite that he found his mind flitting to Harriet Ames and cursed silently. He didn't want to think of her, not in any relationship sense. She was history, just as Catherine and Thea Carlsson were. But thoughts of Thea brought him back to the abbey. God, he hadn't even found out what kind of sentence those toe-rag thieves had been given. The courts had closed a long while ago and there was nothing on his email notifying him of the sentence. It was just on seven. He had Tim Shearer's mobile number and rang him.

'Sorry to call you so late.'

'This is early,' Shearer said pleasantly.

'You're still at work?'

'Yes, like you I expect.'

Horton asked if he knew what sentence Maidment and Foreland had received.

'Two years custodial. They would have got more if they hadn't changed their plea.'

'Have you informed Brother Norman?'

'No.'

'I'll do it tomorrow.' It would give him a reason to return to the island and while there he'd re-interview Thelma Veerman. He might be able to get more out of her about her husband and particularly his movements on Thursday night.

Shearer said, 'About Jasper Kenton, you asked if he'd been involved in any criminal prosecutions or been called as an expert witness in the courts. I can't find any cases logged in London. Want me to check the Hampshire records?'

'No, Trueman's on to that.'

Horton rang off. Maybe Uckfield now had that information from Bliss. Maybe it wasn't relevant anyway. He had no need to pursue this case, not until told to do so. He had plenty of others that needed his attention. But he had a reason why he couldn't let it drop. He had to find out before anyone else did if the beachcomber, Lomas, had anything to do with Kenton's death, and God help him if he did.

CHAPTER FIFTEEN

Tuesday

'Kenton never mentioned owning a boat and I've never seen him at the marina,' Mike Danby said the next morning with genuine surprise when Horton told him what they had discovered the previous day. Horton had called him early and asked for a meeting. 'I didn't even know he liked boats.'

'It seems to have been a well-kept secret,' Horton said as they walked along the shore at Warsash where Danby had told Horton he had a meeting at the Superyacht Academy at nine. Across the River Hamble on their left, and ahead of them, Horton could see the yachts in Hamble Marina. Behind them was the Warsash Maritime Academy buildings, which provided a range of courses for the maritime industry, including training for crew for the growing number of superyachts around the world. Horton knew that Danby had picked up several clients from there. He thought Danby was probably about to pick up another one.

'Kenton was close-mouthed, but then you've got to be in this business,' Danby added. 'Is his boat at the marina now?'

Horton saw no reason to avoid answering the question. Danby could easily check. He nodded. He could see Danby's sharp brain quickly assimilating this information.

'You're wondering if Kenton could have crossed to the island on his boat with his killer who then returned it to the marina.'

'It's a possibility.'

'Still fancy this Brett Veerman you mentioned earlier?'

'Haven't ruled him out yet. He lives on the island, can sail a boat, and he's a member of the same yacht club as Ames.'

'Doesn't mean a thing. It could just be a coincidence that the body was put on Richard's shore. Maybe the killer just wanted a quiet place to dump it.' He eyed Horton steadily. 'But I can understand why you're making the connection. I'd be following it up if I were running the case.'

Pity Uckfield didn't think that, unless he had returned from his meeting with Dean with authorization to formally question Veerman and his colleagues and staff.

'What did Kenton's clients think of him? You must have got some feedback from those he referred to you,' Horton said.

'The same as we all thought of him. Clever, discreet, thorough.'

Horton threw Danby a curious glance. There was more here, he was sure of it. He didn't think that Danby was deliberately holding back information; rather that *he* was asking the wrong questions. Only he didn't know the right questions to ask.

'You said you met Kenton and Swallows at a security conference. Did they approach you or did you approach them?'

'They approached me, that is Jasper did. It was during the lunch break. Kenton said that as we were based in the same geographical area perhaps there would be opportunities to work together. He already knew a lot about me and my company, but this was day three of the conference so he'd had time to look me up on the Internet. I told you he was thorough.'

Not so thorough as to enrol on a powerboat training course, unless Cantelli discovered otherwise today. 'And you conducted a search on him?'

'Of course. And I did one on Eunice Swallows before our first meeting to discuss how we could work together. Both had excellent references. Kenton especially.'

'From his former employers.'

'Yes, and from clients. There's nothing there, Andy. Kenton's as honest and clean as they come.'

'No one's that honest or clean,' muttered Horton, thinking of deception and the beachcomber.

'You're right, of course.' Danby's green eyes studied Horton closely. Horton held them unflinchingly before Danby continued, 'But Kenton was one of those principled people, very straightforward and reliable.' Then he paused before adding, concerned, 'Have you found anything to indicate otherwise?'

'No, but we're looking. Was he ever involved in any prosecutions? Trueman's checking of course,' Horton hastily added. 'But—'

'You thought you'd take a shortcut and see if I'd picked up any gossip. I'd be doing the same myself if I were in your shoes.'

Horton's sensitive ears twitched at the slight emphasis on the word 'your', making him wonder if Danby knew about the beachcomber, and the fact he'd kept silent about it. They walked on.

Danby continued, 'You're looking into the possibility that someone Kenton testified against could have sought revenge. It's one scenario, except that, as far as I'm aware, Kenton has never appeared in the witness box.'

Horton's expression registered disbelief. 'Not even for one of his clients when he discovered that someone he was investigating was making a fraudulent claim on the insurance?'

'No. Kenton's exposure of fraudulent claims always led to the culprit holding his hand up and pleading guilty. Like I said he had an enviable track record. He always amassed such firm evidence that even the bugger he was investigating knew when he was beaten.'

'We should have had him on the force.'

Danby smiled, then a cloud crossed his face. 'He was bloody good.'

'But not good enough to escape being killed.'

'No. So why?'

Horton could see by Danby's expression how much he missed the job. Horton liked him, but did he trust him? He would have done, except for Richard Ames.

Danby went on, 'Maybe he cocked up on a surveillance operation. Like I told you I wouldn't have put him on one. That's the obvious motive. Or he could have unearthed something incriminating that his killer didn't want exposed. He was damn good at forensic computing — perhaps he uncovered another cybercrime.'

'Another?' Horton said, his interest heightened. His mind flashed to Brett Veerman and the thought that he might be involved in a drugs scam. And one that was connected to a European country, hence possibly Harriet Ames's involvement. Could he be right?

'Yes. He unearthed a major one at his former employer, Wimco. It would have left the pharmaceutical company highly vulnerable. As you know, Andy, hacking is no longer the nerd in his basement doing it for fun or spite or in order to sell a few names and addresses and sensitive bank account information. Hacking's become automated on a huge industrial scale — often with state sponsored agencies behind it — and attackers are aiming for an increased competitive edge by stealing company secrets and that's what they were after at Wimco.'

'Did he tell you this?'

'No. I got it from the Vice President; he was the first client Jasper recommended to me. Humphrey Naughton. Naughton couldn't speak highly enough of Kenton.'

'I'm amazed they let him go.'

'No one's indispensable.'

'Including me. Bliss thinks I'm highly dispensable.'

'You know where to come if she boots you out.' Danby consulted his watch and turned back. Horton fell into step beside him. 'I don't think they wanted Kenton to leave but he was adamant he wanted to set up on his own.'

'Were any criminal charges brought against the perpetrators?'

'They didn't get them. Wimco didn't pursue it — bad publicity, share prices plummeting, that kind of thing. Kenton had shut the stable door just before the horse had bolted. Wimco reviewed its policies and Kenton helped them to put better procedures in place. And you're thinking that he might have done the same for one of his clients only this time it *was* going to be investigated and the person undertaking the criminal activity didn't want his scam exposed, so he traced Kenton and silenced him.'

'It's a possibility.'

There was a brief pause before Danby said, 'I asked you before how he was killed and you wouldn't tell me. Can you tell me now?'

'You'd better ask Ames. He seems to be calling the shots in this investigation.'

Danby eyed him curiously. Horton explained, 'We're to go easy with the investigation on account of His Lordship being involved in delicate overseas negotiations and we don't want the media getting hold of a sordid murder on His Lordship's property.'

'Why don't you like him, Andy?' Danby asked quietly.

'Why should I?' Horton quipped, but Danby's words were a warning for him to be more careful not to betray his emotions as far as Richard Ames was concerned. He added, 'I don't like the way this investigation is being soft peddled.'

'But that won't stop you going at it.'

Horton shrugged an answer. 'How did you get Ames as a client?'

'Chas Foxton recommended me. He and Richard know each other from the yachting set — Monaco, not the Solent,' Danby added.

'And who's Chas Foxton?'

Danby eyed him incredulously. 'Gracious Grove. The 1980s pop group. They were classed as one of the New Romantics, like Spandau Ballet and Duran. You must have heard of them.'

'Vaguely.' It wasn't Horton's type of music, but he did remember them. They had been so big it was impossible not to.

'Chas now runs a successful media and entertainment company. He's got half a dozen record labels with some big-name stars. Tammy Freiding is one. We were handling her protection at the Isle of Wight Festival in June when I saw you and Harriet Ames there on a case. I mentioned it to you.'

'So you did. You were staying at Ames's house with Tammy Freiding. So how did you get Chas Foxton as a client? It's hardly the circle CID moved in.'

'No, but James Westrop was, and he recommended me to Chas. You remember Westrop, wealthy entrepreneur, had his place turned over in North Hampshire and his daughter kidnapped and ransomed.'

Horton did. It had been a frantic case, a race against the clock to save a sixteen-year-old girl, and they'd succeeded, or rather Danby had, by working out the perpetrator had been a boyfriend she'd met at a music festival. He'd then set a successful trap for him. Fleur Westrop had been returned to her family unharmed, and shortly after that, Danby had been offered a lucrative job working for Westrop, which he'd agreed to take as a consultant and not as an employee.

'James and Chas are friends. They were also business associates then, but Chas has since diversified into festivals and concerts all around the world. He's been a client for four years and James for eight, and if I don't get a move on, I won't get this next potential client.'

As they picked up their pace Horton asked Danby how soon after meeting Kenton he'd got his first referral from him for close protection work.

'Almost immediately. That was Naughton, as I said. Then Jasper referred another former colleague who used to work with him at Finecare Pharmaceutical. He's a top medical consultant, and no, it's not Brett Veerman.'

'But he might know Brett Veerman,' Horton said quickly. 'And he might know something about Veerman and passed that information on to Kenton.'

Danby frowned as though he hadn't considered this and was annoyed with himself for not making the possible connection. 'I'll ask him and let you know.'

Horton would have preferred to interview this consultant himself but he could see that Danby wasn't going to permit that.

'What's his name?'

Danby halted by the large complex of buildings. 'I'll give it to you, *if* he claims to know Veerman.'

'OK.' But Danby knew he'd be able to get that from Bliss.

Horton let Danby go to his appointment. He returned to the station where he was about to make for the incident suite, wondering what Uckfield had got from Bliss, when his name was bellowed and he turned to see the squat figure of the Superintendent at the foot of the stairs. Uckfield jerked his head in the direction of the canteen leaving Horton to follow.

Uckfield bought himself a cooked breakfast and a coffee and splashed out on a coffee for Horton. They took a table at the far end of the busy canteen.

'Anything from forensics on the sail?' Horton asked.

'Not yet,' Uckfield answered, shovelling in a mouthful of baked beans. To Horton he didn't seem particularly bothered. Usually the big man would be hopping mad at the delay and bellowing down the phone for something.

'What about the pistol crossbow?'

'Marsden and PC Kate Somerfield are doing the rounds of all the archery clubs in the area, collecting names of members and asking about pistol crossbows. We'll match them against the names Bliss has got.'

So she'd handed them over last night. 'And they are?' Horton asked eagerly.

'Natalie Jameson, she's being employed as a nanny to a professional couple's first child. They live just outside Arundel and work in London. He's a civil servant, she's an accountant. Kenton was running a background check on the nanny to make sure she wasn't a dope pusher or user.'

'Any connection with the Isle of Wight?'

'None.'

'And?'

'George Swanton, who's suing his employer for breach of Health and Safety regulations after suffering an accident at work. The owners are disputing it and suspect that Swanton set it up. And before you ask there is no connection with the Isle of Wight for them or the other investigation Kenton was working on, which is tracing the assets of a wealthy businessman, Norman Clayton, whose divorced wife claims he's hidden them from her and the courts so that he doesn't have to pay her the alimony she's entitled to.'

'Has he?'

'Kenton discovered a bank account in the Cayman Islands. He'd reported it to Eunice Swallows but they hadn't given the client that information yet. Clayton's in America so he's off the list. And Trueman took a call earlier this morning from the Met who said that Watling was in a business meeting until nine o'clock Thursday night and then went for a drink and something to eat with a colleague. They're checking it out but I think he's in the clear, and he doesn't own a boat.'

'So Veerman's still our best bet. Unless Kenton's death is connected with one of his previous investigations.'

'Bliss is looking at that now.'

Horton took a sip of coffee. 'What are the Swallows business finances like?'

'In good health according to the accounts filed at Companies House. Trueman's now got access to Kenton's two bank accounts, his credit card and three savings accounts.

It will take some time to trace all the transactions, but the accounts all show a healthy balance and that Kenton was drawing a reasonable salary from the business. The property in Emsworth belonged to him outright, there's no mortgage on it and he purchased it four years ago when he moved from London, where he owned an apartment in Battersea. So he'd have quite a stash of money to splash around. Everything seems in order, no unusual payments coming in or going out.'

'How are the staff taking the news of their boss's death?'

Uckfield bit into a sausage. 'Mary Wiggins, the office manager, says Kenton was polite, quiet and thorough.'

'There's that word again.'

'Eh?'

'Thorough. And the two men?' Horton recalled them huddled over their computers.

'Douglas Mead and Peter Snell both considered Kenton to have been clever. They respected him, said that what he didn't know about computers wasn't worth knowing.'

Which bore out what Danby had said. Horton told Uckfield where he'd been and why and gave him a brief account of his conversation with Danby, adding this time, 'Veerman could be involved in a drugs scam.'

'With this alleged lover,' Uckfield sneered.

'Why not? Or alone.' Horton thought he'd leave out any reference to it possibly connecting with Europol and Harriet Ames. That might be one step too far for Uckfield at the moment in his deaf, cynical mood, which, Horton suspected, had been induced by his need to keep the hierarchy happy and not ruin his future promotion prospects.

'We should find out who this medical consultant is and see if there is a connection with Brett Veerman. Can't leave everything to Mike Danby.'

Uckfield sniffed and wiped up the last of his fried egg with a piece of bacon. 'OK. I'll get Bliss on to it.'

Horton continued, 'How sure are we of Eunice Swallows?' If Bliss was her friend, then how much was she confiding in her?

'What do you mean?' Uckfield eyed him beadily.

'Maybe she wanted to ditch Kenton and had help from Mead or Snell.'

'She's got an alibi.'

'Yes?'

'A rock-solid one. She and DCI Bliss were enjoying a girls' night out. They went for a meal and a drink together.'

'Didn't know they were that close.'

Uckfield narrowed his eyes but said nothing, making Horton wonder if there was more to Bliss's relationship with Eunice Swallows than friendship, and if she'd told Uckfield that. Whatever the depths of their relationship it didn't prove that Eunice Swallows was sound. She could still be involved in Kenton's death.

Uckfield wiped his mouth with a paper serviette and said, 'None of the staff have any connection with the Isle of Wight either.'

'Perhaps they don't have to. They used Kenton's boat to get across there and just dumped his body where they thought would be best. Have we checked if any of them can handle a boat?'

Uckfield looked as though he wanted to say *do we have to*.

Horton added, 'And their alibis for Thursday night and Friday morning?'

'They're not serious contenders.'

'Why not? For all we know Mary Wiggins could have been having an affair with Jasper Kenton and her husband decided to kill him.'

'She's not married.'

'Then Kenton could have discovered something about her past, or Eunice Swallows's past, a secret she'd prefer not to have exposed. Have we looked into that?' Before Uckfield could answer, Horton swiftly continued, 'Or it could be something that either Snell or Mead didn't want coming out. Mary Wiggins or Eunice Swallows could be Brett Veerman's lover and his accomplice.'

'You are kidding.' Uckfield eyed Horton incredulously.

'Am I?' Horton knew that Uckfield hadn't seen Mary Wiggins, and as far as he was aware he hadn't met Eunice Swallows either. OK, so Horton thought both unlikely lovers for Veerman, but there could be other reasons why any one of them could have wanted Kenton dead. 'Has Dean given you authorization to question Brett Veerman about his movements on Thursday night or to question his colleagues at the hospital?'

'Not yet.' Uckfield shifted in his seat.

'Thought not,' muttered Horton. Probably still trying to clear it with His Lordship.

'Did Eunice, or any of the others, know that Kenton owned a boat?'

'Eunice Swallows didn't. Bliss is going to check with the others, but she can hardly go firing off questions all at once. It will take time.'

There was that word again, thought Horton with irritation. Time to spin this out and therefore time for the investigation to go cold or the killer to meet with an accident, if Ames and his cronies were involved. Perhaps Ames and his bosses already knew who the killer was and had known all along. They had seen him depositing Kenton's body. They didn't want this killer found. The investigation would have to go through the motions, but if it was stalled and delayed for as long as possible eventually the trail would go cold. Helpful of Kenton to have a sister who didn't care for him as the only living and close relative. No one to kick up a fuss. Or perhaps the killer would be dealt with in a different way. The MI5 way. That either meant death or disappearance, or both. The body of the beachcomber would be found washed up somewhere, *if* he was the killer. And Horton sincerely hoped he wasn't.

'Wouldn't it be easier and quicker, Steve, if we treated this as what it is, a major murder enquiry, and formally questioned everyone and publicly checked their alibis, instead of tiptoeing around like everyone's made of glass?'

Uckfield sat forward, his voice low. 'Yes, it bloody well would, but until I'm told that, I've got no option.'

'On Lord Ames's say so,' scoffed Horton. 'How do we know he's not up to his aristocratic eyebrows in Kenton's death? Yeah, I know, because he's in Russia, so he can't possibly be involved. Has anyone checked he is actually there?' Uckfield opened his mouth, but before a sound could escape from it, Horton continued, 'No, I didn't think so. He could have flown home, bumped off Kenton and flown back.'

'Don't talk bollocks.'

'He might have hired someone to kill Kenton.'

'Why the hell should he do that?' Uckfield cried.

'Why don't we ask him? Oh, we can't, I forgot. He's in Russia and we can't afford to fly you out there.'

'Look, I don't like this any more than you do, but we have to go along with it.'

'*You* do.'

'And so do you.'

'Do I, Steve?' Horton eyed him closely. Why this private briefing? Why the update as soon as he'd entered the station? Was it Uckfield's idea or had Uckfield been told to keep him informed? And if so, why? To see what he did, of course. To see if he owned up to being on Ames's estate and to seeing the beachcomber, Lomas. Horton was getting the distinct impression that no one wanted him to mention Lomas. Were Uckfield's orders coming from someone even higher up the food chain than Ames, from his bosses in MI5?

Uckfield scraped back his chair and lifted his tray. 'Please yourself. You're not part of my team.' He studied Horton closely. He got the message.

As they headed out of the canteen Horton said in a lighter tone, 'I'm going over to the island to tell Brother Norman that the two thieves who stole from the abbey have been sentenced.'

'Fine, you do that.'

Uckfield would know Horton had another purpose to his visit. The Super hadn't given him official permission to speak to Thelma Veerman and Horton knew why — in case it backfired on him. That was Uckfield's way and Bliss's, but she wasn't here, thankfully, so he didn't need to make any excuses to her. First though, he wanted to check in with Walters.

'It's still all quiet on the restaurant attacks,' reported Walters. 'Perhaps he's run out of things to say or paint to use.'

'Do we know what kind of paint?'

'The lab says it's ordinary blue matt emulsion, the type used in homes and offices. It's new paint though, not old, probably manufactured by one of the major paint companies. They're still working on trying to identify the colour and manufacturer.'

'Call on the hardware shops and ask who has been buying dark blue paint.'

Walters eyed him incredulously. 'They won't remember that.'

'They will if they have an automated stock control system and that applies to all the big DIY stores. It will tell them how many tins of dark blue paint they've sold over the last couple of weeks and if our man bought it using his credit card, a store loyalty card or a trade account, then they'll have that information too.'

'He wouldn't be that stupid.'

'Let's hope he is and we can nail him.'

Walters still looked dubious. 'It's a bit of a long shot, guv.'

And one that involved Walters getting off his fat arse. 'Better that than no shot at all. Anything on the suspects you and PC Tina Collins have identified?'

'Nah, all three have alibis. There are no signs of blue emulsion paint on their premises or in their rubbish bins. And please don't ask me to go to the household waste tip,' Walters pleaded.

It wouldn't help anyway, but he wasn't going to tell Walters that. 'I'll save that for later, *if* you don't catch him. Have you called on the other restaurants in the street that's been targeted?'

'No.' Walters sounded surprised.

'Do so. Find out what their security is like and the state of their kitchens. Note any that look dubious on both accounts.'

And depending on how many there were, they might be worth watching. The only trouble was they didn't know when they might be attacked. It could involve surveillance over several nights and Bliss would never sanction the overtime for that. But DC Walters might do it if he thought he'd get a free meal out of it for every night of the week.

'Well get a move on. You've got plenty to do.'

Walters heaved his bulk from the chair and his jacket from the back of it with about as much enthusiasm as a snail crossing a road. Horton entered his office, took one look at his desk and decided to leave everything where it was and head for the Isle of Wight.

CHAPTER SIXTEEN

Cantelli rang while Horton was on the ferry.

'Kenton didn't receive any powerboat training from the companies I've spoken to,' he reported. 'I thought I'd visit the local ones and show his photo around but no one remembers him, and those I've phoned further afield and emailed his photo to say that they've never seen or heard of him.'

Elkins was checking with the marinas on the island to see if Kenton had put in at any of them, but Horton couldn't see how he could have done without some training on how to use the boat and navigate the Solent. And that meant *if* he had gone across to the island, and *if* the marina manager and boat salesman could be believed, Kenton must have gone with someone who knew about boats.

Cantelli said he'd write that up for Trueman and he'd deal with other CID matters. Horton's thoughts turned to his mother, as they so often did these days. He again wondered if his foster parents' neighbours were still living in the same house and if so whether the Litchfields had ever said anything about his background and his mother to them. It was years ago and a long shot, but like he'd told Walters, it was better than no shot at all. Perhaps he'd get time later today to check.

As the Isle of Wight drew closer, Horton rose and walked to the front of the ferry. He stared through the wide windows. To the right of the single berth of the Fishbourne ferry terminal and along the shore westward was a long stretch of woodland. Beyond that was the small creek bordering Ames's land, which he couldn't see from here. He wondered if he should call Harriet Ames and ask her if she knew Kenton. Had she already been asked? Had her father primed her on what to say? Did she know Kenton's body had been found close to her father's house? And was she still pursuing the investigation into the international jewellery robberies that DCS Sawyer of the Intelligence Directorate thought this mastermind criminal Zeus was connected with, and he in turn with Jennifer's disappearance? Did Zeus even exist? Was there any truth in that story? There was the brooch that Jennifer had owned and which the constable who had been ordered to investigate her disappearance had ended up with. The brooch and all photographic evidence of it had disappeared and the police constable was dead, but DCS Sawyer had claimed the brooch had come from a jewellery theft they believed had been perpetrated by Zeus. Was that just bullshit? Horton thought so because he'd searched the stolen arts and antiques database and there was no record of the brooch, according to his admittedly vague description of it.

He turned his gaze in the opposite direction and again, past the Fishbourne terminal, there were even more woods. These belonged to Northwood Abbey. There was a small inlet and then more woods before a stretch of grass, which led up to the Veermans's property. As the ferry drew closer, he could also see Veerman's boathouse. It would have been easy for Veerman to have brought Kenton's boat over here. Easy for him to have killed Kenton and left him under the upturned dinghy. Easy to have returned by Kenton's boat to the Hamble. And easy for him to transport the body in the dinghy on Saturday morning to Lord Ames's shore. No one would have taken any notice of a man sailing a dinghy with what looked like an old sailcloth lying in it. And if Veerman was guilty of killing Kenton, then he had an accomplice, because as Horton had already surmised, that accomplice had then driven Kenton's car to the Admiralty Towers car park at 4.42 a.m. on Saturday morning.

The call for passengers to return to their cars jolted Horton out of his thoughts and on disembarking some ten minutes later he headed for the Veermans's house where he found the gates closed. He pressed the intercom, but there was no answer and no sound of dogs barking. He could see a car on the driveway in front of the garages. It must be Thelma Veerman's because it wasn't Brett Veerman's Volvo. He guessed she was walking the dogs. He left the Harley outside the house and turned in the direction she'd taken him on Saturday, towards the abbey, which was where he was officially meant to be going anyway.

He glanced at the ruins of the old abbey on his right. Behind the grass and moss-covered broken walls, a thin plume of smoke rose in the autumn afternoon. There was not a breath of wind, but clouds were beginning to obscure the sun. The air felt clammy with the threat of rain. There was no sign of Thelma Veerman or her dogs in the fields in front of the abbey ruins or in the abbey grounds. Perhaps she'd be at home when he returned, he thought, heading for the café and gift shop where he found Cliff Yately, the café manager with his right hand and forearm bandaged and in a sling.

'Been in the wars?' Horton said, nodding at it.

'My own fault. I slipped on the wet kitchen floor and landed on it. And it was me who washed the floor. Sprained it. Good job Mrs Veerman was around to put it right. Coffee?'

Horton hesitated. He was awash with caffeine. But when Yately added the words 'home-made cake' he submitted.

'Not the best of jobs to do one-handed,' Horton said, as Yately placed Horton's coffee on the tray resting on the counter.

'You can say that again. But we're short-handed, excuse the pun. Thought I'd at least help out as best I can, and it's amazing how you adapt,' he added, expertly placing the slice of cake on the plate and putting it on the tray. 'On the house.'

'No. I'll pay for it. I'm sure every little helps to keep the abbey going.'

'It does indeed.'

'Is Brother Norman around?'

Yately turned to address the shabbily dressed man in patched dark green corduroy trousers, a checked faded shirt, woollen scarf and gloves who'd emerged from the kitchens clutching a large bucket of slops. Horton smiled a greeting at Jay Ottley, who nodded, but he couldn't tell if there had been a smile behind the hairy fuzz.

'Tell Brother Norman that Inspector Horton would like a word.'

He nodded and ambled off. Horton took his coffee and lemon drizzle cake into the tea room garden where he found a quiet arbour tucked away in the shrubs. His phone rang. It was Cantelli.

'Charlotte's nursing friend's come up trumps.'

'Veerman.'

'Yes. He was operating until 8.35 p.m. on Thursday.'

That still gave him plenty of time to meet Kenton at Hamble Marina, cross to the island, kill him and return to the Hamble alone on Kenton's boat.

'Call the Wightlink ferry and ask if Veerman travelled to the island late Thursday night. If he didn't, then see if you can find out where he was. Thelma Veerman wasn't in when I called there earlier. But I'm going back to see if she's returned.'

Horton rang off and stared around the exquisitely tended, expansive garden. It was deserted. His mind went back down the years and he saw Bernard tending his small patch of earth, planting out the flowers and vegetables he'd grown from seed in the greenhouse attached to the end of the garage. It was a passion that Horton had never understood as a teenager. He hadn't seen the point in spending hours labouring outside, usually in the wind and cold, but he understood the lure of the hobby now, even though gardening wasn't his thing. Even when he'd lived with Catherine, he hadn't done much to their modestly sized garden except cut the grass and usually only when Catherine had nagged him. He'd either been working or sailing. It hadn't left much time for Catherine, he thought with a twinge of guilt. Then Emma had been born and she had become his passion, his obsession and his love. Sipping his coffee he remembered that Cantelli had once said that Catherine was antagonistic towards him because she was jealous of his love for his daughter. And now, looking back on his relationship with Catherine, he knew he had never loved her. He had merely *wanted* to be in love with her.

He drank his coffee and tried to let the tranquillity of the abbey gardens ease his loneliness. He let the silence settle on him, finding it pleasant just as he found the silence at sea relaxing and at the same time invigorating. But his mind began to fill with thoughts of his daughter and the ache of missing her. That was the problem with silence, he thought with bitterness. It made you think, and often about the things you didn't want to think about.

He swallowed his coffee. It was too late now to save his marriage. Besides, there was no longer a marriage to be saved. They were divorced and Catherine had moved on with a swiftness that had hurt, angered and surprised him, and which had made him wonder if she'd been only too glad to have an excuse to ditch him. Her latest boyfriend was a wealthy businessman. He wasn't jealous of his wealth, or the fact Catherine was now with someone else — as far he was concerned, she could do what she wanted with her life — but the thought that Emma, his daughter, was seeing a succession of men with her mother, and that one of those men might eventually become a permanent fixture, supplanting him, caused his heart to constrict in a spasm of hurt and anger. It also made him recall seeing different men with his mother, one of whom he'd always been told she'd run off with. Who had those men been? How many? Or had he simply imagined there were several because that was what he had been told for so long as a child?

'I hear you were asking to see me.' A man's voice jolted him out of his reminisces. He looked up to see Brother Norman.

Horton made to rise but Brother Norman waved him back in to his seat and took the one opposite.

'I thought you'd like to know the two men who robbed the abbey have been sentenced.'

'Ah.'

Horton sensed a subdued energy in the presence of the monk and noticed that there was pain in his eyes, deep and dark. With a jolt, Horton thought he'd seen that expression before. He'd witnessed it in the beachcomber's eyes when the man had handed him his card. The eyes reflected an accumulation of life's experiences. He wondered fleetingly what people read in his eyes.

'Can I get you anything?' he asked.

But Brother Norman again removed his hand from the sleeve of his habit and held it up in refusal. It was a strong hand, thought Horton, recalling the beachcomber's as he'd given Horton that business card with the phoney name on it. It had been suntanned, unlike Brother Norman's pale one, and it hadn't contained any jewellery — and neither, he recalled, had there been any evidence of paint on it or under the fingernails. Surely there would have been if Lomas had really been an artist. But Horton had stopped believing that a while ago.

'Sorry, I've been working in the vegetable garden,' Brother Norman apologized, mistaking Horton's thoughtful frown for distaste as he eyed his grimy hand. 'The earth gets everywhere.' He twisted the signet ring and plucked under his nail with his fingernails as though ashamed there was dirt.

Horton hastily waved aside his apologies. 'I was thinking of a case,' he explained. 'Nothing to do with the robbery here. They received two years custodial each.'

'That long!'

Not long enough if you ask me, thought Horton. 'They both have previous convictions for theft. They would have got longer if they hadn't changed their plea. You don't look very pleased.'

'I don't think prison will make either of them reform.'

'Probably not, but it keeps them off the streets and prevents them from violating others.'

'For a while.'

'You don't believe in retribution?'

'I didn't say that.'

'What kind of sentence would you have given them?' Horton asked, interested.

'They could have come to work here.'

'Community payback. They've both done that and been given chances, countless times. It didn't work.'

'No more than prison will.'

'Some people are habitual criminals; no matter how many chances they are given they will always steal, kill, maim, torture. There are countless reasons why they do it and that's not my jurisdiction. I just help to catch them.'

'Isn't that a rather simple answer?'

'Maybe but it's the only one for a copper,' Horton said tersely. What did this monk know about the real world? How many times had he witnessed evil? How many times had he stared into the eyes of a killer and seen only mockery and triumph? And how many innocent victims had he had to deal with traumatized by their ordeal? None.

Brother Norman returned Horton's slightly hostile gaze with equanimity. OK, so he'd given a slightly flippant answer and one that he didn't necessarily believe in, because if Bernard hadn't taken a chance on him, then he might have ended up doing time. And if Horton hadn't helped Johnnie Oslow, Cantelli's nephew, after he'd committed an arson offence when he was sixteen, then he too might have continued on the downward spiral of crime instead of being a very successful yachtsman. But Horton wasn't here to indulge in philosophical or religious discussion.

Cliff Yately appeared beside them. 'Sorry to drag you away, Brother Norman, but Brother David in the bookshop would like a word.'

Brother Norman rose. 'Thank you for coming to tell me, Inspector.'

'You're welcome.'

Horton made his way back to the Veermans feeling a little irritated by Brother Norman's complacent manner. But then he should have expected it from a religious man — after all they were meant to be charitable; forgive those that trespass and all that stuff. Forgiveness wasn't Horton's job, he just caught the buggers, and he hoped they'd catch whoever had killed Kenton. Although at the pace this investigation was going, he doubted it. He stifled the sense of guilt that rose up in him at the thought that he too might be hindering the investigation by keeping silent.

He was saved from further internal debate over Brother Norman's less than enthusiastic response by a telephone call from Elkins, who said that Kenton hadn't put in at any of the marinas on the island or along the coast.

When Horton reached the Veermans's house the gates were still closed and there was no answer to his summons on the intercom. Frustrated at the thought that he would have to return tomorrow he caught the four o'clock sailing and was back in his office by five.

Cantelli greeted him with the news that Veerman's car hadn't been booked on any late-night sailing on Thursday or any return sailing to the mainland on Friday morning.

'And Brenda, Charlotte's nursing friend, just called to say that Veerman was booked into one of the rooms in the nurses' accommodation on Thursday night. The consultants sometimes stay over at the hospital if they need to be on call for a critically ill patient.'

'Did anyone see him there?'

'Not that I know of, but short of questioning everyone on the ward and in the nurses' accommodation we won't know.'

And that didn't look as though it would happen. 'He could have left the hospital and gone to Hamble Marina.'

'Wouldn't he have been taking a risk if the patient had a relapse and he was sent for?'

'Perhaps he knew the patient would be OK. Or perhaps he briefed a fellow surgeon to stand in for him in case of complications.' Horton rang through to Uckfield and told him he hadn't been able to speak to Thelma Veerman but he relayed what Cantelli had discovered, adding, 'It looks as though he might not have an alibi.'

'Doesn't mean he's a killer.'

'No, but it does mean we should question him.'

'We will.'

'When?' Horton asked, exasperated.

'When I say so,' snapped Uckfield as he rang off.

Horton glared at his phone. Restless and irritated by the lack of activity, he crossed to Walters who had just returned.

'No joy with the hardware stores, guv. But I've identified a couple of restaurants along that road that could be possible targets. They're Indian and Turkish restaurants, and both have crap security systems. I gave the owners a lecture on getting better security, but I don't think they understood a word I was saying. They just threw their hands about and nodded.'

Sounds like Uckfield, thought Horton with bitterness, except the fat man wasn't doing any hand waving.

He returned to his office and spent an agitated couple of hours shuffling paper around his desk. When Cantelli and Walters left, Horton also called it a day. He didn't feel that he had achieved much. But there was something he could do that might give him information and it wasn't connected with the Kenton investigation or the racist slogans in the restaurants.

CHAPTER SEVENTEEN

A small slim man in his mid-seventies with a face like a walnut answered the door and confirmed to Horton that he had lived there for forty years. Horton swiftly introduced himself, showed his ID and told Mr Kimber that he could call the station to check who he was before letting him in. Harry Kimber waved aside such precautions and ushered him into the front room with pleasure.

Horton refused a cup of tea. He could hardly believe his luck. He had hoped that one of Eileen and Bernard Litchfield's neighbours might still be living next door, but he hadn't really expected it.

He settled himself into an armchair in the front room at Kimber's insistence while the elderly man took the chair opposite him. The room was overcrowded with old-fashioned furniture, but it was spotlessly clean and the sideboard to the left of Horton in the alcove boasted so many family photographs that Horton could barely see the surface. He couldn't hear anyone moving about the house and wondered if Mr Kimber was widowed and lived alone. A fact he confirmed when he saw Horton glancing at the photographs, adding that his two sons lived abroad, one in America, the other in Canada.

'You remember Adrian and Tom.'

But Horton didn't, not much. They had been older than him, in their early twenties when he was a teenager and they had already left home. He said as much, causing Kimber to nod in agreement. Horton remembered little of Harry Kimber or his wife. His experience of being pushed from pillar to post and of seeing countless people come and go in children's homes, along with the pain of his mother's desertion, had made him cautious about forming any attachments. Not that he'd reasoned that back then. He'd just tried to shut out other people. A remark that had been levied at him by Catherine and maybe she had been right. His failed marriage and his past were perhaps reasons why he was still reluctant to let anyone get too close. Maybe Thea Carlsson had sensed this and taken herself off before he could hurt her. Perhaps his reasons for keeping his distance with Harriet Ames and with Gaye Clayton were just excuses to prevent him from being hurt and rejected again. Christ, he was sounding like a psychologist. And maybe he was about to break that habit, he thought, over dinner soon with Gaye.

Horton broached the subject of his visit. 'I'm not here in an official capacity, Mr Kimber, but a personal one. It might seem a strange request but I'd like to know more about Bernard and Eileen, my foster parents.'

'They'd have been proud of you, especially Bernard, with you following in his footsteps, so to speak, and becoming a Detective Inspector. You've done well, lad.'

Horton felt a grateful warm glow. 'Thank you.' Then he added ruefully, 'I guess I was a handful.'

'A bit of one, yes. But understandably so, given your background.'

'You know about it?' Horton asked, surprised.

'Only that your mum was taken suddenly. Heart attack wasn't it, and you were left alone and very young.'

So that had been the official version.

'Must have been tough on you.' There was a moment's silence before Kimber continued more brightly, 'So what do you want to know?'

'How long did you know Bernard and Eileen?'

'Years before they moved in next door. Well, Bernard at least, Eileen I met later.'

Horton hadn't expected that. He cursed the fact he hadn't come here sooner. Not that he thought it would lead him any further forward in his search for the truth about Jennifer's disappearance, but any information was better than none. And police work was all about gathering, sifting and putting together information until something emerged, and that was what they should be doing as far as Jasper Kenton's death was concerned. For now though, he was eager to hear more about his foster parents.

Harry Kimber said, 'In fact it was me who told Bernard the house next door was up for sale. He was living in a rented house then with Eileen. But he managed to get a mortgage and he and Eileen had a bit of money put by. They moved in at Christmas 1979 but Bernard and I go right back to when we did our two years National Service together in 1957. We took to one another immediately. Those were the days of the Cold War, the Suez crisis and the Cyprus conflict. Bernie and I were posted to Cyprus in 1959. It was a bit hairy. British rule was coming to an end, not that we knew that then. We knew nothing. We were working class boys from the streets of Portsmouth, our dads worked in the dockyard, like nearly everyone in Portsmouth did in those days. And you followed in your father's footsteps. Bernie and I were glad to get away and have a bit of an adventure, not like some who did their National Service and hated it. We loved it, the more dangerous the better.'

Horton tried to see the gentle giant he had known as a reckless young man without fear. It was difficult, but then he was looking back at it from a troubled teenager's point of view and one who'd had a large chip on his shoulder. Bernard had managed to get him out of many scrapes and had quietly talked to him. He'd never raised his voice or his fists; he'd never lectured him; he'd just left him to consider what he had done and why, and told him he was clever enough to know right from wrong and doing wrong didn't make things right.

'Do you have any photographs of Bernard and Eileen?' Horton felt a real desire to see them, not to help him with research into his mother's disappearance because they couldn't, but so that he could have a better picture of the couple who had saved him from descending into a hellish life of being on the wrong side of crime. And it hadn't just been Bernard who had refrained from lecturing him: Eileen had never chastised him either, even when he had said such hurtful things to her in his anger and pain. She wasn't his mother and he had resented her for that. He'd rounded on her often. Again and again, she had simply repeated that no, she wasn't and could never be, but that didn't mean she didn't love him. She never spoke ill of his mother. In fact, now he thought back she never spoke of her. And with the passing years he'd come to see Eileen as his mother. His heart ached as he recalled her dying days. He was only glad to have been with her and to have had the opportunity to thank her quietly and to tell her he loved her. He didn't know whether she had heard him.

Kimber said, 'I have some pictures of Bernard but not Eileen. She was very camera shy, not like they are today.' He sprang up with surprising agility and crossed to the sideboard. 'Don't you have any photographs of them?'

'No. Eileen must have cleared them out before she moved into the flat.' And now that he considered it, that was strange. And he couldn't remember Bernard or Eileen taking any photographs of them together, or of him on his own.

As Kimber rummaged around in the drawers Horton said, 'What did Bernard do after his National Service?'

'Resumed his apprenticeship in the dockyard, like I did, but neither of us could stick it. He joined the Royal Air Force as a policeman and I joined the Navy as a diver. Bernie was in the RAF Police until 1979 and then joined the Hampshire Force. He was injured while he was serving in Northern Ireland in 1978. Shot in the shoulder while patrolling the airfield at RAF Aldergrove.'

'I didn't know that. He never said,' Horton replied, astonished. And he hadn't known that Bernard had served in Northern Ireland.

'He wasn't the type to talk about it or his job. The wound wasn't serious. Could have been a hell of a lot worse. He could have been killed. Many service personnel were, and civilians, innocent women and kiddies. It was before those terrible bombs were set off by the IRA in towns and villages across Northern Ireland. And all those bombs in December in Bristol, Coventry, Liverpool, Manchester, and just up the road in Southampton. The IRA said they were gearing up for a long war,' Kimber said sadly. 'But then we seem to have just as many, if not more, troubles now. And all in the name of religion. Or so they claim. Still,' he said more chirpily, 'Northern Ireland was where he met Eileen.'

And that was another shock for Horton. 'She was from Northern Ireland?' Eileen had never spoken with a Northern Irish accent and she'd never once mentioned coming from there. Neither she nor Bernard talked about their family at all — or if they had, then he hadn't paid much attention, but then a teenage boy would hardly have been interested in his foster parents' past, only in himself. Horton didn't remember any family coming to visit. His mind raced back through those years. Now that he came to consider it he didn't remember any friends either, except Harry Kimber and his wife. The Litchfields had been a very private couple.

'Eileen was working in Belfast as a typist in the Civil Service. Now where was she from? I can't remember if she said . . .' Then he clicked his arthritic fingers. 'That's it. Me and the wife were going on holiday and she said, "Give the island my regards" or "my love", something like that.'

'She was from the Isle of Wight?'

But Kimber shook his head. 'No. Mary and I were going on holiday to the Channel Islands.'

'Which island?' Horton asked eagerly even though he already knew the answer.

'Guernsey. Beautiful place. You ever been? Mary and I went back a couple of times. We both loved it.'

Was it a coincidence that Eileen had come from the same place that Ballard had told Horton he was sailing to — only he didn't go there, according to Horton's sources. It had to be, surely. And Kimber could be mistaken. "Give it my love", or some such phrase, didn't mean she had lived there or had been born there; she might simply have been there on holiday. Then why did he have this feeling that it was highly significant? Was there something in Guernsey that connected Eileen Litchfield with Edward Ballard? Guernsey didn't tally with the location reference that Dr Quentin Amos had left him, which was Gosport. Same initial, yes, but miles apart in location and topography. He needed to consider this more fully.

'Do you know what Eileen's maiden name was?' He could get it from the Registry of Births, Deaths and Marriages but this might save him time.

'No, sorry. Ah, here they are.' Kimber turned and handed Horton two photographs. A flood of warm affection swamped Horton as he gazed down at the fit, dark-haired young man in his twenties wearing his army national service uniform. There were the deep-set brown smiling eyes in the heavy square face that he remembered. He swallowed and cleared his throat. Standing beside Bernard was a fair, good-looking man with blue eyes and a cheeky grin. Harry Kimber. He heard the elderly man sigh.

'It doesn't do to look back,' Kimber said sadly.

How right he was, Horton thought, turning to the second photograph of Bernard. He was dressed in combat fatigues and a flak jacket and was carrying an automatic self-loading pistol.

'Northern Ireland,' Kimber said. 'Not quite sure why I kept that one or why Bernard gave it to me, but it could have been to show me how tough he was.' Kimber looked sorrowful for a moment, as he thought back down the years. Then he brightened. 'But I knew that anyway, or at least how brave he was. And a little reckless. Bernard always was a bit of an action man, more so than me.' A frown creased his already corrugated forehead.

'I was worried about Bernard during the troubles. IRA bombs going off everywhere, not only there but over here too. Terrible times, they were. You've always got to be alert for terrorism, but I don't need to tell you about that.'

No, thought Horton; extreme views often led to vandalism, destruction, physical pain and murder. He just hoped their racist restaurant vandal would be apprehended before it went any further.

'Can I borrow these for a while? I'll copy them and return them to you.'

'Of course.'

Kimber showed him to the front door. There Horton paused. He wished he had a photograph of Edward Ballard but he recalled the fair, fit man he'd seen talking to Bernard and asked Kimber if he remembered seeing him. His answer was as Horton expected: no.

Outside, Horton let his memory go back to the time he saw Edward Ballard hand that Bluebird Toffee tin containing the photograph of his mother and his birth certificate to Bernard. Had it contained anything else that Bernard had removed before passing on to him? He would never know, not unless he found Ballard and asked him, and he thought he had about as much chance of that as being promoted.

He scanned the long road of terraced houses built in the 1930s while his memory slipped back in time to the day he'd sneaked home early from school and seen Bernard with Ballard. What had been parked here then? Ballard must have arrived in some kind of vehicle. Would he, as a teenager, have noticed any cars though? Yes, if they had been different, flash and expensive like the one he recalled his mother climbing into once, parked outside their flat. That had been an American car he'd thought, but couldn't be sure. Maybe to a child it had just looked big and flash. No, the only thing he would have noticed here was something he was interested in, even as a boy. Of course! Why hadn't he recalled it before? Because it had been autumn and the weather damp and windy and he'd thought nothing of a man dressed in black clothes — trousers and a big black jacket — but now, if he put that with the admiring glance he'd given a motorbike, Horton knew that Ballard had come by bike. What kind though? A Honda? A Triumph? He racked his brains trying to remember. He'd seen Ballard climb on a motorbike. It had given a satisfyingly deep throb as it had roared away. That had appealed to his boyhood fantasy of being able to escape. He'd wished he could ride away from the school he hated and the other boys he fought with, but most of all from the anger inside him. And there it still was like a hard ball gripping his gut, causing his fists to clench. He took a breath. Emotion was no use to him, but reason was and it was only reason that would help him get to the truth. Edward Ballard had ridden away on a powerful motorbike, but that fact didn't help him find out what had happened to Jennifer and why Bernard and Eileen Litchfield had been able to unofficially foster him.

He returned to his boat where he postponed all thoughts of Jennifer, showered and cooked something to eat. He turned his mind to Jasper Kenton. Mentally he ran through all the facts he'd learned about Kenton and his death, trying to find something that would make Uckfield take more direct action. But he knew this was one of those cases that was set to drag on, mainly because Ames wanted it that way. Was that because of the beachcomber? Was Horton harbouring a killer? He had to know. Perhaps he should take his own boat across to the island and motor up that creek. From the sea it would look different and maybe he'd spot something that could give him a lead. He'd need to refuel though because he hadn't been out sailing for some time. He froze. Fuel. What had Elkins said about Kenton's boat? Rapidly he racked his brain. Yes, that was it, the tank was half full. Had it been empty when Rob at the marina had helped Kenton to refuel? Or had Kenton been topping it up? Did it matter? He knew it did. He wasn't quite sure why, but like that nagging personality discrepancy in Kenton that refused to go away, Horton knew that the amount of fuel in that boat meant something significant and he was determined to find out what it was.

CHAPTER EIGHTEEN

Wednesday

'Neither Kenton nor anyone else took that boat to the Isle of Wight or anywhere Thursday night,' Horton relayed to Cantelli the next morning in the CID Operations room. 'I've spoken to Rob at the marina and he says he asked Kenton if he wanted the boat filled up but Kenton said no, just half a tank, and there was only a small amount of fuel left in it when he took it to the pumps. Elkins says there is still half a tank left in the boat and he hasn't found any trace of Kenton's boat putting in to any of the marinas on the Isle of Wight. He must have met his killer here on the mainland and it wasn't at Oyster Quays or the Camber because I've already checked with them. He certainly didn't drive over to the island because the ferry company have no record of his car being on any sailings on Thursday or Friday.'

'So he either crossed on someone else's boat or in someone else's car.'

'Yes. And that's not Brett Veerman's because he didn't cross to the island until Friday night, by which time Kenton was dead. And I don't think Kenton could have been in the rear of his Volvo, bleeding to death since Thursday night.'

'What about Thelma Veerman's car?'

Horton shook his head. 'There's no record of her having been on the ferry.' He'd checked that morning. 'I've told Uckfield that we need to run a check on all those who travelled on the ferries on Thursday night and Friday morning for any connection with Kenton. I'm going to re-interview Thelma Veerman and I want you with me.'

Cantelli grimaced. 'Wish you'd asked me before I had breakfast.'

'I'd ask Walters only he looks as though he's already been on a rough sea for forty-eight hours.' Horton jerked his head at the overweight DC, who staggered in the door with a face like a constipated St Bernard dog clutching his fat stomach.

'Think I ate something dodgy last night at that Turkish restaurant. My guts feel like they're going to explode.'

'Well for Christ's sake don't let them do it here. I take it you were on surveillance last night and no one showed up to spray filthy slogans on the filthy kitchen.'

'No. After my meal I sat outside in the car until two o'clock. Then my guts started playing up.'

'See that they're better by tonight.'

'I'm not going back in there to eat,' Walters protested vehemently.

'Then try the Indian restaurant you mentioned yesterday or get a takeaway and sit in your car.'

'And if I get taken short?'

'Perhaps they'll let you use the restaurant toilet.'

Walters groaned. 'I'm sick. I should be at home.'

'Then go home,' Horton said sharply. 'But make sure you're outside or in one of those restaurants you identified as in desperate need of redecoration and better security tonight.'

Walters nodded gloomily and plodded out. Horton gave Cantelli instructions to book them on the ten o'clock sailing and returned to his office where he rang Thelma Veerman, but there was no answer. Annoyed, he replaced the receiver without leaving a message. He could have another wasted journey if she wasn't at home, but glancing at the clock and seeing it was just after nine he thought she was probably walking the dogs. She had to go home at some point — unless she was away, he thought, but her car had been on the drive yesterday.

He tried her number again at the ferry terminal but still got no answer. Cantelli handed the electronic ticket to a very wet and clearly very unhappy member of the marshalling staff who zapped the bar code on it with a hand-held device and quickly turned away. Cantelli hastily let the window back up and wiped the inside of the door where the rain had beaten in. He looked worried and Horton knew why; it was very windy and the ferry crossing would be far from smooth.

'Just don't let them bury me at sea,' Cantelli said, as they were waved on board.

Cantelli refused all refreshment and took a seat at a table away from the windows, which he'd been told was the best position to avoid the worst of the rolling of the ferry. He didn't look as though he believed that. Horton bought a Diet Coke. He had just reached the table when his phone rang. It was Gaye Clayton.

'I'm sorry, Andy, but I can't find anyone who saw Brett Veerman in the ward or in the nurses' hostel on Thursday night. He was definitely in surgery until 8.35 p.m., and he did have clinics on Friday morning as well as hospital rounds. He went to the private hospital on Friday afternoon just after four p.m. That's all I can get about his movements but my sources tell me he is well liked and respected. He's considered dishy and sexy. Has a good sense of humour and is courteous and polite, certainly charming. In fact, he seems to have attracted a kind of hero worship.'

'I'm surprised he hasn't been mobbed.'

She laughed. 'If he wasn't suspected of murder, I might fancy him myself. There's no gossip about him having affairs though. Do I still get a free meal?'

'Sure, you wouldn't prefer to dine out with Mr Veerman?' he joked.

'Positive. He might poison me.'

'Let's hope the restaurant food doesn't. When are you free?' he said, pleased.

'No time like the present. Tonight?'

'Sounds good. I'll—'

'No. I'll pick *you* up in the Mini. I don't mind a ride on your Harley, but if you're taking me to a posh restaurant I don't fancy turning up looking like a drowned rat with flattened hair.'

Horton swiftly tried to imagine Gaye's short spiky auburn hair flattened and couldn't. He smiled. 'Eight o'clock.'

'Great.'

He rang off with Cantelli eyeing him smugly and for the moment seemingly oblivious that the ferry was out at sea.

'Where are you going?' Cantelli asked.

'Nowhere near where Walters will be,' Horton answered promptly. And after their meal? He didn't like to think that far ahead.

The ferry bucked and rolled. The car alarms on the decks below began to sound. Cantelli's skin paled.

'Close your eyes and think of England.'

'Not sure that will work,' Cantelli said gloomily.

'OK then we'll go over the details of Kenton's murder.' They did but it threw up no new thoughts except that it highlighted the apparent dual personality of Jasper Kenton. Horton told Cantelli he'd also called the yacht brokerage that morning after he'd spoken to Rob in the marina office and discovered that Jasper Kenton didn't even want to give the boat a trial run when he was in the process of purchasing it. 'The salesman started up the engine and Kenton said that it sounded OK to him.'

'That doesn't sound like a very thorough man to me.'

'Me neither. The salesman also confirmed that the boat had just a small amount of fuel in the tank and that he hadn't topped it up. He said there was no need if Kenton didn't want to take it out for a trial run. Kenton said he trusted the brokerage to provide him with a boat they claimed was in perfect working order.'

Cantelli raised his dark eyebrows. 'For a PI, and someone who'd worked in security, he was incredibly trusting.' And that didn't ring true.

Horton rang Trueman and asked him if he had anything on the sail that Kenton had been wrapped in.

'Just got the preliminary report. It's a gaff-rigged mainsail.'

That surprised Horton and worried him a little. A gaff-rigged mainsail was hoisted up by a pole called a gaff. It was shaped like a truncated triangle but with four sides rather than three, with two short sides top and bottom and two longer sides right and left. They were used on more traditional and classic sailing yachts, not the type of dinghy that Veerman had in his garden nor the yacht Thelma Veerman had told him they'd owned before her son had left home.

Trueman said, 'The size of this sail indicates it comes from a yacht no bigger than twenty-two feet. The sail is anything between ten and five years old. It's been used but is still waterproof.'

'Which means that the body was in sea water before being wrapped in it.'

'Yes. There's no number on it, which the lab says suggests it was made as a spare sail or possibly for a boat designed by the owner.'

Not much help then.

Trueman said, 'It could have been lying around somewhere for months, years even.'

Horton recalled the beachcomber's words. '*I search for bits of flotsam and jetsam I find on the beach that I can turn into art.*' Had he found the sail and after killing Kenton had decided to turn him into a work of art? If so, the man was mad and Horton had prevented him from being apprehended. He shifted uneasily as Trueman continued, 'The lab is trying to find traces of earth or gravel on it which we might be able to match.'

'*If* we knew where it came from. How are Marsden and Somerfield getting on with the archery clubs?'

'They're not. No one matches up with any names we have in the investigation so far.'

Gaye's words about the weapon being used by soldiers overseas darted into Horton's mind and he experienced an uncomfortable few moments as he considered that Veerman was nothing but a smoke screen of his own choosing to divert attention from the real killer, the beachcomber, who could be ex-forces. Thoughts of Bernard Litchfield flashed before him in his RAF uniform with flak jacket and guns. But swiftly he pushed them aside and reminded himself of the facts that made Veerman a suspect — which, he thought with some anxiety, were all circumstantial.

Horton asked Trueman to keep him updated on new developments and said he and Cantelli were on their way to re-interview Thelma Veerman.

Cantelli made no effort to hide his relief as they disembarked from the ferry. Switching on the windscreen wipers he said, 'I only hope the wind drops by the time we return.'

'We'll have Thelma Veerman's statement to consider by then; that should occupy us.' But Horton had tried her number twice on the ferry and still no answer. Perhaps he should call Eunice Swallows and see if she had a mobile number for Thelma Veerman, but that would mean explaining to Bliss why he had asked for it, because Eunice was bound to tell her.

Horton gave Cantelli directions to the Veermans's house. If they got no joy there they'd try the abbey.

The gates were closed and her car was on the driveway and still in the same position as yesterday. Horton didn't think it had been moved, unless she always parked in that exact spot. He thought that unusual but dismissed it. There was no answer when Cantelli pressed the intercom and there didn't look to be any signs of life from the house.

Horton climbed out and as he did the sound of the dogs barking came from a distance. She couldn't be far then. It sounded as though they were on the shore. She was probably down there throwing a ball into the sea for them to fetch. But in this weather? It was sheeting down now, but then Thelma Veerman had struck him as the outdoor type. Obviously she couldn't hear the intercom there, and he hadn't come all this way to turn back again.

He tried the gates. They were firmly locked but Horton eyed them up. Calling back to Cantelli he said, 'I promise I won't make a dent,' and swung nimbly onto the bonnet of the car. There was a bar in the gates near the top between the upright wrought-iron prongs. Horton placed his foot on it, tested it, grabbed one of the prongs on the top of the gate, and brought his other foot over, balanced for a spilt second on the top and then jumped over, dropping with both feet to the ground on the other side in a crouched position.

'Hope you don't expect me to do that!' Cantelli exclaimed in horror. 'I'm an ageing police sergeant, not a paratrooper. I'd like to get my thirty years' service in and draw my pension.'

Horton smiled, found a pad to the right of the gate and punched it. The gates began to open. Cantelli drove forward.

'What's this about ageing?' Horton teased, climbing in. 'You're only a few years older than me.'

'Yes, and I'd like it to stay that way.'

But Cantelli's words had triggered something at the back of Horton's mind that Harry Kimber had said about Bernard joining the police force. How old would Bernard have been when he joined the police? Horton made some quick calculations as Cantelli pulled up in front of the Veermans' house. Forty-two? But the age limit then for officers joining must have been younger because the earliest retirement age for coppers had been fifty-five and the oldest sixty-five. If he remembered correctly the oldest eligible age for joining the force had been thirty-five so that an officer could get thirty years' service in order to get a full pension. But perhaps Bernard's time in the RAF Police had counted. There was more tugging at the back of Horton's mind but there wasn't time to think that through now.

'What about the dogs?' Cantelli asked warily, climbing out of the car.

'They're Springer Spaniels, not Dobermanns or Bull Mastiffs.'

Cantelli didn't look convinced that the breed made any difference to the fact that he might still be attacked. They set off towards the shore at a brisk pace, which was made difficult because the wind was barrelling off the sea and the thin slanting rain driving into them. Surely Thelma Veerman wouldn't be playing with her dogs on the shore in this weather, Horton thought. He threw Cantelli a puzzled and concerned look.

'They don't sound very friendly,' Cantelli said uneasily, picking up something of Horton's concern.

Horton agreed. The barking grew louder as they got closer and it seemed to Horton more frantic. His pulse seemed to skip several beats.

'She could have had an accident.' Or worse, he thought, breaking into a run. Through his mind flashed the awful thought that, distraught at her husband's affair and possible involvement in Jasper Kenton's murder, she'd taken her own life. Had Veerman confessed to her, taunted her with it, knowing she would never betray him? What had Gaye just told him? '*He seems to have attracted a kind of hero worship.*' Did Veerman have the same power over his wife who now, discarded by the hero, had thought her life not worth living? God, he hoped not.

He reached the shore ahead of Cantelli. The two dogs looked up. They rushed towards him, barking furiously, then raced back along the beach past the boathouse to something lying on the shore. Horton's heart stalled. He threw Cantelli a worried glance before rushing towards it. The dogs, seeing him coming, stopped barking but didn't move away from the bundle. As Horton drew nearer, they watched him with soulful deep-brown eyes, panting, their tails wagging furiously. Horton's heart was pounding as his feet struck the shingle. The breath caught in his throat as he drew to a halt. He stared down at the figure of Thelma Veerman on the stones. With a sinking heart and a sickening feeling in the pit of his stomach he tested for a pulse in her neck, knowing he wouldn't find it. He didn't. He was too late. There was no need to call the paramedics. He called Uckfield instead.

CHAPTER NINETEEN

'How long?' Uckfield asked Dr Clayton as she stepped away from the body, which was now covered by a large canvas tent. Brett Veerman had yet to be informed of his wife's death. *Unless he already knew because he'd killed her*, thought Horton, although he had no evidence of that.

'Difficult to say in these conditions and with that kind of wound.' Gaye indicated the crossbow bolt in the chest.

Horton studied it again for the hundredth time since discovering the body and although his anger had lessened, his revulsion was still as strong. There was remarkably little blood around the small wound on the grey T-shirt. She was dressed in casual dark grey trousers, grey socks, sturdy walking shoes and a navy blue zip-up fleece, which was open. There had been nothing in her hands and no sign of the dog lead. The bolt hardly looked powerful or deep enough to have killed. There was only about two and a half inches protruding from Thelma Veerman's chest, when the bolt in Jasper Kenton's was six and a half inches. Kenton had been shot at close range and the same applied to Thelma Veerman. The theory that she might have shot herself had been quickly quashed by the absence of the weapon. Cantelli had made a search of the area but hadn't found it. It surely had to be the one that had been used to kill Jasper Kenton, and therefore the same killer. Was that the beachcomber? Should he say something now? But he told himself that Thelma Veerman being killed and being found here must mean there was no connection with Lord Ames, except for Brett Veerman. Could he have killed his wife in such a cruel and callous way, letting her bleed to death? Or was his lover the driving force in these murders? Horton only hoped Thelma Veerman's death had been quicker than Jasper Kenton's.

Gaye added, 'All I can say before I do the autopsy is that rigor mortis appears to be complete. Lividity, as you can see from the blueish colour of the skin, is permanent. I won't be able to tell if it is all over the body until we get her in the mortuary but if it is then that puts her death approximately sometime between four a.m. and six a.m. But it could be a lot earlier than that. No longer than twenty-four hours certainly.'

Horton rapidly calculated. Twenty-four hours took them back to yesterday afternoon, sometime between 2.30 p.m. and 4.30 p.m. He'd been here then and there had been no sign of Thelma Veerman. Had she been lying on the shore bleeding to death when he'd pressed the intercom and walked away? Could he have saved her life instead of heading to the abbey? But there had been no sound of dogs barking, he recalled, so she must have been alive and elsewhere.

He brought his full attention back to Gaye. 'Because she is lying on her back it indicates that she fell the moment she was shot, but with this method of killing, as I explained before, the exact timing of actual death is difficult to ascertain. There is the possibility that she could have staggered about and then fallen, although she would most probably have done so face down.' She eyed the corpse and frowned as she thought. 'I suppose she could have turned in a final effort to get up and fetch help. However, with dwindling strength I would have said it was more likely she would have got as far as to her knees and then fallen forward.'

Horton said, 'Which means if she didn't die instantly then her body could have been brought here and laid out on the shore.'

'Just like Kenton,' Uckfield said, scratching the inside of his thigh.

'Yes, only this time without the sail as a shroud,' Horton answered. He and Cantelli had walked along the shore and it became impassable after several yards in both directions because of rocks and dense woods. So unless she had admitted her killer through the gates of her house, she must have met him or her coming ashore by boat. And if the person piloting that boat had been Brett Veerman then the dogs wouldn't have barked. He said as much, drawing a deep scowl of unease from Uckfield.

'Maybe they were locked up and only managed to get out a few hours ago.'

'But someone must have locked them up.'

'Thelma Veerman might have done.'

'We need to check Veerman's movements from about 2.30 yesterday afternoon until ten o'clock this morning.'

But Gaye interjected. 'He was conducting his out-patients' clinic this morning and was still there when I got the call to come over. I checked. I thought you might want to know.' She threw a glance at Horton. He saw Uckfield note it and eye him curiously.

Horton said, 'But we don't know where he was yesterday afternoon, evening and night.'

Uckfield nodded and asked if they could move the body. Gaye said they could and that she'd conduct the autopsy as soon as it arrived at the mortuary in Newport. With a resigned shrug at Horton, she stepped outside. He knew that their dinner date for that night was off. Uckfield followed Gaye out.

Horton stared down at the body with sorrow. Her face was discoloured and her body drenched from the rain rather than the sea. She'd fallen or had been placed just above the high-water mark so there was no seaweed or sea life attached to it. Had she wanted to tell them her husband was a killer and been silenced because of it? Or had Brett Veerman and his lover conspired to kill her? Had Veerman's lover alone called at the house and drawn her down to the shore to administer the fatal shot in order to secure the love of Brett Veerman?

The canvas tent flap opened and Cantelli entered. 'Is it OK for the undertakers to come in?'

Horton nodded. Clarke had already taken all the photographs and videos he needed and Taylor had mapped the lie of the land and the location and position of the body. He and his SOCO team would come back inside the tent after the body was removed.

Horton stepped outside, thankful the rain had finally stopped, although he and Cantelli were already wet through. Uckfield had returned to his car where Horton could see him on the phone. Gaye broke off talking to Clarke and crossed to him as the undertakers stepped forward.

'Sorry about tonight. I might finish by eight but you might not. Some other time?'

'Yes.'

He watched her walk away to a waiting police car then turned and stared across the rough muddy grey sea. At least this location, like that of where Kenton's body had been found, was private property with no nosy neighbours or sightseers to come gawping. And yet maybe if there had been neighbours they might have got a clue as to who had done this. He made for Uckfield who had come off his phone and was climbing out of his car.

'The hospital says that Veerman left there two hours ago. Trueman's checked; he's on the car ferry. He'll be here soon.'

And would this be a shock to him or had he timed it so that he could find his wife's body?

'And the investigation?' asked Horton.

Uckfield pointedly eyed Cantelli, who moved away.

'We wait until after we interview Veerman. Then I'm to report back to Dean.'

'Steve, we've got to do more.'

'Like what?' snarled Uckfield. 'Seal off the island?'

'We can find out if Brett Veerman came here yesterday.'

'Not by car ferry he didn't. Trueman's already checked.'

'By private boat.'

'That piddling dinghy in this weather?' Uckfield cried incredulously, pointing to where it lay beside the boathouse on the grass.

'No, on someone else's boat. Elkins' unit is checking to see if they can find a boat owned by Veerman, or any sightings of him around the marinas, on Thursday night. I'll get them to extend that to yesterday. And we need a search warrant for here.'

'I don't need you to tell me how to do my job,' Uckfield snapped, turning away as his phone rang. 'Yes, sir,' Horton heard him say before he moved out of earshot.

Horton returned to Cantelli and relayed the gist of his conversation with Uckfield and asked him to contact Elkins. Horton looked up at the sound of a car approaching and saw Veerman's Volvo sweep to a sharp halt in a flurry of gravel in front of the house. Uckfield hastily terminated his call and jerked his head at Horton in a sign to accompany him as he headed towards the car. To Cantelli, Horton said, 'Here we go. Should be interesting.'

'What the devil is going on here?' Veerman demanded. The police officer at the gate wouldn't have told him. 'Are you in charge?' He addressed Uckfield.

'Can we go inside, sir?'

'No, we damn well can't, not unless you've got a search warrant. Where's my wife?'

Was he too angry, thought Horton? Was this role playing?

'What's going on down there?' He pointed to the activity on the shore and then seemed to take in the surroundings: the other cars parked on the driveway, the canvas tent. His skin paled. It didn't look like an act. He seemed to sway. 'Thelma. Is she . . . ? Is she . . . ?' His keen eyes widened as he scrutinized them.

Evenly and quietly Horton said, 'I'm sorry to say your wife is dead, Mr Veerman. We're treating her death as suspicious.'

'There must be some mistake. Are you sure?' He peered closely at Horton and must have seen confirmation in his eyes because he drew in a deep breath. 'I'd like to see her.'

'I'm sorry, sir, that's not possible.'

'I am a doctor, for God's sake!'

'It's a crime scene,' Horton said firmly.

'She's been killed! But who? How?'

'Shall we go inside?' Uckfield repeated firmly and held out his hand towards the front door, clearly indicating that the matter was not up for debate.

Veerman threw a look at the tent and seemed to be deciding whether to disobey Uckfield's instructions. This was a man clearly used to having his own way and *his* instructions followed without question. But then so was Uckfield. Veerman inhaled, ran a hand over his dark hair and threw Horton a slightly hostile look before marching swiftly to the front door. Withdrawing his keys from his overcoat pocket he opened it. No alarm sounded. But Horton could see the house was fitted with one.

'Did Mrs Veerman usually set the alarm before leaving the house?'

'Sometimes. Not always. Half the time she left the door open.' He looked around. 'Where are the dogs?'

'The Dog Support Unit has them, sir. They can be returned to you as soon as you wish.'

'Keep them. They're not my dogs.' He marched through the hall to the rear of the house and the kitchen. Uckfield raised his eyebrows at Horton as they followed. Nothing seemed to have changed since Horton had first stepped inside there on Saturday. The doors leading off the hall were closed. Nothing looked to have been disturbed and there had been no forced entry from the front, or from the kitchen. The patio doors were intact and the kitchen as before. But then Horton didn't think this was a robbery gone wrong and neither did Uckfield.

Veerman crossed to the sink and drew a glass of water. He drank it down in one go, his figure erect, his back to them.

Horton wondered what he was thinking and if the gesture had been designed to hide his expression and give him time to think. He turned and removed his overcoat to reveal an expensive grey suit exquisitely cut and hanging perfectly on his lean, fit body. His appearance was as immaculate as the kitchen and the flat at Admiralty Towers. He wore a white cotton shirt underneath the suit and a plain lemon-coloured tie; not an item of clothing or hair was out of place. He waved them into seats at the breakfast bar in the centre of the modern kitchen but they both remained standing. Veerman decided to stand too.

'Can't you tell me anything about her death?' he asked, scouring their faces as though searching for answers.

'When were you last here, sir?' Horton asked. He thought he saw a flicker of irritation in Veerman's eyes at not having his question answered.

'Monday morning. I caught the eight o'clock sailing from Fishbourne.'

'And yesterday?'

'At the hospital of course.'

'Until?'

'4.30 p.m., then I went to the private hospital where I had clinics until ten p.m.'

That could be easily checked and if it was true — and Horton couldn't see the man lying about something like that — then it meant that Brett Veerman couldn't have killed his wife.

'What time did you come home?'

'I didn't. I stayed in my apartment at Admiralty Towers both Monday and Tuesday night.'

'Why come home now?' In fact, Veerman had come home early. It was just on three p.m.

'Why not? There's no law against it,' he said sharply and then seemed to relent. 'I've come home early because my diary was clear for this afternoon and tomorrow, and I thought it time Thelma and I talked things over. Now it's too late,' he added in an abstracted tone rather than a sorrowful one, thought Horton. It had been too late a long time ago, he thought, recalling his only conversation with Thelma Veerman. It was clear that she and the man in front of him had stopped communicating years ago. They had been two people living together but separately. And beneath the marriage there was hostility, even hatred for each other — or was that too strong a word? Neither of them had expressed hatred in words, looks or gestures, but he felt it. It wasn't open aggression but a simmering seething hostility that went so deep they hardly recognized it themselves. And it was dangerous. He'd witnessed it before. So dangerous that Veerman and his lover could have killed for it?

Horton said, 'When did you last speak to your wife?'

'Monday morning before I left for the ferry.'

'You argued.'

'We never argued.'

Horton thought that was the truth. He envisaged a cold silence between them, worse than a row, which had stretched on for years. 'Do you know what your wife's movements were yesterday and last night?'

'She would have taken the dogs for a walk. She did so at least twice a day, usually four times. I take it this is not a random attack and that it has something to do with that private detective who was killed.'

'Why do you say that?' Uckfield spoke for the first time during the questioning.

Veerman gave him a withering look. Uckfield didn't flinch for even a second. 'I may not be a detective but it doesn't take much imagination or intelligence to link the two.'

Neither Horton nor Uckfield replied. Horton mentally held his breath and knew Uckfield was doing the same. Was Veerman going to confess to having a lover and being involved in Kenton's killing? Or would he concoct a highly plausible story — he'd had enough time to do so. But Veerman said nothing. What was he thinking? wondered Horton. Was he behaving how he thought he should or was he looking back down the years at the time he'd spent with his wife and was now envisaging a life without her? Uckfield let the silence stretch on, but Veerman clearly wasn't going to break it. Uckfield made to speak but Horton got in first.

'Why did you lie about the time you arrived home on Saturday morning?'

'Saturday? What's Saturday got to do with Thelma's death? Oh, I see, of course, the private detective she hired. I didn't lie. Thelma did.'

And now she couldn't contradict that.

'Why would she do that?' asked Uckfield.

'Why do you think? To make you query my movements, as you have done.'

'She believed you had killed Jasper Kenton?'

'I don't know what she believed, Superintendent.'

'Except that you were having an affair. Are you?'

'No.'

Horton said, 'Do you have separate bedrooms?'

'I don't see how that's any business of yours.'

Horton said nothing, neither did Uckfield.

After a while Veerman said stiffly, 'Yes.'

'So you don't know if she was asleep or awake.'

'I don't even know if she was in the house. I didn't look in to say goodnight, but I do know what time I got in and it was just before one a.m.'

Horton watched Veerman carefully. Had he deliberately said that to plant the idea that Thelma might have been out in order to shift the blame away from him? There was bewilderment in his expression but also something else, a kind of arrogance, or was it mockery?

'Where would she have been at that time of night?'

'No idea, probably walking the bloody dogs.'

'Why don't you like them?'

'Why should I? And I don't see that that has any bearing on your investigation.'

It didn't and Horton thought he knew the reason why Veerman didn't care for the animals. Veerman liked a clean, clinical, neat environment and dogs meant smell, dirt, hairs and mess.

Uckfield said, 'Could your wife have had a lover?'

Veerman eyed Uckfield with incredulity and in his expression, Horton saw exactly what kind of life Thelma must have had with him. Veerman thought his wife incapable of having a lover, or of any man wanting her.

'I don't think so, Superintendent,' he answered with a superior tone.

'But how can you be sure?' Horton insisted.

'I knew my wife.' It was said matter-of-factly, without bitterness or sorrow.

'Friends then, perhaps you could let us have names and contact details.'

'I don't know them.'

Uckfield cocked a sceptical eyebrow.

'My wife didn't socialize.'

'But you must have done as a couple.'

'Once, yes. But my wife has become . . . became more reclusive in recent years.'

'She didn't go to the Castle Hill Yacht Club with you?'

Veerman looked surprised and then confused at the question. He answered it warily. 'Not for some years. I hardly go there myself now. Why are you interested in that?'

'Have you and your wife ever been to Lord Ames's house?' Horton asked before Uckfield could prevent him.

'Yes. Why? Look, what has—'

'We'll need to check your movements, sir.'

'Then check away,' Veerman snapped.

'And we need to see your wife's room and go through her belongings. It could help us to find her killer.'

'By all means, when you have a warrant to do so,' Veerman replied icily.

Uckfield eyed him, surprised. 'It would assist us greatly if we could do so now, sir,' he said smoothly.

'My wife has just died. I have a son to inform. Get your warrant and return. Now I'd like you to leave my house.' He made for the door. 'I have calls to make.'

And who would he call first, wondered Horton. His lover? His lawyer? His son?

Uckfield nodded at Horton. To Veerman he said, 'We need a photograph of your wife. We'll need it for our inquiries,' he added when Veerman looked set to protest. 'It will help us to establish her movements before she died.'

'I don't want this in the media,' Veerman said curtly. 'You're not to say anything to the press.'

'We won't, sir, but the press still have a way of finding out about these things.'

'Not from me they won't. And if I believe that anyone in the police has spoken to them, I will make a complaint at the highest level.' Veerman opened the front door.

'We'll let you know when we've finished here, sir.'

'I'll be able to see that for myself. And then those gates will be closed.' Coolly he added, 'Where will the autopsy be held?'

He was a doctor after all, thought Horton. 'At Newport.'

'Then you'll need me to make a formal identification.'

'Tomorrow morning, *if* that suits you, Mr Veerman,' Uckfield said pointedly, with a hint of sarcasm.

'Perfectly. I'll email you a photograph when I can find one.'

Uckfield handed him his card. Veerman took it and the door closed firmly on them.

'He did it,' Uckfield announced, heading for his car.

Changed your tune now, Horton thought but didn't say.

Uckfield added, 'You could have told me what he was like!'

Horton opened his mouth to retort that he'd been telling him that since Saturday, but then realized there was no point. Uckfield would be deaf to such claims.

Uckfield continued, 'He killed Kenton and then he killed his wife, or got someone to do it. He wanted shot of her and he's so damn confident that he'll get away with it. Smooth-talking bastard. He'll make sure there's nothing incriminating in the house. I'll post a local officer here in case he's thinking of having a bonfire. Tomorrow we start talking to everyone who knows him.'

Horton refrained from saying that's what they should have done to begin with.

Uckfield went on, 'We'll find this lover. And maybe we'd better find her quick before he polishes her off because I can't see Veerman wanting someone with that knowledge hanging round his neck for the rest of his life, threatening to incriminate him in murder. I'll pull Bliss out of Swallows Agency. No need for her to be there now. This isn't con-nected with any of Kenton's cases except that one back there.' Uckfield jerked his head at the house.

It had taken him a long time to see it, thought Horton. But he could see another reason why Uckfield had suddenly become so keen on action and Brett Veerman as their main suspect. Thelma Veerman's body had been found on her own land and not Lord Ames's property and that, as far as Uckfield was concerned, meant the motive had nothing to do with His Lordship. Furthermore, Uckfield didn't have to tip toe around the investigation now or kowtow to the Chief Constable.

Uckfield said, 'I'll get a warrant tomorrow and we'll take that place apart. We'll also go over both of their cars, his and Thelma's, and that boathouse. Dennings can oversee the search this end and Bliss the search of his apartment in Portsmouth, as well as his consulting rooms and the ques-tioning of his colleagues. We'll find this ruddy lover of his.'

Horton said, 'Thelma Veerman told me Kenton was trawling the Internet looking for reports on the confer-ences and seminars her husband attended to see if there was any one particular woman who appeared regularly at the same places as Brett Veerman. Kenton was also examining Veerman's social and professional network website profiles. We should do the same.'

'I'll get the Hi-Tech Unit working on it.' Uckfield made to climb into his car but Horton forestalled him.

'I don't believe Thelma Veerman lived such a reclusive life as her husband claims. She must have had friends and we might be able to get details of them from her mobile phone records. Eunice Swallows must have the number. Thelma also visited the abbey frequently. I'd like to question the monks to see if anyone saw her there.'

'Get on to it now. I'll get a house-to-house organized here, which shouldn't take long as there aren't that many properties.' Uckfield called out to Sergeant Norris, leaving Horton to head for Cantelli's car. Horton gave Cantelli instructions to head for Northwood Abbey. On the way he brought Cantelli up to speed with the interview with Veerman, describing his attitude to his wife's brutal murder. Cantelli agreed it was defensive and unhelpful, but ventured that it might be the result of trauma.

'Doctors see death all the time but don't always believe it can happen to them or someone close to them,' he ventured. 'But I feel sorry for Thelma Veerman if what he says is true. Must have been a hell of a lonely life.'

Horton agreed. The only comfort she had found seemed to have been with her dogs and the monks.

CHAPTER TWENTY

'She used to come here to pray quite regularly and sometimes she'd join us for the services,' Brother Norman told them after expressing shock and sorrow at the news of Thelma's death. They were sitting in a quiet private garden enjoyed by the monks behind the dormitory and orchard. There was a gap in the trees and Horton could see out to the Solent in the late afternoon. It was so peaceful and tranquil that he could almost believe the outside world didn't exist or that time had been suspended. It seemed at odds with the brutal scenes he and Cantelli had just witnessed and it made Brett Veerman's words and attitude to his wife's death seem even harsher.

Horton had said nothing about how Thelma Veerman had died and Brother Norman didn't ask. He knew they wouldn't be able to tell him that. Horton had asked for him at the tea room because he was the only monk he really knew. He had been hoping to have a word with Cliff Yately about Thelma Veerman — she had treated his sprained wrist and he might be able to tell them more about her — but Brother Norman had told them Yately had finally capitulated to his injury and had taken the day off, probably after overdoing it the day before.

'Did you see Mrs Veerman yesterday?' Horton asked.

'Yes. She was in the chapel for Sexts at one o'clock. But I didn't speak to her.'

'How long does that last?'

'It's the fourth service of the day and short, just a hymn, three psalms, a reading and a prayer. Fifteen minutes at the most.'

'Did you see where she went afterwards?'

'No. I'm sorry, I didn't. We go straight into dinner for 1.15 p.m. I can ask my Brothers if any of them saw or spoke to her.'

'Please. If she was in the chapel she wouldn't have had the dogs with her.'

'She might have tied them up outside. They're very well behaved and are used to coming here. They would have sat quietly until she came out.'

'Did she ever confide in you or in any of the monks?'

'She certainly didn't to me and I wouldn't ask, but I'm always willing to listen when someone wants to share their troubles or concerns with me.'

Horton thought it was a hint to him. But he wasn't used to sharing his problems or his thoughts with anyone. His childhood had taught him that was a foolishly dangerous thing to do and a lesson once learned the hard way was one that couldn't be forgotten and was often impossible to shrug off.

Brother Norman continued, 'And even if she had confided I wouldn't betray that confidence, even in death.'

Cantelli nodded. Being a Catholic he'd understand that.

'Can you tell me anything about her?' Horton asked with a plea in his voice.

'I know she was a nurse.'

That was new information at least, and it explained why she had tended to Cliff Yately's sprained wrist. It was probably how she had met her husband.

Horton said, 'Did she tell you that?'

'She demonstrated it when one of the Brothers fell ill tending the garden. That was two years ago and she's helped us ever since. Not on an official paid basis; she wouldn't take payment. We used to give her apples from the orchards, vegetables, eggs and pork instead, though she wasn't fond of the latter after seeing the pigs reared here. If anyone needed medical advice or was poorly then she was only too willing to help. She enjoyed it too. I think she might have liked to return to nursing. It's such a tragic loss. Are there family?'

Horton searched his face to see if he already knew the answer to that question. Maybe he did and had perfected the art of looking innocent. Surely he knew there was a husband. Thelma must have told him that or spoken about him, and she had worn a wedding ring. And what mother didn't boast about her children? Many, he thought with regret, recalling the countless criminals he'd met over the years and the mothers who neglected, hurt and abandoned their children. But Thelma Veerman hadn't been like that. Only he didn't know that for certain. In fact, he realized he knew nothing about her.

'There's a husband and son,' he answered, looking closely for a reaction.

Brother Norman held his gaze, and in it, Horton thought he saw a hint of something that he couldn't put his finger on. It wasn't amusement but it was close to it. It jarred at something in the remote recesses of his mind, but he knew he wouldn't be able to retrieve it. Then the shutters came down and Brother Norman's face resumed its usual calm, genial, gentle expression.

'I will pray for them,' he said.

Horton wasn't sure that Brett Veerman would want or deserve the Brother's prayers but maybe he was being uncharitable. The son most certainly would. But how did he know that? Perhaps the son was a chip off his father's block and both had left Thelma feeling isolated and unloved. A feeling Horton knew only too well and one that caused a tightness in his chest even after all these years. His mind flicked back to Bernard again and the fact that he had been injured in Northern Ireland, and alongside that, the new knowledge that Thelma Veerman had been a nurse. Then suddenly something clicked. His heart skipped a beat. Could Bernard have been treated at the Royal Naval Hospital Haslar at Gosport? Bloody hell! Was it possible? But Bernard was Royal Air Force, not navy. Had the hospital treated members of other services? Had Jennifer been on her way to see Bernard on the day she'd disappeared?

'Is there is anything else I can do for you, Inspector?'

Brother Norman's voice penetrated Horton's whirling thoughts. Hastily he pulled himself together.

'I'd like to email you a photograph of Thelma and I'd be grateful if you would show it around and ask if anyone saw her yesterday.'

'Of course, but we all knew Thelma so no need for the photograph.'

Horton rose. Cantelli put away his notebook. 'Beautiful place,' he said. 'I'd like to bring my family over to take a look around it.'

'You're welcome any time, Sergeant. I wish you well with your investigations.' He didn't shake hands.

As they headed towards the car park Horton caught sight of Jay Ottley in the piggery. Knowing how uneasy Ottley was with people Horton said to Cantelli, 'I'll meet you in the car.' He didn't want to alarm Ottley by questioning him mob handed.

Ottley nodded a greeting and straightened up. 'Just giving them their supper.'

'They look as though they're enjoying it.'

Ottley scratched his beard with his gloved fingers and his dark eyes looked lovingly on the sow and her litter of six.

'Is the sick pig better now? I saw you and Brother Norman with the vet on Friday.'

'She's mending.'

'Must be hard to part with them,' Horton said.

But Ottley shrugged. 'They're not pets. They're here for a purpose.'

Horton asked him if he had seen Thelma Veerman yesterday afternoon.

'I did.'

'When?'

'Just after Sexts.'

'What did she do?' Horton knew he'd have to ask precise questions. Ottley wasn't the type to volunteer information. Probably not used to conducting conversation, having spent so much time conducting monologues with his pigs. The thought made him consider Thelma Veerman locked in a marriage where conversation had also died. Perhaps that was what had made her steadily more reclusive, withdrawing into a world of her own, and the world of the abbey.

'She walked over to the café,' Ottley said.

'Why?'

'Mr Yately let her keep the dogs outside while she went into worship. They were tied up. They had a drink,' he added almost defensively as though Horton was going to accuse her of cruelty.

'What did she do next?'

'Spoke to Mr Yately and then went off over there.'

'There' was the direction of the footpath back to her house.

'Did she talk to Mr Yately long?'

'A few minutes.' Ottley looked anxious to return to his pigs.

Horton didn't think he'd get any more from him. He didn't think it kind to spoil Ottley's day by breaking the bad news about Thelma Veerman's death. Brother Norman could do that. Tomorrow he'd ask Brother Norman for Yately's contact details and speak to him to find out whether Thelma was anxious about anything or whether she had mentioned she was going somewhere other than home. Horton wondered if maybe Cliff Yately and Thelma Veerman had a bit of a thing going. He wouldn't have blamed her if she had.

In the car, he phoned through to Uckfield and told him they had a sighting of Thelma Veerman and a time that she'd left the abbey and headed in the direction of home the day before, at about 1.30 p.m. That had been at least an hour before he'd called there the first time and there had been no answer, so perhaps she had walked further on towards Ryde.

But there had been no answer when he had returned, so she'd either still been out, or had returned and left again, or was down on the beach bleeding to death. He asked Uckfield if he needed them to stay over for the results of the autopsy, which wouldn't be due for some hours yet, but Uckfield said not.

'Trueman's checking into her background. Dennings has arrived. He'll handle the incident suite and investigation this end. I want you and Cantelli in the briefing tomorrow morning, nine thirty. And we keep this away from the media for as long as possible — not because Veerman says so,' Uckfield added hastily, 'but because the ACC does and we don't want the press hounds connecting this with Kenton's death.'

'Or His Lordship,' muttered Horton, knowing exactly why Dean wanted it kept quiet. There would be no public appeals for last sightings of Thelma Veerman, just as there hadn't been for Jasper Kenton.

'We're dismissed, Barney. Let's head for home.'

Cantelli looked pleased even though it meant another fairly rough crossing. They boarded the six o'clock sailing. It felt a lot later. Cantelli looked as tired as Horton felt, his fatigue deepened by sadness. The death of Thelma Veerman was somehow unreal. As he and Uckfield had discussed earlier, he had half-expected Brett Veerman's lover to be killed instead of his wife, because it was too risky for Veerman to allow an accomplice to murder to live. That could still be the case.

In the comfortable silence that fell between them on the journey, Horton let his thoughts roam back to the two things he'd considered earlier about his foster father. That he'd joined the Hampshire Police unusually late, and that after being injured in Northern Ireland in 1978 he could have been treated at the Royal Naval Hospital Haslar. He knew that Bernard and Eileen had been married shortly after Bernard had been injured. He'd checked with the Registry of Births, Deaths and Marriages. It had been Christmas Eve 1978 and Eileen's maiden name was Ducale. He hadn't had time to request her birth certificate but he would. Could Eileen have visited Bernard in the hospital at Gosport? Had Jennifer been on her way to see Eileen or Bernard, or both of them, on the day she'd disappeared? Or had she been returning from there? Had Eileen or Bernard known Jennifer?

He gazed out of the window at the darkening day. If Jennifer had been meeting either of them then they must have known about her disappearance. The Eileen he had come to love would have been concerned about her friend and her son though, and that further convinced Horton of two things, which he'd already considered. That neither Eileen nor Bernard had known Jennifer had a son until four years later when he had been fostered by them. And that neither had known she had disappeared. So if Jennifer had been visiting them at Haslar Hospital then Eileen would have waved her friend off not knowing that harm had come to her until Ballard had shown up and told her of it and the fact she'd had son. Perhaps Jennifer had never mentioned her son in order to protect him. But from whom?

Cantelli dropped him back at the station where he collected his Harley and headed for home, this time with thoughts of Thelma Veerman's lonely life haunting him. The wind was howling through the masts and shaking and slapping the halyards. It was a sound that would have kept many people awake, but Horton had grown so used to it that he no longer noticed. He stood under a hot shower for some minutes, trying to wash away the image of Thelma's body on the beach, but he knew it wouldn't leave him for a long time.

He cooked an omelette, thinking with regret of a very different meal and evening he should have been spending with Gaye Clayton. Maybe she was thinking that too. Had she finished the autopsy yet? It was just gone eight o'clock, the time she should have been collecting him in her red Mini. He reached for his phone and called her.

'I'm still on the island,' she said, with what Horton hoped was a trace of disappointment in her voice, but perhaps he just wanted to hear that.

'I suspected you might be. What did you discover?'

'Lividity was present throughout the entire body and flies had laid their eggs in the soft tissue; in fact the eggs were just beginning to hatch.'

Horton's stomach turned over as he thought of the omelette he'd just eaten.

'The time of death is between ten and midnight but she was probably shot a few hours earlier, say 6.30 or seven p.m. Tuesday night. As I said to Superintendent Uckfield though, these are estimates.'

'She was seen at the abbey at 1.30 p.m. and I called at her house twice. The first time at about 2.45 p.m. and the second about an hour later, and there was no answer and no sound of the dogs at either time.'

'Perhaps she'd gone out to meet her killer and taken the dogs with her.'

'And the dogs wouldn't attack someone they knew.'

'They could have been drugged.'

God, he hadn't thought of that. And by the time the dogs had regained consciousness their mistress was already dead. They'd stayed by her side barking to attract attention.

Gaye was saying, 'There's no evidence that the victim was drugged but you'll have to wait for the results from the forensic toxicologist. And there is no evidence that she was restrained or sexually assaulted or that she was rendered unconscious by a blow to the head and then shot.'

'Was she killed where we found her body?'

'There are no scratches or marks to indicate that she was moved but it's possible. I didn't find anything unusual or significant on her clothes but the forensic examination of them might reveal something. The bolt was fired at almost point-blank range with a great degree of accuracy. Your killer knew exactly where to aim. The victim didn't turn or run away. Before she realized what was happening she'd been shot. The killer then either waited for her to die or left her knowing she would.'

And whichever way you looked at it they were dealing with a cold-blooded bastard, someone without compassion, feeling or conscience.

Horton said, 'I'll call you about that dinner.'

'When you're ready,' she answered.

He rang off. She at least knew the demands of the job, which Catherine had never really understood. Few did, although Cantelli had found himself a gem in Charlotte.

His thoughts again conjured up the solitary figure of Thelma Veerman, her grey-blue eyes, sharp, but also suspicious, the air of superiority about her that now he knew had been developed as a protective shield to disguise her shyness and to stop others from probing and getting too close to her for fear of rejection, as her husband had rejected her.

As he cleared away, listening to the rain drumming on the boat, he wanted Veerman to be guilty of killing Jasper Kenton and Thelma Veerman, not only because it was cleaner and simpler, and because he thought Veerman arrogant, superior and cold-hearted, but because it exonerated him in keeping silent about Lomas, the beachcomber. Because if Veerman and his lover hadn't killed them, who had?

He laid on his bunk trying to recall what he had seen at the Veermans's house on Tuesday afternoon. Had there been anything unusual or different? Only that Thelma's car was on the driveway, but that wasn't unusual. And he hadn't heard anything to arouse his suspicions. Perhaps if he'd observed the shore from the ferry on his way back to Portsmouth he might have seen a boat approaching the house. He certainly hadn't seen one on his arrival.

Then there was the fact that Kenton had travelled to the Isle of Wight by car ferry on the Friday before he was reported missing. Why? And how many other times had he crossed to the island recently? Did it matter? And still nagging relentlessly away at him was the purchase of that boat, the fact that he'd received no training in handling it, that he hadn't even wanted to take it out for a trial and that he'd had it refuelled but hadn't used it. But above all was the discrepancy in reports of Jasper Kenton's personality and Horton thought it was about time they got to the bottom of it.

CHAPTER TWENTY-ONE

Thursday

'I'd like to interview Jasper Kenton's sister,' Horton announced to Uckfield after the briefing had finished.

'What the hell for? She didn't kill them.'

'I know, but the description of Kenton given by the marina manager and the salesman bothers me. It's contrary to everything we've been told about Kenton.' And that amongst other things had preoccupied Horton during his many wakeful moments throughout the night. Uckfield had confirmed at the briefing that everything that could be done was being done. The house-to-house would be conducted. The warrants would be through later that morning. Dennings would oversee the search of Veerman's Isle of Wight property, the boathouse and the couple's cars. Bliss would coordinate the search of the Admiralty Towers apartment, Veerman's consulting rooms and the questioning of Veerman's colleagues at both the National Health Service and private hospitals. The latter two of which would be conducted by DC Marsden and PC Kate Somerfield.

Kenton's bank accounts had been handed over to the economic crime unit to analyse. Trueman had reported that

Kenton's phone records hadn't revealed any calls to Thelma Veerman's number but the records of his calls were still being analysed. Trueman had also applied for access to Thelma Veerman's mobile phone record. Eunice Swallows had given Bliss the number.

Horton had suggested that the dogs could have been drugged.

And as they were still with the Dog Support Unit on the Isle of Wight, Dennings would arrange to have them tested. But it might be too late, thought Horton, as whatever they had been given could now be out of their system. He had asked about the Veermans's son and had ventured that he should also be questioned. He would be able to tell them more about his parent's relationship. Trueman had revealed that John Veerman was on board RFA *Argus*, the Royal Navy's primary casualty receiving ship. It was on counter-drugs patrol around the Caribbean. He was being flown home.

Bliss now eyed Horton in her customary cold, suspicious manner. 'I can't see how you talking to Kenton's sister can help find his killer or Thelma Veerman's when they haven't spoken for years.'

'Did she tell you that?'

'She told the local police and she also told Eunice Swallows, who spoke to her on the phone after she'd formerly identified the body.'

'Do you know why they fell out?'

'Who said they did? They just drifted apart.'

'I'd like to know more about Kenton. And I'd like Cantelli with me,' Horton said to Uckfield. Bliss looked as though she was about to refuse but Uckfield got there first and he outranked her.

'OK, but don't be all day about it.'

Horton made his escape before Uckfield could change his mind or Bliss could persuade him to. Walters had been designated to continue working on the restaurant attacks after another fruitless late night spent watching them and to attend to CID matters. He seemed to have recovered from his stomach upset.

Horton asked Cantelli to call Louise Durridge to tell her they were on their way. He didn't want a wasted journey. He turned to Walters. 'Chase up forensic to see if they've got more on the manufacturer of the paint that was used on those restaurants, and if so, follow it up. Yes, I know you've checked the major hardware stores but there must be other shops in the area.' Then he paused on his way to his office as an idea struck him. Walters had already identified those restaurants whose security systems were doubtful and those whose kitchens looked in need of redecoration, but had he returned to the three that had been vandalized?

He turned back. 'Find out if any of the restaurants attacked have received a quote for redecorating. If they have, get whatever information you can on who's quoted them. Find out what jobs they've carried out before. This could be a straightforward con man trying to drum up business.'

Horton fetched his sailing jacket from his office and eyed his phone, hesitating over whether to call Harry Kimber. Early that morning, before the briefing, he'd discovered from his research on the Internet that the Royal Navy Hospital Haslar had expanded its remit in 1966 to admit members of all three services — the Royal Navy, Army and Royal Air Force. So Bernard Litchfield *could* have been a patient there. And Eileen *could* have been visiting him. And Jennifer *could* have been heading there. Horton was sure that Kimber would have visited his closest friend in hospital. He might be able to confirm that Bernard was actually in the hospital at that time and for how long.

Cantelli popped his head round the door to say that Louise Durridge would see them at her place of work, a dress shop in the small market town of Marlborough. Harry Kimber would have to wait.

Horton calculated that it would take them about eighty minutes to get to Marlborough, in the north-east corner of Wiltshire, and another eighty to get back, plus about an hour at the most to interview Louise Durridge, so they should return by mid-afternoon. But Horton's timescale soon went by the wayside when first they were held up because of an earlier accident on the M27 heading towards Southampton and secondly because of heavy traffic on the M3 to Winchester. He was beginning to wonder whether they would ever reach Marlborough or if they were doomed to spend the entire day on the gridlocked roads of Britain. Eventually, Cantelli drew into the market town and began searching for a parking place in the middle of the wide and ancient high street.

'Did you know that Marlborough was granted a Royal Charter by King John in 1204 enabling it to achieve market town status?' he said, scouring the road keenly, ready to pounce if someone looked even remotely like they were returning to their vehicle.

'No, but I believe you. Anything else I should know?' Horton asked — apart, he said to himself, from the fact that one of Lord Ames's estates bordered the attractive old market town.

'They've got a very posh private boarding school here.'

Horton knew that.

'Well outside the remit of a sergeant's pay and even a Chief Constable's,' Cantelli added.

But not that of the Ames family, because Horton had also discovered through his research on the Ames family history that Richard Ames's younger brother, Gordon, had attended Marlborough College. It had been founded by a group of Church of England clergymen in 1843 with the prime purpose of educating the sons of clergy. Perhaps Lady Marsha and Lord William Ames had hoped some of the Christian influence of the past would rub off on their younger son. If so, they had been sorely disappointed. Gordon Ames's life had spiralled out of control somewhere between the mid-1960s and early '70s and he had died abroad in 1973, leaving Richard Ames, the current Lord, the only surviving child.

Horton wondered what Ames had made of the death of Thelma Veerman. He must have been told by now and that meant that Mike Danby would also know, even though he'd not been on the phone to inquire about it. Why should he though? Kenton's death being connected with Ames was now highly unlikely. His Lordship could get on with his trade negotiations with Russia in peace.

Cantelli finally found a parking space and they located Louise Durridge's spacious and tastefully decorated dress shop just off the high street. Cantelli apologized for their lateness, which she dismissed with a nervous smile.

'I know what the traffic is like,' she said, excusing herself from her assistant, an elegant lady in her late fifties. She showed them through to the back of the shop where to his left Horton caught sight of a row of well-lit changing rooms with enough mirrors to terrorize anyone suffering from Eisoptrophobia. They stepped into a back room that, despite the fact it contained rails of clothes, a steam iron and ironing board as well as a sink, fridge, coffee machine and kettle, was spotlessly clean and tidy. A door to the right indicated the toilet, which, Horton thought, her customers must need if they took as long as Catherine to buy clothes. From what he'd seen on entering, this was just the kind of place that would have had her salivating at the mouth. And at prices her new boyfriend could easily afford, but then he wasn't a public servant, a phrase that had become something of a dirty word of late and which Horton bitterly resented. There was another door beside the fridge that led into a back yard for deliveries.

Louise Durridge offered them refreshments, which they accepted, Cantelli plumping for tea and Horton coffee. He eyed her keenly. She was younger than her brother by four years but she could easily have passed for late thirties. Her dark hair was cut in a short neat bob framing a lean and attractive dark face with minimal make-up. She was dressed smartly in a light grey shift dress that reached her knees and showed off her figure, rounded in all the right places, but not fat. Her legs, clad in black stockings, or tights, were shapely and she wore black court shoes with a small heel.

'How long have you had the shop?' Cantelli asked, as she gestured them into two seats at a small table and flicked on the kettle.

'Eight years. I stock all the latest designer wear. It's very successful,' she declared proudly and a little defensively, Horton thought. 'It's a wealthy area and being so close to the College I get mothers, aunts, sisters and even some of the students in here.'

'From Marlborough College?' Cantelli said, displaying his recently acquired knowledge.

'Yes. It's half term next week so I'm expecting to be busy today and over the weekend.' She handed Horton his black coffee in an expensive-looking porcelain mug. And as if to prove her point the shop bell buzzed.

'We won't keep you long,' Horton replied. 'And we do appreciate you giving us the time.'

'That's OK, only I'm not sure I can help you much. I don't really know anything about Jasper's life. I hadn't seen him for years.' She handed Cantelli his tea and put milk and sugar on the table in front of them.

Cantelli said, 'When was the last time you had contact with your brother?'

She stood back and eyed them both. Again Horton thought she seemed nervous. 'I don't remember exactly. It was a long time ago.'

But it was a lie. Horton saw that instantly and so too did Cantelli, not that he betrayed it and neither did Horton. They both remained silent, sensing that it would prompt her to disclose more. And she did.

'Jasper and I . . . well, we were different,' she stammered.

'You fell out?' Cantelli prompted gently.

'Not exactly.' She took a breath. 'We just didn't have a lot in common.' She eyed them anxiously. 'I understand from Ms Swallows that you're investigating his death. Do you think . . . . is there any reason to believe . . . ?'

'He was unlawfully killed, yes.'

'Murdered?' she breathed.

Cantelli solemnly nodded.

She studied his face for a moment then let out a long slow breath. Pulling out the third seat at the table, she sat down as the shop doorbell again buzzed and loud female voices reached into the back room. She seemed not to notice.

After a moment she resumed. 'Jasper was the favourite. A boy and clever. He was quiet, studious and obedient. He always did what people wanted or expected him to do. Me? I was the dunce. I was noisy, clumsy and rebellious.' She gave a timid smile as though it was a joke but Horton heard the bitterness and sensed the pain it had caused her. She looked down at her immaculate manicured fingers. 'I know I shouldn't speak ill of the dead and all that but . . .' She trailed off.

'What happened?' Horton asked quietly.

Her head came up and in her eyes Horton saw years of anguish.

'I left home as soon as I could, just before I was seventeen. I couldn't stand hearing about how wonderful Jasper was and how well he was doing any longer. He'd got high grades in his A levels and was destined to go to university. He was a credit to his parents. The sun shone out of his every orifice. So when Stuart Hayes told me he had a friend in London who was looking for someone to share, I went like a shot.'

'Stuart Hayes?' Cantelli said, surprised.

'Yes. You remember him?' she asked with an expression that Horton thought was pleasure as he racked his brains trying to recall the name, which was obviously familiar to Cantelli.

'If it's the same one, he was the drummer in Gracious Grove, the 1980s band,' Cantelli answered.

'That's right.' She beamed at him.

Horton showed nothing of his racing thoughts. It was the group Mike Danby had mentioned because his first client James Westrop had recommended Chas Foxton, also a previous member of Gracious Grove, to Danby. And Foxton's pop star clients had stayed at Lord Ames's Isle of Wight residence. Interesting. But significant? He didn't yet know, but he felt a frisson of excitement.

'How did you know Stuart Hayes?' he asked her, keenly interested. Cantelli threw him a curious glance.

'I went to school with him; we were in the same class. Jasper won a scholarship to the grammar school but I went to the local comprehensive.'

Horton tucked away this interesting piece of information for examination later, uncertain where it would lead them, if anywhere. But perhaps more would be revealed as she continued.

'I got a job in a boutique in London and loved it. I began to spend more time with the boys in the band. That's when I met Mason Petterson, another member of the band and, well we became more than friends.' Then her smile faded. 'It took Jasper two months before he turned up and two weeks to get hired by them.'

That wasn't on his CV. And Danby certainly hadn't mentioned it. Why? Because he didn't know or he didn't want him to know? Horton's interest deepened. His police antennae told him this meant something. Quickly he recalled what he'd read and what Trueman had told him about Kenton; he was certain there wasn't anything about him having a degree.

He said, 'Your brother didn't go to university.'

'No. He preferred to stay with the band. My parents were furious, not with Jasper but with me. They blamed me for corrupting him and ruining his future chances. They didn't want to have anything more to do with me. Jasper said not to let it worry me. He'd talk them round. I believed him. Jasper could be extremely persuasive.'

She said it with a passion borne of bitterness tinged with resignation and regret. Horton's mind raced with thoughts as she continued.

'The band got bigger and more famous. Mason and I got engaged. He even bought me a ring.' She looked sad and her head dropped but quickly came up again. Not before

Horton saw a ring on the third finger of her left hand. It looked expensive. A large ruby set in a cluster of diamonds. 'But Mason and I spilt up,' she said hastily, her gaze flicking between them uneasily.

Horton saw at once what she meant. 'Jasper used you to get the job. He targeted you to get in with the band.'

She studied him open-mouthed because he'd so quickly understood. Recovering she said, 'Yes. Jasper used everyone to get what he wanted. That's what he was like. He was very charming but very ruthless. He'd let no one and nothing stand in his way.'

And here was yet another side of the dead man's personality that no one had mentioned. Alongside the thorough, patient, painstaking, quiet man, and one who had been described as reckless, impulsive, and chatty, Horton now added persuasive, manipulative and cunning. If he put what she was saying with what Danby had told him about how they'd met, a thread was beginning to form. It was possible that Kenton had singled out Mike Danby and probably before him Eunice Swallows. Why though? What was it that Kenton had wanted? Was it access to Chas Foxton via Danby? If so, where did that leave them with Brett Veerman as a suspect? Time to consider that later.

'What did Jasper want from the band?' he asked.

'What do you think? Money. He even used our parents.'

'He sponged off your parents?'

She smiled sardonically. 'No, Jasper was too clever for that. He never took a penny from them. He was the hard-working, clever and very dutiful son. They adored him.'

'Then how did he use them?' asked Cantelli, clearly as intrigued as Horton.

Women's voices came from the room behind them as they began to try on clothes.

'They went to their graves thinking Jasper was a saint. My mother died first. I came back for the funeral and my father barely spoke two words to me. It hurt.' She stared down at her hands then took a breath and her head came up. 'I got into a relationship with a married man, had his child, he ditched me. Then my father died three years after my mother. Jasper found where I was living and asked me to come to the funeral. The quarrel wasn't between us, even though I resented him. I refused. He told me that Dad had left everything to him, but that he didn't think that fair and he was prepared to split it equally. It wasn't much he said. The house had been remortgaged to pay for health care bills and Dad had spent much of his savings. Jasper said there was about ten thousand pounds left in the estate. There should have been more and there probably had been and that had gone to Jasper. But five thousand pounds was a lot of money to a single parent and I took it.'

'It was money to keep you silent,' said Horton. But if she had been that hard up, why hadn't she sold the ring Petterson had given her — unless she had and the one she was wearing now was from another man, her husband. Except she wasn't wearing a wedding ring.

'I can't prove anything,' she was saying, 'but I think Jasper took money from my father's account gradually over a period of time, either without his knowledge or because Jasper had spun him some yarn when he was ill. And Jasper put the money somewhere no one would find when it went to probate.'

And Horton was beginning to see how Kenton could have done that. He had been an expert on computer fraud and cybercrime and although this was in the 1980s and 1990s, when the Internet was in its infancy, before cybercrime and Internet fraud had become the epidemic it now was, Kenton had cut his teeth on siphoning funds from his parents' account so that they wouldn't notice. He'd been honing his skills before hitting the big time later. And Horton wouldn't mind betting that was what he had done with the band's money. Kenton's ability with a computer had existed long before many had even tapped at a keyboard, manipulated a mouse and stared at a screen.

With a wry smile she said, 'I don't think he will have left me anything in his will.'

Horton didn't even know if there was one. Dennings had said nothing about finding it in the apartment and if Jasper Kenton hadn't made a will then Louise Durridge might be in for a windfall.

'Have you any idea who would have killed him?' she asked somewhat anxiously as laughter came from the room behind them. But Horton also caught the sound of a movement outside. And he glimpsed the silhouette of a man behind the window. There was someone in the yard. Louise Durridge looked troubled.

'Do you?' he asked.

'No,' she answered quickly, but perhaps she did and there was only one man she would protect, he thought, rising swiftly and crossing to the door. The man who had given her that ring. With his heart pumping, he wondered if he was about to come face to face with the beachcomber. Louise Durridge sprang up. Her skin paled. Horton threw open the door and found himself facing a well-built man in his late forties with longish greying brown hair who, disappointingly, was not the beachcomber Lomas.

'It's OK, Louise,' the man said as he entered the room. Then to Horton he said, 'I'm Mason Petterson and although I'd like to have done, I didn't kill Jasper Kenton.'

CHAPTER TWENTY-TWO

'Jasper Kenton came to see you,' said Horton, but Petterson was prevented from answering as Louise Durridge's assistant put her worried head around the door.

'We're rather busy,' she said agitatedly.

'I'll be with you in a moment.' Louise Durridge turned her anxious eyes on Horton — not, he thought, because she might be losing sales but because she was afraid for her lover.

Petterson said, 'I don't know how he found me but he did. Louise and I have told no one and everyone believes me to be Joshua Jenkins, Louise's partner.'

But Jasper Kenton was skilled in tracing assets and people. Chas Foxton would have been easy to find. He was a public figure. Horton didn't know about the rest of the band but he soon would.

Petterson took Louise's hand and continued, 'After the band split up, I followed another passion of mine, painting. And I became successful, which was helped no doubt by my already being a public figure. I had a name and that brought punters into the art gallery and sold my paintings. But it also pissed me off because I felt people were buying them because of who I was, not for what they were. I took to drinking in a big way. Then one night during an exhibition

I lost it. The media loved that. There were pictures of me all over the newspapers, completely off my head, ripping up my paintings. I stopped painting, drank more, until one day I tried to end it all by throwing myself off the Clifton Suspension Bridge in Bristol. I was talked down by a kindly fireman. After that I took myself off to the Priory Clinic. It took me five years to rebuild myself. I changed my name and rented a remote cottage in Wales in the Brecon Beacons where by chance I met up again with Louise. She was on holiday and her car had broken down. The mist was coming in. Her mobile phone wasn't working, she had no idea where she was. I recognized her at once but hoped she didn't recognize me — not because I didn't want to see her; I did. But because I didn't want to see Jasper, or anyone from those days, and I certainly didn't want to be involved with any revival or some such crap.'

'There are revivals?' asked Horton.

But Cantelli answered. 'Yes, and a thriving fan base. My wife was a big fan, still is.'

'And there are royalties?' asked Horton.

'Yes. But I haven't touched a penny since I left the clinic. And neither have I spent any of the money from the sale of any of my pictures except for those I paint under the name of Joshua Jenkins. The other money is in an account in the name of Mason Petterson.'

'And it's still there?'

'I guess so. I haven't checked.'

'Because if you did you knew that Jasper would find you. Why so desperate for him not to locate you?'

Petterson threw Louise a glance. 'He showed up here in March.'

Horton saw that Petterson had to answer the question in his own way and time.

Louise picked up the tale. 'Jasper came to the shop. I told him I hadn't seen Mason since 1987.'

'He specifically asked about him?'

'Yes. Jasper must have followed me when I went home.'

Or maybe he didn't have to because he would already have discovered where Louise lived and all he had to do was mount a surveillance operation. Something Danby had said Kenton wouldn't be good at, but Horton thought Danby, like everyone else, had underestimated Kenton's skills, intelligence, cunning and deviousness, not to mention his greed. And Kenton had deliberately fostered that opinion, or any other he wished to assume depending on who he was communicating with. Horton's mind flicked to Kenton's performance with the marina manager and salesman at the yacht brokerage.

'He was friendly and pleasant,' Petterson resumed. 'There were no threats. He said he was glad I was OK and pleased I'd got together again with his sister. He said he was also pleased to see how well Louise was doing and that was it. He left.'

'But you were worried.'

'Yes. I knew that he wouldn't go bleating to the media. That wasn't his style. But everything Jasper did had a purpose and an ulterior motive.'

There was that thread again. 'Did he steal from the band?' Horton asked, recalling how Louise had said he'd muscled in on them.

'He might have done, who the hell knows.'

'I thought the band had a manager,' said Cantelli.

'We did. He got us gigs and made sure we had the right press coverage and the right interviews lined up. Jasper handled the merchandising, royalties and everything else we couldn't be bothered with including licensing and opening the right investment accounts. None of us questioned it. Jasper was straight. I didn't question anything until I met Louise again and she told me about her brother. Before we spilt up, I'd believed she was jealous of her brother and that she was insecure and unstable.'

'And I wonder who told you that,' said Horton knowingly.

'He even showed me evidence. A computer record at the local mental institution with her name and a record of violence against him and their parents.'

Louise took a breath. Mason Petterson squeezed her hand. 'I didn't tell Louise I knew this. I just ditched her.'

'Didn't you check it with Stuart Hayes?' asked Cantelli.

'No, because Stuart had already told me how much Louise hated her parents. I thought it fitted and I was too wrapped up in the band, too bloody pleased with myself, too damn cocky and too spaced out on drink and drugs. I could have any girl I wanted. They were throwing themselves at me and the others, so why should I stay engaged to a mental case? I thought I'd had a lucky escape. I'd nearly got married to a fruitcake. That's how it looked to me. Louise went off and that was it.'

'So why didn't you think she was a fruitcake when you met her in Wales?' asked Cantelli.

'Because by then I'd been classed as one. I thought she would understand what I'd been through. As we talked we realized what Jasper had done. She told me about her suspicions about Jasper siphoning off money from his parents and I began to wonder if he had done that with us. It didn't matter if he had; there was plenty of the stuff sloshing around. It was the lies and trickery that disgusted me.'

And that was what disgusted Horton about his mother's disappearance. Sometimes — in fact often — it was the lies you ended up believing, because they'd been told so many times, they became the truth. He again recalled Bernard's words: '*You have to find the truth for yourself. And even then, you must ask whether it really is the truth, or what someone is persuading you into believing.*' He hadn't understood them then, but he did now.

Petterson continued, 'Louise and I decided that we would leave things in the past and start again. We did for six years before he showed up in March.'

'So what do you think his purpose was?'

'I'm not sure. He gave nothing away. Said he was pleased to find I was OK and that was it. He never contacted me or Louise again.'

'You never tackled him about the lies he told.'

Louise shook her head. Petterson said, 'We just wanted him out of our lives. We thought about moving and would have done if he'd come round again but he didn't. Blackmail wasn't his style. And even if we had moved, he'd probably have found us. But he can't now. You're sure he is dead? I told Louise she should identify the body just to make certain, but she couldn't cope with it.'

'We're sure, Mr Petterson,' Horton said firmly.

The shop bell buzzed again. Louise Durridge rose. 'I'd better help out in the shop, if that's all right?'

'Of course,' Horton replied. After she'd left Horton asked Mason Petterson if he was in touch with any of the other band members.

'No.'

'Do you know what happened to them?'

'Stuart Hayes died ten years ago of cancer. Chas Foxton is a millionaire record producer, Gary Grainger some kind of property millionaire and Nigel Swaythling is a big action movie star in Hollywood. I don't know what happened to Sam Tandy, our lead singer, after he followed a solo career when the band spilt up. He had some success, but then like me the drink and drugs got the better of him. He could be dead for all I know.'

'And did you tell Jasper this?'

'No and he didn't ask.'

So Kenton wouldn't have got any new information from Petterson. He already knew where Foxton was and what he was doing. And unless he had simply tracked down his sister and her boyfriend to apologize for splitting them up, which he hadn't, then he'd have left disappointed. Or perhaps not. Petterson was one more name crossed off his list. How many of the others of the group had he visited or contacted?

Horton signalled to Cantelli that the interview was over. As they rose Horton said more as a matter of form than because he thought it pertinent, 'Where were you both last Thursday night and Friday morning?'

'At home Thursday night. On Friday, Louise was here in the shop and I was in my studio — well it's a shed in the garden — painting. We didn't kill Jasper.'

No, Horton didn't think they had.

Petterson showed them out of the rear exit. In the car, Cantelli said, 'So has this anything to do with Kenton and Thelma Veerman's deaths?'

Good question. It's what Horton had been thinking. 'It might do. Kenton was professionally engaged to find out if Veerman was having an affair and that could still be the reason why he was killed, because if the affair was made public it would ruin Veerman's reputation. Alternatively Kenton might have unearthed some kind of drugs scandal that Veerman and an associate are involved in and which could link back to one of the pharmaceutical companies Kenton used to work for. But it also seems clear that Kenton was working on his own private investigation in tracking down members of Gracious Grove and there is a connection between them, Mike Danby and Lord Ames. Foxton is one of Danby's clients and he uses Ames's Isle of Wight home for his stars when they're appearing at the festivals over there. Tell me about Gracious Grove.'

Cantelli started the car and pulled out into the traffic. 'Charlotte was mad about them, especially Sam Tandy. They wore these weird clothes.'

'Didn't everyone then?'

Cantelli smiled. 'Dark suits with flouncy white shirts and long flowing cuffs sticking out of the end of their jackets like some seventeenth-century dandy, but their music was good. If you liked that sort of electronic melodic male sound. Catchy tunes. Must have made a fortune. Had hits both sides of the Atlantic and did that film score for *Devil Death Threat*, the all-action movie that broke all box office records, not to mention that advert for chocolate, amongst others. Good disco music — not for me, I was no disco king,' Cantelli hastily added. 'But Charlotte loved dancing. I used to mooch around the best I could. Charlotte will go into a swoon when I tell her I've met Mason Petterson. Why would Kenton want to make contact with them if he siphoned off money from their accounts?' Cantelli headed out of Marlborough along the top road across Savernake Forest.

'Maybe to check they hadn't discovered it.' But there was more to Kenton the computer and IT security expert.

'He sounds like a nasty piece of work to do that to his sister,' said Cantelli.

'And I think he's done more than that over the years to others. Oh, not the same lies but the same method. Planting false information to get whatever he wanted, such as promotion over a colleague who was more suitable for the position than him until something emerged about this colleague and he or she was side-lined; getting someone the sack and then stepping into their shoes. If Trueman delves deep into Kenton's employment record that's what he'll find.'

Horton recalled what Danby had told him about the healthcare company Kenton had worked for and how he had unearthed a major cybercrime. This discovery had earned him an unequalled reputation and promotion, as well as probably money, and Horton wouldn't mind betting that the whole thing was a scam to make him look good and to cream off money. Kenton used others to get what he wanted and he was patient and thorough. If he had singled out Eunice Swallows to work with her, why? Because she had clients he wanted to get into? And why pick Mike Danby for referrals for close protection work? Because Kenton had wanted access to Chas Foxton? Horton explained his thinking to Cantelli and then reached for his mobile phone. He called Danby.

'I need to speak to Chas Foxton,' Horton said when Danby came on the line.

'Why?' Danby asked, surprised. Then he swiftly answered his own question with another. 'Is it connected with Jasper Kenton?'

Had Danby known all the time? Or was it just an educated guess? For a copper the latter wouldn't have been such a mental leap especially as Danby knew what Horton was investigating. 'Yes, but possibly not his death. I have an idea that Kenton was tracking down members of the band that he once used to work for.'

There was a small silence at the other end of the line before Danby replied, 'I didn't know that.'

It could be a bluff but Horton didn't think so. 'Did he ever pump you for information on Chas Foxton?'

'No. But I also work for another member of the band, Gary Grainger. And before you ask me, Kenton never pumped me for information on him either.'

Perhaps he didn't need to if he'd accessed Danby's computers.

Danby said, 'Gary's in the West Indies so you can't speak to him and Chas is flying out to Switzerland today but I'll see if I can get hold of him. I'll call you back.'

Horton relayed the information to Cantelli and then, accessing the Internet on his mobile phone, he keyed in the name of the band and was soon logged on to the official website of Gracious Grove. He read how the band had been performing gigs for some time at the places that mattered in the 1980s, the Blitz in London and the London Scala Cinema, but it was their appearance on London Weekend Television that catapulted the working-class lads from Swindon to fame.

'There's some photos of them as they were and recently,' he said to Cantelli. 'Gary Grainger looks affluent and he's put on a bit of weight but not as much as Chas Foxton. I'm not sure Charlotte would fancy either of them now. She might still go for Nigel Swaythling though. No, you keep your eyes on the road. Very distinguished looking, slim and photogenic. I remember him now. I've seen him in a couple of action movies. I didn't make the connection between him and the band. There's an obituary on Stuart Hayes and the only picture they have of Mason Petterson was taken at one of his art exhibitions before his breakdown.' And Petterson didn't look too pleased at being at the bash.

'There are some of his paintings, not the sort of thing you'd hang on your living room wall unless you want to be permanently depressed,' he said, scrolling through the dark brooding images that looked like blobs of black paint on a canvas, which reminded Horton of Walters and his search for the paint vandal.

Horton turned his gaze on Sam Tandy. Just as Petterson had told them Sam had launched a solo career after the group had broken up, but the blurb said he'd never repeated the same level of success. In the mid-1990s he'd dropped off the radar altogether. Horton rang Trueman and asked him to check the databases for the whereabouts of Sam Tandy, former member of Gracious Grove.

'You starting a fan club?'

'They've already got one.' Swiftly he brought Trueman up to speed with their interview with Louise Durridge and Mason Petterson. 'Have you tracked down any fans of Brett Veerman?'

'Half the hospital staff by the sounds of it, according to Marsden. Dennings hasn't found anything incriminating at Veerman's Isle of Wight property or in the boathouse but samples have been taken from the latter and the cars. Eunice Swallows has given me the link to Kenton's reports on Brett Veerman, which I've read, but they're cursory to say the least and make no mention of his searches on the Internet for newspaper reports, photographs, articles or papers presented at conferences, or any mention of anyone who appears regularly with him. The Hi-Tech Unit are doing their own searches. If we had Kenton's computer we'd be able to interrogate that.'

And that was precisely why they didn't have it. The killer had taken it. Horton would need to talk to Uckfield about conducting a deep investigation into the two pharmaceutical companies where Kenton had been employed to see if they could uncover fraud and in order to do that Horton knew they would need the assistance of the International Fraud Intelligence Bureau, City of London Police.

He said, 'See if you can establish the whereabouts of Nigel Swaything.'

'The actor?'

'Yes.'

'I know exactly where he is. He's in Budapest shooting the next Garth Johnson film. I read about it this morning in the newspaper.'

Was he there last Thursday, though? Horton thought he probably was. He rang off and almost instantly his phone rang.

It was Danby.

'If you want to talk to Chas Foxton you'd better get a move on. He'll stop off at my boat at Hamble Marina on the way to the airport.'

'That's a roundabout way to get to Switzerland if he's flying from London.'

'He's going from Southampton and, before you ask, he's flying by private jet.'

All right for some, thought Horton. 'We'll be there in forty minutes.' To Cantelli he said, 'Better get your autograph book ready. We're going to interview Chas Foxton.'

CHAPTER TWENTY-THREE

'We felt sorry for him,' Chas Foxton said, eyeing Horton and Cantelli in the main cabin of Danby's motor cruiser. Foxton had piled on even more weight since the photograph Horton had seen on the website. His face was so fleshy that it made the eyes, that girls had once swooned over, look small and mean. And although his casual clothes — tan suede jacket and loose-fitting pale blue shirt — were expensive, no amount of money spent on good tailoring could disguise the enormous protruding waistline. Horton wondered if Cantelli was shocked or disappointed. If he was, he didn't show it and neither did he display signs of unease at being on the water, albeit in the relative calm of the marina.

'Why sorry?' asked Horton, keenly interested.

'He was just one of those guys you thought weak and pathetic. Wouldn't say boo to a goose. Always wanting to please people.'

Yet another view of Jasper Kenton which conflicted with Louise Durridge's and the marina staff. Although that could simply be Chas Foxton's interpretation of anyone who quietly and painstakingly got on with their work, never seeking praise or crowing about what they had achieved.

'Always had his head stuck in a computer. Bit of a geek, even back then before they became fashionable,' Foxton added.

'He seemed to have done all right for himself, before he got killed,' Horton answered a little tersely. He knew Danby would have told Foxton that the police were treating Kenton's death as suspicious — hence their wanting to interview him — but how much more he'd said he didn't know.

'Yeah, that surprised me. People like Jasper don't get themselves killed.'

Don't you believe it, thought Horton. 'People like what?' he probed in a neutral voice, disguising his dislike of the self-centred, arrogant man in front of him. He could see Danby eyeing him with a secret smile. The ex-detective knew exactly how he felt.

'Jasper was kind of nondescript. You didn't notice him even if he was there.'

Cantelli looked up from his notebook. 'He could have changed since those days. The 1980s were a long time ago.'

Horton didn't know if Cantelli had said that to remind Foxton that he was no longer young, slim and handsome. Cantelli's expression was devoid of emotion, but Foxton's mouth tightened and the slit-like eyes in the folds of his flesh narrowed. He'd caught the meaning alright.

'Well he hadn't changed much the last time I saw him and that was a hell of a lot more recent than 1989,' he said abruptly.

'How recently?' asked Horton, alert at this news.

'Five months ago. June.'

'You had an appointment with him?'

'Of course I didn't. I had my boat at Oyster Quays and he was on the pontoon.'

Horton registered the boat. 'What was Kenton doing there?'

'No idea. I didn't ask.'

No, thought Horton, Foxton wasn't the type to bother making polite conversation or take an interest in a former acquaintance.

'I was heading for the Isle of Wight Festival where I had acts performing.'

'You moored up at Lord Ames's house,' Horton said, recalling what Danby had previously told him.

'Yes.'

Horton threw Danby a swift glance. Danby indicated with a slight shake of his head that he'd said nothing about Kenton's body being found on Ames's shore.

'Where is your boat now, sir?' asked Horton.

'Monaco. No point in having it here in winter. Sometimes not much point in summer either with the weather we get.'

They could check but even if the boat was in Monaco and it hadn't been used to dispose of Kenton's body it showed that Foxton could handle a boat. And he could have borrowed one. Danby's?

Danby was studying Horton closely and a flicker in his expression showed he was following Horton's thoughts precisely. If Foxton hadn't borrowed Danby's boat — which Horton thought unlikely — maybe he had access to another boat or owned more than one. But why kill Kenton? Because Kenton had stolen money from him or because Kenton knew something about the band? No, about Foxton, who he'd made contact with *after* visiting Mason Petterson. Perhaps Kenton had unearthed an underage sex scandal surrounding the former pop star. And maybe Kenton had been working on that for a long time, hence his approach to Danby, gathering evidence or even planting evidence to finally squeeze money from those in the band who could have been innocent of such charges.

Foxton was saying, 'The helicopter took Katia Milani over for the festival and then returned for Spanking Blazes.'

'Mega pop stars,' Cantelli explained to Horton. Then to Foxton, 'My daughters Ellen and Sadie are great admirers of them.'

'Then I'll get you their autographs.' Foxton nodded at Danby, clearly giving him instructions to obtain them for Cantelli. Then his small blue eyes shifted back to Horton. 'I took Tammy Freiding over on the boat because she doesn't do helicopters and neither do I, nor the kind of plane that can land on the Isle of Wight. I prefer flying in something that has more than four seats and more than one pilot. So I went by boat. I was about to leave Oyster Quays when Kenton hailed me.'

'Were you there, Mike?' Horton asked.

'No. I had two men with Chas and of course Geoff was with him.'

Geoff was the big guy standing on the pontoon keeping watch, for what Horton wasn't quite sure. There were no marauding fans in the remote marina on a mid-October afternoon nor anyone destined to assassinate or kidnap the wealthy pop tycoon. Geoff, built like Mr T in the 1980s hit television series *The A-Team*, had been introduced as Foxton's chauffeur, but was also obviously his bodyguard.

'What did you talk about?' asked Horton.

'Can't say I remember. I wasn't really taking any notice. Truth is I just wanted shot of him.'

'Didn't you like him?' asked Cantelli.

'He was OK.'

'But?' Cantelli pressed.

'But I've moved on since those days. Look, when you get to be as powerful as I am you get all sorts of people after you touting for jobs, asking for money, sidling up to you for contacts, favours . . . I thought Jasper wanted some of that.'

'But he didn't?' asked Horton.

'No. He just said it's been a long time, you've done really well, I'm pleased for you, that stuff and how are the rest of the boys in the band? I said that apart from Gary who's made it big in property investment I have no idea — oh, except Nigel who's a poncey actor in those all-action movies and we joked about how he'd even tremble if he saw a spider run across the floor. The others I've not heard from in years. I knew that Stuart was dead and that Mason had freaked out in an art gallery and booked himself into detox. Sam probably blew his mind years ago.'

'Drugs?'

'Yeah, big time. Coke, Heroin, LSD, the lot.'

Mr T stepped onto the boat, which bucked violently at his weight and alarmed Cantelli.

Foxton eased his portly body out from behind the table with a series of grunts. 'I've got a plane to catch. I'm sorry he's dead, but like I said, we weren't close.'

Horton slid out of the seat. As the large man heaved his blubber up to the cockpit, Horton said, 'Did you have any cause to think Kenton was ripping you off?'

'Everyone was ripping us off,' Foxton tossed over his shoulder. 'I can't see why Kenton would have been any different. He was a whizz at computers so he could have been doing anything behind our backs and creaming off money. We were earning it so fast it was impossible to keep track of it.' He stood in the cockpit. 'But if he did make money then he must have spent it because he didn't look like he'd made mega bucks.' To Cantelli he said, 'I'll make sure you get those autographs.'

Danby showed him off the boat, which swayed and bucked again, causing Cantelli to turn pale. 'Did Kenton engineer that meeting?' he asked as they watched the three men walk down the pontoon.

'Sounds like it,' Horton replied.

'Perhaps he wanted to remind Foxton that he could find him if he wanted to.'

'To put the wind up him you mean? If Kenton was putting pressure on Foxton, I'm certain Foxton would have seen to it.'

'Perhaps he did, by killing Kenton or having him killed.' Cantelli voiced what had been going through Horton's mind earlier. 'Perhaps Kenton met Foxton on his boat or a boat at Oyster Quays.'

'Not according to the marina staff.' Horton had shown Kenton's photograph there and drawn a blank.

'Then here and he moved Kenton's car into the Admiralty Towers car park when he discovered that Kenton was investigating Brett Veerman. He could have got that information from Kenton's computer.'

'But would Foxton be able to do that? Kenton must have set up a password.'

'Perhaps he got it from him before killing him.'

There had been no evidence of torture on the body but it but it didn't have to be physical; maybe the threat of it was enough for Kenton to tell all.

Cantelli said, 'It would be a good way of pointing the finger at someone else. And Foxton could have had help.'

'If Mr T parked Kenton's car he'd stand out a mile despite any blurry video images. But Foxton could have got someone else to do his dirty work. As he said he's a very rich man.' Horton watched Danby shake Foxton's hand. He headed back towards them as the two men crossed to the Bentley Continental.

'He's not your killer,' Danby said, joining them on the pontoon. 'His boat *is* in Monaco. I can give the name and details if you want to check, and he doesn't have another boat here and neither did he borrow mine. He was at a concert in London on Thursday night until the early hours of the morning with me and there are hundreds of people who can confirm that. I had a meeting with him in the Savoy, London, in the morning where he and a couple of the acts stayed on Thursday night.'

But Foxton could have arranged to have Kenton killed as Cantelli and he had just been discussing. Horton asked Danby how Kenton and Swallows had teamed up.

'Much as Kenton and I did. They met at a security conference. Kenton was looking to go in with someone. His skills and Eunice's complemented one another. They'd both been working alone. Kenton had been operating in London for about a year and Eunice in Havant for about three years. After they got together Kenton moved down here and they worked for a while from Eunice's offices in Havant and then moved to the premises in Portsmouth.'

And Horton wondered how much research Kenton had done in deciding who might be his best partner. They left Danby to shut up his boat and headed back to the car.

Cantelli said, 'Maybe Kenton tracked down Foxton and Mason to see if they or any of the others had discovered his fraud from years ago. He could still be creaming off money from the reissuing of the CDs and DVDs and the royalties from the movie and advertisement music. He wanted to check he was in the clear.'

'But that doesn't explain Thelma Veerman's death.'

'Perhaps she witnessed Kenton's killing.'

'If so, then why not tell me on Saturday when I interviewed her?'

'She might have been too scared.'

'Or perhaps she was protecting someone. And that brings us back to her husband. Kenton making contact with the band members could be a side issue. Oh, I don't doubt he was up to something because what we *have* learned about Jasper Kenton is that everything he did was for a purpose, such as buying that boat, and behaving the way he did.' And Horton knew that was the key to his death. He just had to find out how to use it to get to the truth, which was easier said than done.

As Cantelli pointed the car back to Portsmouth, Horton mentally ran through some of the facts, or rather the things they'd been told about Kenton. Facts they were short of. Except that Kenton *had* travelled to the Isle of Wight the week before he was killed and Kenton *had* been engaged by Thelma Veerman and *had* been investigating her husband. Eunice Swallows had confirmed this and the date when her agency had been appointed. But had Thelma Veerman lied about when she had met Kenton?

'Barney, find out from the ferry company if Kenton travelled to the island any other times over the last year, and get the dates.'

Something Trueman had said also resonated in the back of Horton's mind. Thelma Veerman had said that Kenton had trawled the Internet for the conferences and seminars that her husband had attended, but according to Trueman, Kenton had barely got started. If Thelma Veerman had lied about that then had she also lied about researching private investigation agencies on the Internet at the library in Ryde? Was the investigation of her husband a fabrication, a collusion between her and Jasper Kenton? Had Kenton befriended the lonely Thelma Veerman and persuaded her to hire him as a private detective? Why? The obvious answer, according to what they had just learned about the dead man, was because he needed her.

His mind was racing as it tried to pull the pieces together. *'Everything Jasper did had a purpose and an ulterior motive.'* That's what Petterson had said and Kenton had befriended Thelma Veerman for a reason. He'd also bought that boat and put on an act for a purpose and Horton was beginning to see what that could be. Quickly, before he could lose the thread, he voiced his thoughts to Cantelli.

'Kenton was a crook dating back to his schoolboy days if we believe Louise Durridge, and I do. But he was a quiet crook, the kind that was very clever, and very patient. With the growth of computers, then the Internet, he learned how to manipulate information, set up multiple identities and accounts. Patiently and painstakingly, he planned and plotted his career, seeking out the right people he could use to get more money from until he could disappear and begin a new life somewhere. And that's where the boat comes in. He was going to disappear on it.'

Cantelli looked baffled. Horton didn't blame him; he hadn't quite worked it all out but he was close.

'But not to sail off into the sunset.'

Cantelli caught on. 'He was going to do a Robert Maxwell.'

The media tycoon who had disappeared from his yacht off the Canary Islands leaving behind a business empire with over three billion pounds of debt. 'Yes, except Kenton's body would never be found. The boat would be located drifting in the English Channel, everyone would say he'd never owned one before, knew nothing about charts and piloting a boat, and had been too damn cocky. It was a tragedy destined to happen.'

'He'd assume a new identity.'

'Yes, and with access to God knows how many offshore accounts with goodness knows how much money stashed away, including that from Gracious Grove and probably his former employers. But I'm betting that somewhere, in either this country or abroad, Kenton took lessons on how to handle a motor cruiser and not in his own name. Perhaps he planned to have a private light aeroplane waiting at Sandown or Bembridge airport, or he could have bought himself another large motor boat from elsewhere in the country, using a false ID and from funds in a bank account in a false name, maybe not even the name he intended ending up with. He could have several false identities and accounts set up abroad.'

'But he ends up dead. So who killed him? Did someone find out he'd stolen from them?'

Probably. But was that enough to kill for? And why kill Thelma? Because they both knew the killer's identity? And was that killer Brett Veerman? Did Kenton want a share in Veerman's drugs scam or was it information he was after? Information that he thought Thelma Veerman could give him. Had her husband treated someone that Kenton was very keen to locate? And did that person have a connection with Lord Ames, hence Kenton's body being dumped there? Was it the beachcomber, Lomas, who had led a quiet undisturbed life roaming the beach looking for flotsam and jetsam, until Kenton had shown up? Then Horton had arrived and soon Thelma was dead. Lomas hadn't seemed afraid when Horton had met him but if he was correct and Lomas had been living in one of those three stone derelict buildings, then he had cleared out pretty quickly. Lomas hadn't known that Horton was a police officer though, not when they had met, but had someone told him that since, and could that person be Danby or Ames? If he had hindered a murder investigation and if his silence had led to the death of Thelma Veerman then it was time to take up Danby's offer, if it would still be open after this.

'I need to talk to Veerman again. It's OK, Barney, I'll go alone and I need you to say nothing about it to Uckfield. I can't explain why yet. I don't want you to get into trouble.'

'You're not going to do anything foolish?' Cantelli said, horror-stricken.

'I'm not going to lay one finger on him if that's what you mean. I need to ask him about Thelma. I'll tell you after I've seen him. Brief Trueman about the interviews. Find out how many times Kenton travelled to the Isle of Wight, and dig up everything you can on Sam Tandy.'

Horton stopped at the station long enough to collect his helmet and leathers from his office and to learn that Walters had identified the fly-boy painter. He'd touted for business at all three of the targeted restaurants and had been back to provide them with a quote. Horton had called out over his shoulder as he swept out of CID, 'Bring him in for questioning.' He made it out of the station without being stopped by Uckfield. Bliss's car wasn't in the station car park so she was still at the hospital overseeing the questioning of Veerman's colleagues.

At the ferry terminal Horton dashed across to the ticket office in the heavy rain and hurried back to the Harley just as the ferry was coming into its narrow berth. He held out his ticket and watched as the marshalling steward zapped it with his handheld electronic device and moved quickly across to the lane where cars were queuing. He seemed in a hurry. Maybe he just wanted to get out of the driving rain. Horton didn't blame him; he was looking forward to that himself. Then something tugged at the back of his mind. It had been raining on Thursday night when Kenton had been shot. Kenton had been found dead on the Isle of Wight and his car had been discovered over here. His eyes fixed on the steward as he went hurriedly down the line of vehicles. Could it be? Was it possible?

He climbed off the Harley and hurried to the steward, reaching for his warrant card as he went. Showing it, he said, 'Don't you check the registration number on the ticket against the vehicle?' The steward looked uneasy and Horton could see him weighing up how much to tell him. 'Please, it's important. No one will get into trouble.'

'We do mostly, but sometimes in the rain and the dark, and when we're running late, the pressure's on to load as quickly as we can.'

And that's what had happened. Sometimes Kenton had used his own name and vehicle licensing number and sometimes not, choosing instead to use one of his false identities, which is what he had done on the night he was shot. Because after that night he was going to disappear. Probably on the Friday or Saturday. That last visit to the island was to make sure that the trail he left immediately before his death couldn't be traced back there because he had been confident that he would get what he wanted from the person he was seeing, which was either Thelma Veerman or the beachcomber or perhaps both. Thelma's job was to lure the beachcomber to a rendezvous and once there to leave him with Kenton, not knowing that Kenton would be killed.

Horton felt a stab of triumph. He called Cantelli as soon as he was on the ferry.

'Kenton *did* cross to the island by car ferry on Thursday night and in his own car.'

'It's not on the list of any of the five sailings that Trueman checked running from five p.m. until the last one at just before midnight.'

'It won't be, not under his vehicle registration or his own name. Jasper Kenton used a false ID and a false vehicle registration number when he purchased his ticket online. They don't always check the number on the ticket with the vehicle travelling. On one of those sailings there's a car and a passenger who doesn't exist.'

'I'll tell Trueman. Andy, I've spoken to Wightlink. Jasper Kenton travelled to the Isle of Wight by car ferry in March, twice in April, once in June and twice in September.'

'And I bet he went even more than that using a false ID. Anything on Sam Tandy?'

'Still checking. I'll call you the moment I get anything. Oh and Uckfield wants to speak to you. I told him that you had to see Catherine about the arrangements for having Emma next week for half term.'

'Thanks.'

'Be careful.'

'When aren't I?'

'Never,' Cantelli said with a sigh of exasperation.

Horton rang off.

CHAPTER TWENTY-FOUR

The gates were closed. Horton pressed the intercom. Brett Veerman answered.

'Could I have a word, sir? I'm alone. It's urgent.' Horton hoped that Veerman wouldn't refuse.

There was a fraction's pause before the gates swung open and Horton took the Harley up the gravel drive, drawing to a stop in front of the house. As he climbed off, Veerman stepped out closing the front door behind him. Clearly Horton wasn't going to be invited inside. He didn't think it was because Veerman had anything to hide. Perhaps his lawyer had advised him that the police couldn't enter again without another search warrant. Or perhaps his son was inside and he didn't want him to be troubled or to over-hear their conversation. Horton didn't care where they talked just as long as they did.

The heavy rain had given way to a light drizzle. Veerman was wearing a rain jacket but no hat. Horton removed his helmet.

'What is it now, Inspector?' Veerman said wearily and tetchily.

'This isn't a formal interview, sir. If you don't wish to speak with me then that's fine. I'll leave.'

Veerman eyed him steadily. He'd been curious enough to allow him to enter the premises so Horton was guessing he wouldn't turf him out now. Veerman gave a curt nod and turned away in the direction of the rear of the house. Horton followed. He could taste the salt in the air coming off the sea. He let the silence stretch on until they reached the shore where there was no evidence that Veerman's wife had died only a few yards from where they were standing. Horton felt a pang of guilt and turned to study the man beside him. His face was drawn, his mouth tight and there were dark circles under his eyes. On the ferry Horton had been thinking a great deal about this confident, cool man with the superior manner and his immaculate flat that showed no evidence of any woman having ever set foot in it. And of the fact that there were no rumours or gossip of him playing the field but his staff and patients worshipped him, and he was considered something of a dish. If Horton dismissed everything that Thelma Veerman had told him as a lie, where did that leave him? With the fact that she had known about her husband's flat, known he had no lover and that there had been no mysterious texts or phone calls.

'You're not having an affair, are you?' Horton bluntly announced. 'But you didn't mind your wife or us believing it.' Veerman eyed Horton sharply.

'There's no evidence of a lover ever having been in your apartment,' continued Horton, recalling that bland, pristine interior. 'But you knew that your wife had engaged a private investigation agency to check up on you because you'd seen Jasper Kenton following you.'

He'd been meant to. Kenton had engineered that. He'd intended killing Thelma, who would know too much, and framing her husband for her death. Veerman's eyes looked troubled before he swung his gaze away from Horton and out to sea. Horton pressed on.

'You never expected the flat to be searched by the police though,' Horton continued. 'Otherwise you might have planted some female items, clothing, perfume . . . And you didn't expect Jasper Kenton to be found dead, or his car to be in your car park. And because you didn't know if your wife had been home when you arrived in the early hours of Saturday morning, when you first heard the news that he was dead, you wondered if she could have been involved. But why would she kill a private investigator she'd hired, and a man she was having an affair with?' Horton registered Veerman's surprise but thought it phoney; behind it was contempt.

He continued, 'You couldn't have killed him either, but you didn't mind us thinking you might be involved, along with a lover who you were supposedly protecting. But as I said, you have no lover. You just thought you'd go along with it.'

Veerman was eyeing him steadily. 'Why should I do that?'

'Oh, several reasons,' Horton said airily. 'To make yourself appear more dashing and glamorous, to make you seem mysterious and exciting, to hurt your wife or to get even with her for having a lover. Yes, that stung your huge male ego because you couldn't believe that anyone would be interested in your plain, nondescript and unimportant wife.'

'I didn't come out here to be insulted.' Veerman made to turn back.

'Or did you think it would hide your real problem?'

Veerman's body stiffened. He turned. 'What problem?' he asked sharply, his eyes narrowing.

'You tell me.'

'Why should I?'

'Because the time for pretend is over, Mr Veerman. If we're to find who killed your wife then we need the truth. No more lies and games. No more secrets.' He held Veerman's gaze, silently willing him to tell the truth as the wind whipped around them, whistling through the rigging on the dinghy. Suddenly Dr Quentin Amos's words shot through his head: *Secrets and lies. Someone's kept silent for a long time. They might want it to stay that way . . . there is always evil below.*

'You're right. There is no lover,' Veerman said stiffly.

Horton dragged himself back to the man beside him and the present, but with the residue of a thought lurking in the back of his brain from the past.

'I'm impotent. Or if you want the medical term for it, I suffer from erectile dysfunction.'

Horton had suspected it must be something like that because he'd been recalling what Thelma had said when they'd walked towards the abbey together, about how cold her husband was, how withdrawn he'd become. He'd worked out that if Veerman didn't have a lover, either male or female — and there had been no evidence to show he had one, or had ever had an affair — there had to be another reason.

'Have you sought medical help?'

Veerman gave a hollow laugh. 'Doctors are the last people to want to see a doctor. However, I did undergo a health check to rule out the obvious possible causes, without explaining the problem, of course. I won't bore you with my medical history but my heart is healthy, I don't have diabetes, I'm not suffering from multiple sclerosis or Parkinson's disease. I'm not obese as you can see and I don't smoke or drink to excess. And neither do I take any drugs that could produce the side effects of erectile dysfunction. I concluded that the likely cause must be stress related and that it would pass. Foolish I know, and it hasn't passed. I've not gone down the road of trying any of the PDE-5 inhibitors — Viagra, Cialis and the like — because I'd either have to steal them from the hospital dispensary, get a prescription from a doctor who would then know about my problem or buy them on the Internet and risk being made seriously ill by contaminated and fraudulent drugs.' He ran a hand through his dark hair. His eyes were troubled. 'I just let it go on, hoping it would sort itself out, which is something I chastise my patients for when they leave it too late to consult a doctor. I also blamed Thelma for it. She hated living here and she hated me, but she wouldn't divorce me.'

'Because she was a Catholic.'

'No, because she wanted money and a great deal of it. I wasn't prepared to give her that. I never loved Thelma and she never really loved me.'

So they had stayed locked in this cold, hateful marriage. Then Kenton had come along, got talking to her, befriended her, had discovered which buttons to press, had made love to her and she'd poured out her sorrows to him. Kenton had promised he'd get evidence that would make Veerman only too happy to divorce her and with enough money to make her comfortable for the rest of her life. A life he said they would spend together. Horton could hear him now: *'Tell me everything you can about your husband, the more information I have the better . . .'* And gently he'd steer her towards what he wanted to know.

'What did she tell you after my visit here on Saturday?'

'She accused me of killing him, but said she'd say nothing to the police if I agreed to settle a huge sum of money on her. I was to give her this house, which she'd sell, because she hated it, and more. I told her not to be ridiculous; I didn't even know the man. But she said I'd killed him because I was jealous. I laughed. I said I'd be only too pleased if she'd found herself someone other than those bloody monks and those filthy dogs.'

Horton thought Veerman's 'problem' went deeper than stress. But his words struck a chord and one that was chiming loudly. He brought his attention back to Veerman who was saying, 'I told Thelma she could have a divorce tomorrow on the grounds of her adultery, but that didn't suit her. She wanted *me* to divorce *her* and she wanted a settlement that I was not prepared to give in exchange for her silence.'

'So you killed her, hoping we would believe it was the same person who had killed Jasper Kenton.'

'Of course I didn't.'

Was that the truth? Was anything Veerman was saying the truth? 'Did you ask her how and when she met Kenton?'

'No.'

Pity. But it had to be on one of those trips to the island that Cantelli had told him Kenton had undertaken.

Veerman added, 'I wasn't interested and she didn't say, but the only place it could have been was at that abbey she was so fond of. Since she started being their unofficial nurse she spent more time there than here.'

Horton recalled what Brother Norman had told him about tending to one of the monks who had been taken ill in the garden. 'That was two years ago.'

'If you say so. I only know that she went there every day, often three or four times a day, not only to walk the dogs but to see to anyone who was sick. With my work and her obsession with the monks our paths hardly ever crossed, which suited me. I bought the flat as I told you for ease of use, when I needed somewhere to stay over when working late, and to be alone.'

And maybe because he wanted to hide that asset from his wife in case of a divorce. Perhaps Veerman had other property or assets that he had no intention of telling his wife about and hoped the courts wouldn't find. He might even have put property in another name — his son's, for example. But that could be checked later, if it needed to be checked. And he didn't think it did.

Now Horton saw what Kenton had been after. It wasn't anything that Brett Veerman knew. He had just been the lever Kenton had used to get what he wanted. He'd formed a relationship with Thelma Veerman because of her intimate knowledge of the monks.

Veerman turned back towards the house. Horton fell into step beside him. 'I didn't kill my wife,' he said. 'But if you and your colleagues believe I did then I suggest you get your evidence and formerly charge me. Meanwhile I have a lot to do.'

And Horton didn't think grieving was one of them, although Veerman would put up a convincing show of it. He took his leave and headed for the abbey on the Harley feeling disturbed by his thoughts. There was still the chance that Veerman had deliberately steered him towards the abbey because in this case nothing seemed as it appeared. How could a monk, a religious man, kill two people in cold blood? But then nothing should surprise him having been in the job for so long. He knew people were capable of anything if driven hard enough or if the motive was powerful and overwhelming. And was the motive here the need *not* to be discovered, not to be exposed to the public again and Kenton had threatened that? Because Horton thought that Kenton had been on the trail of Sam Tandy. Or was the killer protecting Tandy?

His thoughts occupied him as he travelled the short distance to the abbey where he drew up in the car park and checked his mobile phone. Cantelli had tried to call him. He rang him back.

'We've identified one vehicle which travelled to the Isle of Wight by ferry last Thursday evening on the seven p.m. sailing and the same vehicle returned on the four a.m. sailing on Saturday morning.'

'That has to be Kenton's,' Horton said with excitement. The ferry would have arrived in Portsmouth at about 4.30 a.m. The killer then drove into the Admiralty Towers car park and entered it at 4.42 a.m.

'It's registered in the name of David Lane, Five Jasmine Grove, Luton. The local police have just confirmed that no one of that name lives at that address. The property is empty. I've checked with the ferry company and the ticket was a day return so whoever drove Kenton's car back from the Isle of Wight would have had to buy another ticket to return to Portsmouth Saturday morning. He did. This time using the name Adam Rooney. He didn't have to give an address because he bought it at the ticket office and paid cash. And there was one foot passenger on the five a.m. sailing from Portsmouth to Fishbourne. We're searching for an Adam Rooney but my guess is he's phoney.'

Horton thought so too. In fact, he knew it. He quickly relayed what he had discovered from Brett Veerman and his idea that Kenton had used Thelma Veerman to identify Sam Tandy, living and worshipping in the abbey.

'But in order for Thelma to be able to identify Tandy there must be something distinctive about him. Some distinguishing mark. Something that Thelma would have seen when she nursed him or treated him for some illness or accident. Something that wasn't immediately visible, that was covered up so that Kenton, no matter how many times he came here, couldn't see.'

He thought of the long habits the monks wore with the cowl draped around their heads, the gown reaching the ground, their hands tucked in the wide sleeves. There was a great deal covered up. Whatever scar or physical defect Tandy had couldn't be on his face because that was visible and so too were some of the monks' feet, often clad in sandals. Horton's mind darted to the beachcomber's suntanned feet in tatty sandals. But he hadn't seen anything remarkable about them. And the beachcomber was too old to be Tandy but, as he'd considered before, there was the possibility he had killed to protect Tandy.

Something stirred at the back of Horton's mind. Mentally he recalled the beachcomber stretching across a tattered business card with strong bronzed hands that hadn't looked like any artist Horton had come across, although admittedly he hadn't met many. But he had seen Mason Petterson's hands with his long, slender fingers and there had been paint under the nails. His mind leapt to Louise Durridge's manicured nails and the ring on her finger that Petterson had given her years ago and suddenly he was transported back to 1967. His body went rigid. His heart beat fast as his mind raced, trying to make sense of what he was thinking. Images flashed before him of Brother Norman's slender hand coming out of the sleeve of his habit when Horton had come here to tell him about the sentencing of the men who had robbed the abbey. A glimmer of sunlight, a smile, before the hand had gone back into the sleeve. Brother Norman had been wearing a ring. Horton had never seen him wearing it before, he was certain of that. The breath caught in his throat as he tried to recall exactly what the ring had been like. His thoughts had been occupied by paint on an artists' hand. Brother Norman had apologized for the dirt under his fingernails from his gardening. Then it came to him. It had been gold, a signet ring, and there had been a stone in it, deep red. And he'd seen that ring before.

'Andy, are you there?' Cantelli's concerned voice broke through Horton's thoughts.

With an effort he pulled himself together. 'Yes.' He hurried towards the café. 'Check Sam Tandy's medical records, photographs and bios on the website for any physical disabilities or scars. Let me know the moment you find anything.'

He rang off. The café was closed but there was a light on inside. Horton banged on the door and soon a figure hurried to answer his summons.

'Can I help you, Inspector?' Cliff Yately said, worried. His hand was still bandaged and his arm in the sling. Behind him Jay Ottley emerged from the kitchen, a tatty leather hat low over the brow of his grizzled greying long hair and his gloved hands carrying a large bucket of slops.

'I need to see Brother Norman urgently,' Horton said.

'I can ask in the abbey for you.'

But Ottley interjected, 'I saw him walk down to the old abbey about five minutes ago.'

'Thanks.' Horton dashed out and ran towards the ruins. His head was spinning, his body fuelled with adrenalin, his heart hammering fit to bust. He drew up at the small field that led down to the moss and bracken-covered ancient wall. Leaping over the gate he raced across the grass towards it. Dusk was falling and the wind was blowing chill off the sea. He could hear the waves rushing onto the shore. Frantically he searched for an entrance and finally found a small gap where the brickwork was crumbling. As he squeezed through it he registered it hadn't been used much, which confirmed to him that there must be a way onto the shore from behind the abbey.

He paused. The tide was on the rise but it wouldn't be high water yet for about four hours. To his right the shore led towards the Veermans's house, but that was hidden from view and not accessible by the beach. He turned left and with a growing sense of urgency ran along the shingled shore to where it curved inwards. There he drew up sharply. Rapidly he took in the lean figure bending over a small dinghy with an outboard engine on the rear. Behind it was a timber boathouse, the door ajar. Horton couldn't see inside but he knew that it must once have contained an old sailcloth that had ended up wrapped around Kenton's body.

The man straightened up. He turned and nodded knowingly with a smile curving the thin lips. The serious, solemn and rather sad monk with the hood hiding the sides of his face had vanished and in its place was a confident, younger-looking man. Horton thought his heart must have stopped beating. The air became still. The wind dropped and his brain swiftly rearranged all his theories and speculations.

He'd been wrong. Kenton hadn't found Sam Tandy. He'd found someone else. Someone connected with Lord Ames, and that was why his body had been placed on Lord Ames's beach. Because in front of Horton was one of the two remaining men he'd been seeking who featured in a photograph taken on 13 March 1967.

CHAPTER TWENTY-FIVE

'Jasper Kenton traced *you*, not Sam Tandy,' Horton said, eyeing Antony Dormand closely, trying desperately to make sense of what he was seeing. Dormand looked so different out of the black habit that Horton could hardly believe it was Brother Norman. The casual dark trousers, black high-neck jumper and black waterproof jacket made him appear taller and fitter. The beginnings of a close-cropped beard and the absence of the cowl around his face also showed more of the resemblance to the young man with the beard in the photograph from 1967. There was no meek stoop about him now. How long had Dormand been a monk here? What had brought him here? Was he, in fact, a monk or just masquerading as one? So many questions assailed Horton that they made his head ache. It was difficult to know where to start.

'I doubt that, Inspector Horton. Even you couldn't trace me without a little help and I wasn't sure you were going to work it out in time.'

Time for what? Before Dormand made his escape, Horton guessed, judging by the boat beside him. 'The ring, you mean.' Horton's eyes fell on it. 'You weren't wearing it when I first came here.'

'No. Hands are so important, don't you think? They don't lie.'

Horton studied Dormand carefully. He caught a hidden meaning behind his words which registered in his teeming brain but which he quickly filed away to be analysed and dealt with later. 'You knew I had the photograph.'

Horton tried to keep his voice steady although his heart was pounding. 'Otherwise there would have been no point in you putting on the ring when I came to tell you about the sentencing of the two thieves.' In that photograph from 1967 Dormand had his hand draped over Rory Mortimer's shoulder and he'd been wearing a ring. Horton remembered how Dormand had held up his hand refusing the offer of a drink, and how he had seen in Dormand's face something that had jarred with him. He'd also sensed a subdued energy in the monk's lean body and seen something deep and dark in his eyes that had reminded him of the beachcomber, Lomas, and which he'd considered had reflected an accumulation of life's experiences. He wondered what Dormand's life had held before he'd ended up here.

'Did Richard Ames tell you I had the photograph?' Horton asked. Or had it been Ballard? There was also Professor Thurstan Madeley who had pulled together the archive project on the sit-in protest of 1967, but who had omitted to include the photograph Ballard had left Horton on his boat. Madeley had pointed Horton towards Dr Quentin Amos, who could also have made contact with Dormand. When Dormand didn't answer, Horton continued. 'Did you put Jasper Kenton's body on Richard Ames's property?'

Dormand's lips twitched in the ghost of smile and behind the cool blue eyes Horton registered a steeliness he hadn't seen before and which sent a cold shiver down his spine.

Ames must have picked up Dormand's activities from his security sensors. It would have been dark then but Ames's security probably had infrared sensors. Ames must have believed that Kenton had unearthed Brother Norman's true identity and been killed because of it, which was why he'd ordered the softly-softly approach to the investigation and let him believe Brett Veerman could be involved in order to protect Dormand and his new identity. But if Ames and Dormand were working in cohort then why would Dormand dump the body there? Why not dump it miles away and make sure it sank to the bottom of the sea? Because Ames had no idea of Dormand's new ID and Dormand wanted Ames to know where he was. But if that was the case, then why hadn't Ames sent someone to deal with Dormand? Maybe he had, Horton thought with a shiver. The beachcomber, Lomas. Only Dormand had dealt with him first.

Lomas and Ames had been on the trail of Antony Dormand and Dormand had discovered this. Lomas had been living in one of those stone buildings close to Ames's house, which Horton had inspected and found remarkably empty, too empty. So maybe he hadn't been there but inside Ames's house. Lomas had seen Horton approach on Friday and make for the woods. All Lomas had to do was head through the rear of Ames's property, let himself out the back entrance, jump down from the pontoon and hide around the side of the creek until he was ready to make his encounter with him. Lomas already knew who he was. Ames would have told him.

Lomas had then returned to the house and had been inside it when Uckfield had sent Danby inside to check nothing had been stolen. Danby was probably oblivious to his presence. Was Lomas still there or had he made off after the discovery of Kenton's body on the shore under Ames's instructions? Or had Dormand killed him? Perhaps Lomas had been here to flush out the man everyone seemed to be looking for — Antony Dormand.

Horton eyed Dormand coldly and with anger churning his gut. Was this the man who had killed Jennifer and had condemned him to a lonely and cruel childhood? His fists clenched and his body stiffened. Or had Lomas been working independently? Was Lomas the man that Ames and his cronies wanted Horton to flush out? And who Dormand was after? Was Lomas his mother's killer?

Horton still couldn't make sense of it all. He needed answers to the multitude of questions swimming round in his head. 'Did you know I was on that shore the Friday before you dumped Kenton's body there?'

Dormand said nothing, which indicated to Horton that he did. And if Ames hadn't told him directly then either Lomas had done so and had come here after seeing him on the shore or Dormand had managed to hack into Ames's security system.

'The beachcomber I saw on the shore on Friday, who is he, Dormand? Is it Rory Mortimer? The sixth man in the photograph?'

'No, he's dead.'

'How can you be sure?'

'I killed him.'

Horton was taken aback.

'Under orders, of course.' Dormand seemed completely unperturbed. 'Mortimer was a traitor, as were Royston and Wilson, selling secrets to the Russians.'

'You killed them too!' Horton cried, unable to believe what he was hearing, but afraid it was the truth. 'And Zachary Benham? Was he selling secrets?'

'No, he was trying to unearth them and died doing so.'

'In a psychiatric hospital. What was he doing there?'

'We don't know. I suspect someone would like to find out.'

Horton felt confused and angry. 'But all that was years ago,' he insisted. 'It's history and the Cold War is over.' But he remembered Quentin Amos's words about it never being over, not as far as terrorism was concerned, and Horton knew that all too well.

'There are other threats,' Dormand answered, echoing Horton's thoughts. 'Some more dangerous and deadlier than we have ever faced in our history. It can start in a very small way and if not contained, if information is not gathered, analysed and imparted in the right quarters, and certain parties eliminated, it can escalate out of all control.'

Horton thought of the hate crime of the paint sprawled on restaurant walls. It had been trivial, carried out by someone who just wanted to earn a quick and crooked buck. But it could have been deadly serious.

Dormand continued. 'It can end in bloody carnage and the slaughter of innocent people. Cast your mind back to 1978, when Jennifer disappeared, what was happening then? If you don't know then read it up and you'll soon see what Jennifer was involved with.'

But Horton already knew. Harry Kimber had given him that information: '*November 1978 . . . it was before those terrible bombs were set off by the IRA in towns and villages across Northern Ireland . . . and then all those bombs in December in Bristol, Coventry, Liverpool, Manchester, and just up the road in Southampton. The IRA said they were gearing up for a long war.*' It was the height of the troubles in Northern Ireland.

'You're saying that Jennifer had intelligence on the IRA?'

'It's a dirty business, Inspector, as you no doubt know or are finding out.'

'And my mother was involved in this dirty business in 1967. She'd been working for the intelligence services, feeding information to them on the members of the Radical Student Alliance.'

Horton recalled what he'd read. There had been the mass anti-Vietnam War rally in Grosvenor Square in 1968, the violent student protests at the London School of Economics in 1969, a British Minister's home had been bombed in 1971 and there was a massive expulsion of Soviet spies in 1971. And if Jennifer had been in some way linked to the troubles in Northern Ireland then Horton recollected the horrific bombing of Aldershot Barracks in 1972 that had killed six people and the bombs that were set off in Manchester City, Victoria Station, Kings Cross and Oxford Street in 1973. And in 1973 Jennifer had left London with her small son.

Horton said, 'So you'd had enough. Is that why you came here, to escape? To hide,' he goaded.

'An intelligence agent can never hide.'

Horton narrowed his eyes. 'You mean Jennifer couldn't hide even when she fled London with me and tried to start a new life in Portsmouth with nothing and knowing no one. Who was she running away from?'

'I think you might need to rephrase that.'

Horton froze. He felt sickened. This was incredible. It couldn't be true and yet if he pieced together the fragments of information and facts he'd discovered over the last year he knew it could be. It completely turned on its head all his thoughts and preconceptions and memories of his mother. 'Who was she running to?'

'Or for. That is something we'd all like to know.'

Horton eyed him keenly, looking for the lie, but he saw none. 'And is that who I am supposed to find and lead Lord Ames and his colleagues to?' Pictures flashed through Horton's mind: the wealthy man with the big car, the man with the boat. Had the latter been Edward Ballard? Had they both been Edward Ballard? Then he considered what he'd discovered about Eileen and Bernard. Eileen had worked for the civil service in Northern Ireland during the troubles; she'd left there and come to Portsmouth when Bernard had been shot and injured. The code that Amos had bequeathed to him, which could be the location reference for the Royal Navy hospital at Gosport where Bernard had been taken and where Horton now believed Jennifer had been heading the day she disappeared. To rendezvous with Eileen. To give her information about the IRA or to assist the IRA.

His head was spinning. He said, 'We never had any money and my mother had to work as a croupier in a casino and leave me to fend for myself at nights. There was no one she was in the pay of.' He eyed Dormand closely. What could he see in that expression? 'Don't tell me all that was a cover!' he cried, astounded. *My God it couldn't be*! He recalled the damp, smelly, crowded terraced houses in Portsmouth where he'd lived with his mother before they had been rehoused in the tower block. 'You think this person she was reporting to killed her?' And he was certain that couldn't have been Eileen Litchfield. Dormand didn't reply. 'She went to meet him on that day in November. Who is he?'

'That is something we'd all like to know.'

And had Dormand been hoping to find him here? Had he thought he'd found him in Lomas and had been deceived? Had Ames thought he'd found him in Dormand and realized he was wrong?

'Why? It happened years ago.' But maybe Horton understood. Swiftly he answered his own question. 'Because he has highly damaging information about you and Richard Ames?'

'And others.'

Horton exhaled. Nothing he remembered was how it seemed. He didn't know any longer which memories he could trust.

'Is that why you're leaving — because this man is not here, because your cover is blown or because you killed Lomas?' Horton wasn't sure of that, but it was possible. Whoever Lomas had been working for, Ames had been keen to keep his presence quiet. Dormand was eyeing him evenly but his expression didn't betray his thoughts.

Horton continued. 'You didn't kill Jasper Kenton though. You just moved his body.' Dormand had placed it on Ames's shore in the early hours of Saturday morning, not because he wanted to draw Horton to the abbey — Horton had already been here several times in connection with the recovery of stolen goods — but as a message to Ames that he had killed Lomas and was prepared to continue to kill rather than be exposed or be killed. Horton took a breath. 'Who took that photograph from 1967?' he asked.

'Jennifer.'

Ames had denied she had but then Ames was a liar, as might Dormand be. These men lied whenever it suited them. But if it was true then had Jennifer given the picture to Edward Ballard or had the picture been found in their flat after Jennifer had disappeared? By whom though? Someone working for the Intelligence Services or someone responsible for killing Jennifer? How had it ended up with Ballard? Had Ballard been her contact in London or Portsmouth? Had he discovered that Jennifer had been betrayed or had betrayed them but that she'd left behind a child — him? When Ballard discovered what had happened to her he had taken him from the children's home and placed him with Eileen and Bernard Litchfield.

'Is she dead?'

'I would say most certainly, wouldn't you?'

He would. But so too were Jasper Kenton and Thelma Veerman. He might not be able to do anything about Lomas but he could about Kenton and Thelma Veerman. His weary brain picked up what Dormand had said earlier: *'Hands are so important, don't you think? They don't lie.'* The monks often kept their hands hidden in their sleeves — not so easy for others — but which of them was it: Jay Ottley, who always wore gloves, or Cliff Yately, who had sprained his wrist and had his hand bandaged and his arm in a sling? But it wasn't only hands that didn't lie; it could also be the shape of the face and much of a face could be hidden behind a beard as Dormand's had been in that old photograph. 'Where's Jay? Or should I say Sam Tandy?' Again Dormand remained silent.

Horton continued. 'Kenton wanted Jay Ottley's money, or rather the royalties that have been accruing in Sam Tandy's account for years. Kenton had located the account, but hadn't got access to it. In return for keeping quiet about Jay's new life, Kenton said he would leave Jay in peace. So what disfigurement does Jay Ottley have on his hands that Thelma Veerman had seen?'

'His left hand. An accident when he was in his late teens left a permanent weakness and a scar.'

'Don't tell me, with a pistol crossbow.'

Dormand inclined his head in acknowledgement.

Horton continued. 'Kenton tracked Tandy to the abbey but he needed Thelma Veerman to identify him. He wormed his way into her lonely empty life, having discovered that she provided nursing care. Did Thelma see Tandy kill Kenton? Is that why he had to kill her?'

'That was a shame. Thelma was innocent but Kenton was a crook and blackmailer. If Jay had left it to me, I would have seen to it and no one would have been any the wiser.'

Horton believed that. 'You removed Kenton's clothes, wrapped him in an old sailcloth and took him to Ames's land in the early hours of Saturday morning, after which you returned to the abbey and drove Kenton's car to the Fishbourne ferry terminal for the four a.m. sailing to Portsmouth. You bought a ticket in the name of Adam Rooney. Kenton had a return ticket in his wallet under a false name and false registration number so that he couldn't be traced after Sam Tandy had signed over his millions to him. In the rear of Kenton's car you found a camera and video along with a laptop computer and phone, all of which contained information on his investigation into Brett Veerman. You decided to leave the car where Veerman had a flat. You wiped the car clean, of course.' And Dormand would have been an expert at that.

'And did you find Thelma's body here on Tuesday afternoon, after she'd met Jay?' Did he drug her dogs? Yes, he must have done, probably with some medication he had got from the vet for his sick pig. 'On Wednesday afternoon or morning you took her back to her house by that boat with her dogs and left her there.'

'Just tidying up as I've been trained to do.'

'Why didn't Jay Ottley just sign over the money? He didn't need it. Two people would be alive today if he had done so.'

'He thought Kenton had come here to take him away. Jay could never leave. Too much LSD had left him with hallucinations, one of which was that if he stepped outside of the abbey grounds demons from hell would come after him and eat him alive.'

'He'll have to leave now when I charge him with double murder. He'll get treatment.'

'It's too late for that.'

Dormand's words sent a chill through Horton. 'Where is he? Where's Sam Tandy?' he asked, fearing the worse.

Dormand glanced beyond Horton to the boathouse. He turned. His blood ran cold. 'He's dead?'

'Perhaps by now he is. When you asked at the café where you could find me, Jay would have thought you'd come to take him away.'

That confirmed to Horton that there was another way through the abbey gardens to the shore and a much quicker route than the one he'd taken. Could he trust Dormand to be telling the truth though? Was he just saying that to divert him so that he could make his escape on the boat, which was clearly his intention?

'Did you kill him?' Horton tossed a concerned glance at the boathouse.

'No. He killed himself. With his pistol crossbow which he kept here.'

Horton again looked back at the boathouse.

'You have a choice, Andy Horton. Either stop me from leaving or try and save Sam Tandy's life.'

Horton studied Dormand evenly for a few seconds, then turned and ran to the boathouse. He pushed open the door and saw the recumbent body of Jay Ottley stretched out amongst the lines, sails, oars, life jackets and rusting bits of boat. Ottley's eyes were wide open and even in death he looked haunted. Swiftly Horton checked for a pulse, knowing he wouldn't find one. Ottley had made sure of that. The bolt from the pistol crossbow was embedded in the right side of the head and the weapon was lying close to Ottley's right gloveless hand. The scar from his accident years ago was visible in the palm of the left hand.

The sound of a boat's small engine alerted Horton. He raced out and peered into the black night and could just make out the dark shape of Dormand in the dinghy heading out into the Solent. Dormand raised his hand in farewell.

Horton stepped forward, but what could he do except call the coastguard?

He reached for his phone but hesitated. Would they be too late to find Dormand? Would his body be washed out to sea? Or had he or others planned his escape route? Was there a speed boat waiting to take him somewhere? Would the coastguard find the small boat empty and drifting? Just as Kenton had planned his phoney death, perhaps Dormand had already planned his. He scoured the sea for the small dinghy and thought he saw it heading out towards Ryde.

'Just tidying up like I've been trained to do.'

Horton stared back at the boathouse. Had Jay Ottley really shot himself or had Dormand, a trained assassin, killed him? Had he been tidying up? Was he tidying up with his own death? No one would know what he had told him about the past and Jennifer. And Dormand had let him live because he was the bait.

Horton let the sea lap at his feet. He couldn't see any boats now, only a few tiny lights in the distance. He wasn't sure how long he stood but after a while he stabbed a number on his phone and called the coastguard. He reported a possible man overboard from a small dinghy. Then, taking a breath, he called in.

He didn't tell Uckfield all of it and he wouldn't. He had an appointment with Lord Ames for that. Or rather Ames would find him. The official story would be that Sam Tandy, known as Jay Ottley, had killed Jasper Kenton and Thelma Veerman and Brother Norman had conspired with Ottley after their deaths to help move their bodies in order to delay and confuse the investigation. Brother Norman, unable to live with his conscience, had killed himself at sea. Sam Tandy, alias Jay Ottley, had committed suicide by firing a pistol crossbow into his brains after Horton had shown up and asked for the whereabouts of Brother Norman, believing that the police were on to him. No one would know Brother Norman's true identity except him and Lord Ames.

Horton's phone rang but he ignored it. It would be Ames. There were now only two men left alive from those days of the Cold War, of spies, betrayal and the dirty tricks of 1967: Lord Richard Ames and another man whom Jennifer had worked with or for. One of those men had lured Jennifer to her death.

Horton stared out to sea. He was several steps closer to finding him but there were bigger and more dangerous steps yet to take. The trail began in Guernsey with Eileen Litchfield. But it didn't end there. It didn't even end in Gosport where his mother had gone on that foggy November day in 1978. No, it ended with the troubles in Northern Ireland and that was where he would begin. He turned and headed back up the shore to wait for the approaching police cars.

THE END

Thank you for reading this book.

If you enjoyed it please leave feedback on Amazon or Goodreads, and if there is anything we missed or you have a question about, then please get in touch. We appreciate you choosing our book.

Founded in 2014 in Shoreditch, London, we at Joffe Books pride ourselves on our history of innovative publishing. We were thrilled to be shortlisted for Independent Publisher of the Year at the British Book Awards.

www.joffebooks.com

We're very grateful to eagle-eyed readers who take the time to contact us. Please send any errors you find to corrections@joffebooks.com. We'll get them fixed ASAP.

Milton Keynes UK
Ingram Content Group UK Ltd.
UKHW041447090724
445399UK00023B/206